Eight Gods: Book I

Green Dragons

by Lanegan Bicchieri

This book is written for family and friends and
the people who have held open doors for me and been patient
when I was low and people who I've never met.

And to Pops, who reminded of parallel construction and semi-colons.

And to Mom, who got me On Writing.

ISBN 978-0-692-89244-2
LCCN 2017909736

paolobicchieri.com

Seattle, WA.

Author's note:

It's important to know that eight gods will destroy the world as it is known. They'll devastate it with their hands, and with their footfall they'll manifest ancient doom, but the craters and sinks and holes will be carved with armies, too.

People will bring about their lords' ruin as fast as they can.

And they will call it heaven.

Book I

"The pelt-wearer, gate-keeper, bell-ringer, demon-feller. The steward, smither, scholar, stalwart blockade of light. Come now into his arms and he will take your task in stride and take you far away and along."

The Luminary Inscriptionate, found written on the Caprican Bell

Chapter I

Tiny orchestras played in his mind in a way wholly unlike orchestras do. If an orchestra has sections playing together in harmony creating something beautiful, digestible for the audience, these cerebral performances were dischordant and rancorous. They still played their own part for the final piece, but they were misshapen and juvenile. But they were all in crescendo. In his mind they brewed like ale, fermenting and morphing forward. Swirling like cosmos.

And around him they did, too. He limped, but strode, through visions of terrible change and ruin. Smiles with jeweled teeth like pirates in smoky villages, thunder clapping and mewling cries near and far. The vagabond just kept on ambling. Perseverance in adversity is power. His journey is surreal but his mission fueled by that power, wings gusting around him and feeding the flame. His journey to Caprica, an almost unique one, plowed forward.

It was a dream but dreamscape gives nostalgia a chance to shimmer in radiance, a dark memory becoming fractal and fine. It can gain influence and new connotations.

∞∞∞

This memory feels like a portal to true love, now. The sleeping soldier remembers it in his dreams often.

High, thick brush rose on each side of him. He was five-years-old. The high brush was an orchard of brambly, thorny eller-

1

wright. The boy could not see over the peaks, just the dense rows making walls to his left and right. It was fun, leaving his cramped home to come run through the labyrinth plants. Like leaving the pantry for the castle maze.

The land was full of short, brown, dying grass and sagebrush. The air was dry but still the life of the plants sustained, and it was all a part of the place any ways.

The boy wore a rural outfit: brimmed sun hat, a yellow sleeveless shirt, and brown short pants. After he sees himself, and feels the character of the West Lands, loves the roots, then in the dreamy memory he hears his father. He sounds like he's being hurt, a short, desperate inhale with a cold gasp. He watches himself trot through the channel between the plants, beginning to look for his dad. There are too many rows, and in his youth he's so unnerved and overwhelmed that he is ready to cry.

Then he hears a big laugh, nearer than the gasp now. The boy crosses trough a space between rooks of ellerwight and sees his father. He's alright, with a smile on his face.

In the dusty grass his dad is sitting with a bag, a machete and a pipe. There is smoke near his head is, resting, and his gaze is cast down away from the sun. He's shirtless and wears a bigger pair of the same brown short pants as his son. With a sigh he looks up, sees his son, throws wide his arms and the boy rushes to his sanctuary.

"Are you okay?" the boy asks. He sits on his dad's thigh, his father sitting criss-crossed.

"I'm fine, son," his dad gushed. "Stellar."

"Oh, alright," the boy said. "Good."

The ellerwright surrounding them, that thick, gorgeous plant, and his father holding him let the boy feel safe and good. Their love was unique and in the orchard it was all that mattered. His confusion and fear fled him like a cross to a ghost.

Then the journey through the portal, all the years in between, hits hard. Like stepping from a clean and kind space into a pool of hot mercury.

Chapter 2

The morning bell rung and crashed into Porter's more often than not hung over and slumbering mind. The sound was his, but it also wasn't, it was a confusing identity. Either way, this morning the chime was an assault. It rang on his hollow body and caused an internal clamor. He left his dream with his sheets and got up.

Running a calloused, groggy hand over and through his tawny and short hair the man rose with the people of the city. The morning bell of Caprica was one of many aspects of the city that created a character of fastidiousness and wholesomeness for every denizen. The morning bell was instated after the Roaring Thunder of 311, a storm that destroyed about half of what was then a small Western trading outpost, to remind citizens that there were still crops to tend, pigs to slaughter and now smoldering debris to remove (and a half-destroyed general store to reconstruct.)

Porter walked into his apartment washing quarters which held the disheveled old wash bucket his father had left him, filled to the brim with cool well water. Porter thought of his father as he splashed the water over his tired eyes; it was one of the few odd items left behind by an odd man. Though his father had been reigning second captain of the king's army, a position Porter ascended to himself, Pod Rosset had always been an estranged man. He was not estranged to liquor, however. Agatha's Ale, Caprica's earthiest and eldest brew made by Agatha Arantastile, now her blinded and aging grandson Arthur Arantastile, had been his favorite.

Water ran through Porter's hair as he dumped the remainder of the reserve over his head. It was so hot, the same sun as his youth but no longer novel, and beads of salty water trickled over his brow and down to the cement basin below. The tattoo of a green dragon on his right breast, now fading and stretched with the expansion of his body, caught his eye in his reflection again. It made him wince.

The man lunged in half-doze to the closet and grabbed his white tunic which like an old wife was familiar and necessary. His sometimes dark skin, the shade of a legume now, contrasted the tunic, as old as it was. Porter then donned his chain mail, and next the sterling breast plate with the hammer and bell of Caprica, resting over his hidden ink, and fastened it at his shoulders and at his sides. Caught in muddled thoughts of last night and last nights too long ago Porter dressed and snatched his maroon cape that hung, always, by his door on his way towards the same, contrived, tired routine. Porter feared he was becoming much like this routine.

The door needed a hard shove to shut, as it did most days, and creaked on its leather hinges, as it did most days. The enormous sun that bore over Caprica hung high this morning, and found its way to pierce Porter's field of vision. He brought his hand to his brow so he could look at the city.

Porter's apartment sat on the second floor of the old Dermio Building, often refurbished, on the Northern end of the city. It had been the city's first bakery, owned and installed by Bruce Dermio's family in 450, right after the fall of Reprico and during Caprica's contending of becoming the next Crown City-State of Man, no easy contest, and though the business boomed selling Dermio's Danishes for years, their expansion to the bed and breakfast market, hence the construction of five additional floors which almost bankrupt the family of four. They had no market on the edge of town at the top of a hill, and they were forced to sell to Florio Yuvaton.

Yuvaton was a trader from Ollete, which was an out-skirt town, nestled in the Bastions of Tellor, huge pinnacles of earth making a mountain ridge. Yuvaton claimed that it was one of many "inter-towns", a place that people from all across the world could call home, and went so far as to claim that he knew of elves who lived just "a hop and a skip away, I say, I say". But whether it was his incredulous stories or his stone like baguettes he also failed as a proprietor, but not before finishing the furnishing of each room with a black bear rug that Yuvaton said were "so much like Ollete I could cry, I could cry."

Yuvaton sold to his brother, also named Florio, who sold to the town crier Holnin, who, after being reprimanded for buying such an inaccessible place for the new town hall, sold to a local farm boy who planned to make his bid in the world of entrepre neurship with nothing but a functioning headquarters and his cousin's recipe for Dlower Delight, a soup that allegedly resembled the creatures of the Ennabon Forest when they took up their flowery form as they slept. This led to some of Capricas first legal battles, pitting boy against cousin. Tort war raged for at least a year, and just to evade his legal expenses the boy gave the building, and a remainder of one hundred and fifty opal to his lawyer Hunter Frogg.

Frogg, a man unlike other Capricans by origin, though from where none could say, stood at six foot six and weighed no more than his bones. He resembled a skeleton, due to his size but also to the skin drawn tight around his skull, with frozen blue eyes for staring down clients, and the black cloak that he wore day in and day out. Frogg was Porter's landlord.

The year is 1020.

Boots thudded against the wooden stairs as Porter came down the last few steps to the earth below, and they were Frogg's. His steely displeasure was painted on his face like marble. In other words, things continued to go exactly as they did every day.

"Rosset," Frogg croaked as he shot an arm in front of Porter, barring the stair well. Porter looked down and saw a bit of dead wrist rubbing against his breast plate, and looked up only to be shunned away by Frogg's luminous and frightening eyes. "You'll need to pay rent, you know."

"Hunter, I paid rent not more than a week ago," Porter sighed.

"Is that so? You're calling me a crazy man, then?"

"No sir, but I would advise you slide a hand into your purse and see if there's not another four hundred twenty opal, and eighty blue, than you expected," Porter said.

Both men remained silent as the gaunter one rummaged through the satchel slung over his shoulder.

"Ah, well, of course. I'd advise you to watch your tongue, Porter, because living in the Dermio is a privilege granted to few," Frogg said. The sun shone over Porter's shoulders and onto the coin that rested in the man's withered hands.

"I'll do my best, sir," Porter replied. At the rates and location of the Dermio Building, there certainly were few who had such a privilege to live there. Porter was tired of shifting around the downtown houses, and on his crown pay, with no family or wife to speak of, he was happy to have a place remotely his own.

The early part of the day was Porter's least favorite due to the requirement of his dressing in full Caprican official uniform. It was an understandable practice to rouse support and morale for poor town members who often felt only the disparity of their livelihoods, but *Tellor* it was so hot most mornings. The colder seasons of Caprica were just windy and rainy, and a stoic three quarters of the year held a consistent heat and humidity unlike anywhere else in the West.

Porter yanked a rag from his back pocket and dabbed at his brow as he smiled like a government prop ought to at the vendors down Trainer's Row. His morning routine was to make a round from his hill to Trainer's Row, the Northern end of the city's merchant designated three blocks, through the surrounding neighborhoods so as to include their farms and stables, offering assistance where needed, and back to the Caprica head office for a written report.

Porter finished his loop and greeted Ula, the secretary to the king's mouth, a one Bord Honsan, to whom he delivered his written report. Ula was plain and kind, often giving Porter his tasks for the day with the smile reserved by plain, kind women. There's an ancient importance to the role of these women.

As Porter was unfastening his breastplate, Bord flew into the office in his own general demeanor, fascinatingly distraught. The man assigned to handle the numerous responsibilities of the sovereign ruler who presided over the land of the Western men ought to be a bit more adjusted, but it seemed that every day this foggy and white haired representative was caught off guard, rushing and anxious.

The door slammed behind Bord and the man struggled to juggle a stack of papers, to push his long white blonde hair out of his face, and to reposition his purple head band. Trippably long Caprican sage robes adorned the man from neck to toe.

"Porter, oh my dear Porter, there's work to be done

today," Bord said, cutting Ula's not-so funny story off. He spin Porter around about face.

"Is there not always at least a few things to do, Bord?" Porter asked. "Wouldn't be a job without a few things to do."

"Today is unlike any other! Today we must see the king's stables swept and the horses tended, his majesty's quarters thoroughly, I mean THOROUGHLY, scrubbed and cleaned WHILE he is out of the premises, and, man, at least twenty other tasks that I, I just don't see getting done!" Bord said.

"I think we can figure it out, old friend," Porter said as he slung his arm around his nervous compatriot's slender frame. He searched through his papers, "It seems as though Soranin and I are to give a rousing speech to his majesty's newest troop at mid-day, no?"

"That is one of the most IMPORTANT tasks of the day, yes," Bord said.

"Why don't I arrange for the stables to be swept, his majesty's quarters to be thoroughly-"

"Thoroughly!"

"Right, thoroughly, cleaned, and then I'll adorn this shining plate yet again and mount once more to join Soranin for this initiation, and we'll rendezvous later, hm?" Porter suggested as he gathered his armor.

"You'll be back as soon as you're finished with this rousing, correct?" Bord asked in a tone ripe with self-pity as Porter crept to the door.

"You can bet your neat purple head band on it, Bord," Porter said with a wink as he ducked out, before Bord had any other distressing but unsurprising news to divulge.

"Tellor craft your light," Bord said, smiling.

"It is crafted," Porter said, nodding.

Nervous stammering behind him, Porter moved from the office towards the king's compound.

Chapter 3

Bord shouldered himself the task of reminding Porter of Tellor every day, most of the day. Being a man of the government, Porter understood it was in the sage's job description to do so. The custom is benign and comforting, yet hegemonic in design.

Tellor the bell ringer above the clouds. Tellor the forger of music and light, the passionate defender and champion. Also known as The Champion, The Crafter, The Infuser. Tellor seemed to be a talented guy, or so his books and sages proclaim. Men don't have a creed or tome that details Tellor; Tellor always has been, concrete, and everyone in the West agrees on the goodness of his truth.

The bell of Caprica exists because of Tellor, as does any of Caprica at all. As does any of the world for that matter. He rang it into existence with the globular bell he carries upon his tremendous back, and he creates our world each day by hammering at his forge. Each stroke is a new moment to be seized, and his disciples remind each other of this with their affirmations. Muttered by some under breath, shouted by others with a beat on their hairy chests, like Tellor would; his followers come silent and shy and some corrupt with pride.

Seen each day was Tellor's finest handiwork, the Bastions of Tellor. The noblest being had, due to his nobility of course, not set his creations into the world to suffer. These enormous mountains formed a likeness of the pauldron he wore on his shoulder, an earthen defense to the treacherous lands that lay to the East. Unknown and unseen, most believed the world to become blackness, void, past the mountains. Cowering in uncertainty was enough for many.

In Tellor's name some call it a castle, but truly the Caprican city-state, though ruled by a king, had a far more sprawling, beauracratic government headquarters than a single castle, which may conjure notions of unadulterated fantasy. The head office operated as a front gate to the enormous royal complex, and Porter was checked by two men of the army at the bronze gate that was drawn up to allow vetted, authorized visitors into the wide and extravagant court that flowed beyond the thick doors.

It's easy to forget dusty and worn Trainer's Row lies not far from the gates. The court had statue after statue of kings and heads of state, those that had operated while kings grew, followed each by a fantastic carved wooden art piece, or perhaps shrubbery in the shape of a creature or a dream. Farrowberry bushes, spiny things with the most exquisite purple berries, speckled with dots of maroon, Caprican standard colors, lined the walking path. From the court one could head to the king's arena where games ranging from bouts of archery to log tosses were held, or into the Caprican royal library where tomes and texts that held hand written work from those faceless scholars who write tomes and texts were watched over with vigilance, though these days few fingered through their papery words.

One would probably follow the stone path to the foot of the king's quarters, by far the most impressive building in all of Caprica. The building was made of white brick, and though the first story was thin and had but four windows around the circular floor, the second story of the building was a beautiful wonder. The chamber opened up and out, like a saucer, and two doors stood on either side of this core of the building; the second floor was a vast balcony. The balcony was adorned with sitting tables, four gardens, with more farrowberry bushes, the royal blood's favorite botanical sight, and a wood-fire oven. The reason the building was the most impressive in all of Caprica was that the architect had followed the first floor-second floor pattern for a total of eight flights. The Tower of Indecision, since from a distance it seemed that the building itself could not decide whether it was one size or another, had features and fixtures making it more than fit for a king and his family. Their chambers lie at the top most out stretching floor.

Porter gazed up and thought, yet again, that looking straight up from underneath the thing made it seem quite intimidating. On the eighth floor balcony there was a mounted periscope, right there next to the falconry, that the king employed often. Porter smiled as he glared through the sun to see him using it today.

From the court one might also take the path to the Southern end of the facility, a basin that housed an enormous sta ble and dirt court. The court housed exercise facilities, racks ofcruel weapons, and a small barracks for the newest troop being brought up at the time. This was where Porter was headed; the newest group of forty young men from surrounding villages, and even a few city-slicking Capricans, were either true patriots aspiring to make a name for themselves in a sanctified rank of men, or just looking for a decent wage and less-decent food.

The king's army was a vast one, though no true wars were fought since the falling of Reprico. The troops, in a squad of a few men, were sent to make check points throughout the villages and townships that belonged under Crown rule and to the land of Western men. This area included the city state of Caprica, ruling body, the port city Roiling Tide, the Southernmost city of Khu'ron, and "the gem of the land," Jobelnon. Several townships existed in this area, and even more villages, and a few dotted nomadic tribes as well. All of them well within the rule of Caprican King Kalan Ernhart, son of Remirin and sole ruler of the lands to the East of the Bastions of Tellor. Not to mention Ollette.

The rural, outer realms have, historically, been home to uneducated but spirited tribal people. Squads must remind them of their place when they refuse to pay the new taxes. Quashing riots in a militarized fashion, then, became the practice. Few citizens appreciated the taxes supporting this, since in a near-comedic if not demonic way it was a cycle, but Tellor asked obedience, and in their faith they were reclined.

Porter had, when he was a young man of the armed service, found himself spending many a day, and well into the night, reading the story of the Ernharts and their exploits during the falling of Reprico, when men still battled each other for Western dominance, before it became an agreed upon cabal. It became clear that only an elected city-state could rule freely, and though the four cities all did their damndest to appeal to the people, no one could forget Dorigin Ernhart's charity to the people of Reprico as they moved all they had left to either Caprica or Roiling Tide. Were it not for his family's good will and determination to see the city evacuated safely during those bloody times when Repricoans still fought their political battles, Rossets very well could have found themselves as farmers or ditch diggers. If the archives didn't inform Porter of this, he could just remember from the countless times his father sung the praises of the Ernharts and their "golden souls, they got golden souls" from the bottom of his tankard. As a boy Porter heard the kids call them the "Barnyards," a timeless bit of juvenile word play.

Porter strode into the stable, again stirring himself from his thoughts, and slung a bag of oat grain over his shoulder to give to his horse, Kettlestep. The rusty and gifted animal was nearly as old as Porter, and had been selected by him when he was a boy during a patrol with his father to the town of Marryfarm, a place famous for napping in straw and excellent live stock. The chestnut horse seemed glad to see Porter, and as the feed rained from the bag into the horse's feeding bucket, Porter's commanding officer strolled into the stable. The Caprican sun shone at his back, but Porter heard the man's "hallo!" and knew the thundering voice.

Captain of the king's army, and certainly deserving of the title and fame, was Soranin Redbell. The man was just forty, and had a head of curly red hair and a chin of the same. Broad shoul-dered, wore his armor for the sake of it, and donned in a flowing silver cape, he was a man with that irresistible warmth which ensnares and pulls forever. Born of a high family in Caprican history, the same family that installed the morning bell, Soranin was the oldest of six and destined for the army, but none knew how high he would rise in his service. His cool head during battles and somehow old wisdom served the man well during the many small battles that Caprica had served in the last twenty years, all of which Soranin played the focal point, the piercing ballista through riots and would-be usurpers.

"Porter, ready to forage the finest from this teeming group of ne'er do well knaves?" Soranin said. He grinned as he fingered the hilt of his two handed broad sword, Joi'den. The name comes from a Southern origin story which told of a troll named Joi'den coming through their city-state and giving them the gift of fire.

"I'd be just as ready to watch another riveting log show with Bord. When shall we begin this festive chat?"

"As soon as you armor and mount up, brave Second Captain. Here," Soranin said as he passed a flagon to Porter. "Some liquid courage?"

"It's not courage I need, just patience," Porter said, but took a long drink of Soranin's companionate drink, Skell Brew. Fermented with skell, the bitter long grass from Ollette, it is sold in a sort of sealed jar which it was buried in, and Soranin moves the bitter drink to his flask when his home has gone to sleep and their eyes don't judge.

Kettlestep, Porter, Soranin and the enormous blonde Clydesdale horse Nin'tei (we're told the name of Joi'den's trollish lover) rode into the dusty training field to greet three training officers who had already organized the unruly, unwound, unshaven, often pock-marked youth into ranks before them. Soranin strode to face the men, Porter close behind on his left and wishing he had more Skell Brew. Soranin paused; it's said charisma lies in the waiting.

"Caprica's army isn't for vast battles any more, no. You won't find yourselves bracing the Bastions of Tellor waiting for the Foothill Rebels to shower you with arrows so that you may retaliate with a heroic dive. You won't find yourselves staked outside Roiling Tide waiting for smugglers to bring in some rebellious war machine, a gulping hulk from the mind of a rude sadist. Not a single one of you will find yourselves in the ruins of Reciprico, rooting out dissenters and hanging them for war crimes. If you're looking for blood, you've come to the wrong place," Soranin cleared his throat, thanked his horse for patience, under breath.

"What you are is a shield. A finely polished device that serves not only this city-state but three cities, eight townships, fifteen villages, and every other soul who enters our realm with good will in his heart! You are shepherds, you are suns in the night for any villager who may happen upon you with need, sorrow, or grievance. I will keep you polished, I will keep you looking after your flock, and I will keep you burning bright. There is no question that you will stand straight, be kempt, be loyal, and serve Caprica and the entire West to the best of your ability because Tellor knows I will strike you down if you do not or cannot, and if it isn't me the bell ringer himself will temper you to an early grave. We may be in a time of peace, but service doesn't rely on violence or desperation, and if you thought that you'd be a hero or at least get free food, I'll remind you..." Soranin roared as he rode to the front line, bent his head down, "the food tastes like skell."

The three officers began to bark at the men to hold their heads higher and to stand heels in, and the two captains began to mosey towards the stable.

"How was it today?" Soranin asked.

"Impressive. The 'food isn't skell' needs to have some more power to it, perhaps threaten with ration shortages or something. Clever, though."

"Bah, I never know how to round those damn speeches out to scare them. The food is pretty good."

◇◇

Porter sat in his apartment later that evening after all of the menial tasks were tended to and Bord had been swaddled like a babe. Often Porter would read and drink, watch the walls maybe, that other thing sometimes, but tonight only he read. Porter wouldn't speak of it much, it was far too strange in the year 1020 because folks resigned themselves with contented eating and sloshing silly with drink and worst of all deciding the thoughts of anyone but their own kin weren't worth listening to, but he wondered about the rest of the world. That was really what it was, mostly. Wondering what there was outside of the Western Lands, outside of farms and fields that Porter knew he would never truly be alone in so long as King Ernhart could still spy him with his periscope. There was nothing wrong with Ernhart, Porter thought, nor periscopes. In fact, he thought the man a benevolent ruler, and seemed to treat everyone with the best intentions. Porter just wondered what else there was over the mountains was all. Perspective for periscopes.

Pod Rosset believed that a man needed to "see more to be more," he would often tell his son over dinner. Porter's mother's family never moved to Caprica when the city became elected city-state. So she remained in the earthy shack her family owned with her shadows and a few pieces of bad furniture. Whether it was excuse to leave the family or not, Porter never knew, but he had few memories of his mother and she had never visited. His father was comfortable in the pseudo-suburban life, but his mother came from a community to the South. It wasn't quite Khu'Ron, and all Pod would say is that his mother's home was not on any Caprican map. Speaking her name in that small shed of a home that the two Rossets lived in just outside the city's walls as a boy was like touching ice, or biting steel. Striking, foreign and not recommended.

Theoretically Pod had traveled, but mostly he encouraged Porter to go see these supposed mind-blowing beauties for himself. South of Khu'Ron, East of the Bastions of Tellor, places beyond the sea and other sights the folks in the West Lands knew were just pretend. More people with beautiful ways and stories, he sometimes said. Pod would always start with a "here, read this book." He insisted there were more colonies than just those that presided in the hills of the Bastions of Tellor. Pod was important to Porter but that's because sons are fathers to themselves second, after their dads get a crack at it, and the first time they have fathers the bonds become like stone crosses in their bones.

Long known to be the only hospitable place for humans to call home, the West Lands then were home to all civilized folk. Those rebellious tribes in the Bastions of Tellor foothills were squashed during Irvin's reign in 800, and any who remained had certainly come West in chains. Caprica practiced less slavery than other city-states but no city-state is free of its shame, and no poor people are free of their shackles.

Pod liked to prod certain points: how could we believe we were the only men in the world? We knew so little of it! And to believe they all lived in this section of the world, these West Lands? You think all the commerce in Rolling Tide comes from fishing up dredges of those awful Slinky Fish that they muck up in the bay? That Khu'Ron sends ambassadors to the desert for fun, or that Ollette is called the bridge to the land for old time's sake? Pod said, "Hey, if you don't buy it that's entirely too fine by me, but you ought to see for yourself by the time ya croak." By the end of most nights this was his creed and the main topic of discussion. Porter often told his father he truly didn't buy any of it, and really would rather discuss something else, but still read the books. And heard the stories. And the messages did take hold, and somewhere in his mind the labyrinths of conspiracy and curiosity merged with understanding and reality.

The only story or theory or allegory Porter particularly cared for, craved to be truth, was the one with the green dragons. His adoration of this tale certainly had to do with the fact that at as a newborn boy his parents had decided they would take it upon themselves to brand him with a drawing that Pod had mocked up himself, because he'd SEEN one. "What, you've never seen one?" he would ask, just because he loved hearing the sheepish "no" of West Lands folk. The folks would scratch their beards and watch Pod light up a just-made cigarette, preparing himself for a story.

"I had just come down the other side of the mountains, the last being Old Yit and it opens into a huge plain, ya see, and it flew just over head like it didn't care who saw but of course it did or you'd have seen it by now. Wings from here to here," he'd take his cigarette as far as his short arms could sail it, "and horns as gold as all the gold in a Khu'Roni desert at dawn. It flew so fast and so low it set me on my back, broke a vase I'd stole from an elvish township to boot, and all I could see was a big gold belly fly above me, and by the time I'd spiraled 'round on all fours to get another look all I could spy was the huge spikes on its back and its long green tail trailing after it.

And when I made it to the next tavern I chatted with an old fella who told me those things run in packs! Tight-knit. Bonds like korekwood, rallying together to blitz across the sky. Man, those green dragons did it."

"Did what, Pops?"

"Made sure I knew there were things out there that'll take the wind right out of ya, beautiful and magnificent things. You've gotta see 'em, Porter. You do. If Tellor created truth, it was upon those wings."

Porter read, often times the same books. Most of the readings in the library were written about agriculture, economy, alchemy, mining, trading, construction, or geography. There was one genre Porter had killed with overreading; history. Though the history section was indeed massive and took a good half of the library, most were minutes of meetings, speeches, treaties, or things of a more political nature. There were a few though, about as many as there was an entire works of fiction section that had some information that seemed to bolster his father's tougher-to-be-lieve theories. None of the stories or legends were about his mother's people – they didn't belong in the West Lands libraries, it seemed. That left that hollowness in Porter.

He got up and walked along the stairs down to the dirt road. He needed to move if all these thoughts were going to corrupt his drinking and wall-watching. All the thoughts of time gone, and exposition exposed, and preface to prefecture and things that don't matter to him anymore. But the hollowness persists, and matter is all they seem capable of tonight.

There were nearly no books that proposed people did not sail to the West on the massive ship the Roiling Wave, of which the remains are said to lie at the bottom of Heavy Bay, from their unnamed home land which had been flooded from the Heavy Storm. A prophecy of storm gave some the time to get on a boat. The rains chased the ark all the way up to the lip of the land, trying to polish off the few lucky souls that escaped its dark grip, but fell at the sight of the land, crafting the Heavy Bay. Then everyone knew what humans had been doing since. Farming and growing, until we had the West Lands as we know them today, arid and tough.

The Bastions of Tellor: A Complete Text spoke to some contradiction, though. Porter would read the chapter over and over, the one that mentioned something besides the gorgeous tumbling hills and the fauna that could be spotted on the solstice. People indeed testified to the short lived towns that men had raised there, the rebels, only to be called treasonous for not moving into the borders of the West Lands and slaughtered in a few short months by King Irvin Ernhart's army. Those not destroyed moved within the borders, in iron, and some of their testimony, as recorded in the text, spoke of "thriving communities in the hills" with "peoples from Tellor knows where". Now most historians said it was only Ollette, a township that flourishes just inside the mountains and did then too by the Ernharts as a sign of good grace, but it didn't answer the question another testimony raised. A young farm boy, in a chain gang shuffling down a mountain, was quoted saying "The tall ones were good to us. Brought us sweet foods and spreads for our oat. Nothing like we'd ever had in Holladale, no sir." It wasn't much, but those cherubic words knotted the labyrinth well for Porter. He worked frequently and furiously, and desperately, to unknot, as nights spent in sick dreams infused with brew turned into weeks spent tossing, turning, and reading.

◇◇

Bord's list was longer, perhaps even more pointless, and more aggravating, Porter thought as he took a sip from his flagon. Frogg was crueler this morning and the sun was hotter, no doubt about it, Porter knew. Porter knew one more thing as well: today was the Rough Bout.

Only a week had gone by, he thought with a pang of guilt about the lethargy of his literarily steeped life, since Soranin and he had addressed the new group of soldiers. Knowing this, Porter could confirm that today was the Rough Bout; the new recruits first chance to prove their grit, test their mettle and such brouhaha, by melee with men of the king's service.

The Rough Bout had been instituted by Gulliver Mayne, one of Caprica's most loved and most berated army captains. He was a tyrant, in short. His legend is a funny one; a man standing as tall as a wooly bear, with a beard to match, but with a voice befitting a swan suffering a nasty cold. He had a head shaved all but clean spare a small bun on the back of his head. The man thought, with King Ivan Ernhart's endorsement and approval, a training exercise could not only bring up a troop in skill but bring a community together, jangle some opal from pocket to pocket, and give him a chance to beat people to drudges of person soup in front of an audience. Mayne, by the end of his life, was known to switch the black piece of cloth tied around his head from eye to eye.

Now in theory Porter enjoyed the notion of roughing up some young men who just fit their breast plates and could barely raise their training swords and shields, banging and bashing them to his delight, exercising out all his doubts, anxiety, and general apathy that had always accrued since the last pseudo tourney. The feeling of using an axe, even one compiled of haggard wood instead of the familiar weight and bite of the axe made of metal he employed, made his biceps tense and a joy stir inside of him that he felt far less than the hollowness.

The Rough Bout was, every year, much less enjoyable

17

than he played it in his mind, biceps and all. The bout was long, as long as the Bastions of Tellor were wide, and took place outside in the dusty, arid courtyard. Porter was lucky to have one or two matches himself, and then was expected to stand and wait, bedecked in his entire suit of plate, cloak flowing heroically in the non-existent wind as the sun slow cooked the man of the king's army to the marrow, while the Rough Bout, perhaps a ten-plus hour event, finally came to a close, whereupon Porter was expected to assist in the tidying up, the paying of vendors and the general menagerie of items expected of a man of his position. One of the days Porter regretted not aiming for a high position on the bureaucratic pecking order.

The bout was also one of the few days the doors opened wide and cast a long net to the village folk to come and see the good grace of King Ernhart. His majesty allowed the purchasing of overpriced food and drink, the smell of Billy Yak and horse manure to waft like an ambling peasant into unsuspecting nostrils from said vendor's carts, and the viewing of the least cared for or used area of the entire compound. The king's home was a nice passing by view, though, as were the bushes of delectable fruits unavailable to such peasants and peons.

The heat made Porter's stomach begin to roast at the notion, also a longing, not to mention the long broil of it all, but the worst part was the "come one come all" theme of the combatant list; it was not only the king's army who were asked to test the new men.

In Caprica the king had two major military task forces. His Royal Army, wherein Porter held the station of second captain, and the King's Sword. The King's Sword were the knights of Caprica. The King's Sword were a group of ten men who swore to protect the king from "the vile, the unholy, the unclean, and from destruction, my liege." The King's Sword was a bunch of insatiable, incomparable and erroneous boobs (If you asked Porter or Soranin, any ways).

Porter entered the courtyard just before the Rough Bout was set to begin; he was thankful that Soranin, as captain, was the man who set up the event because it allowed for Porter's long nights of self-cruelty transition into mornings of public service.

Beginning the day with a tall mug of Agatha's Brew let the horrible process of mollifying the body be put on hold, too.

The battered and beaten banner that seemed to scream "THE ROUGH BOUT" in red, blue, and misshapen block letters was just being pinned above his head at the entrance to the brown rectangle that was the stage for today's merriment. Just below that banner was a less glorious banner, though also battered and beaten, which read "HAVE THESE NEWTS GOT THE MAKINGS OF GREATNESS? CAPRICAN SCONES, MUFFINS, AND GENERAL GOOD-ES TEN OPAL ALL DAY".

All to Porter's right the vendors adorned their stands with last pieces of flare and zest, sweat on their collective brow, while others to his left stoked their fires that would create meaty Wooly Bear pies, crumbly farrowberry scones, chewy Muffin Malignant, sold first and best by Marryfarm Malignant Maladies, who sell treats far less malignant than their advertising might suggest. Porter enjoyed their comic spin on Caprica's signature Hopejule Sweet Bread, the Hope Fool Teet Bread, which tasted like a sharp cheese with rosemary. Even the rare Hot Boiled Bubble Brew. was wonderful, though elusive. But Porter saw the old men setting their stand now. It was run by two tall, gray haired men who, on a good Rough Bout, would travel from the hills near the Bastions of Tellor by way of the Noon Road, which collided with Diandre's Road, upon their Billy Yaks and deliver to the sprawling throngs their ancient recipe of spice infused ale that was nearly scalding when served right. Scintillating spice, meat sliding off bone, treats sweet enough for Tellor's hall, and only once a year.

Porter kept his gaze forward the best he could, with tickling scents doing their best to pull him astray and to rob him of all but two blue: a few bucks, really. He knew the haphazard con-glomeration of traveling vendors and bumbling townsfolk could and would lend itself to a much more enjoyable day for Porter, but he had to bully up on the King's Sword and, if Tellor winked his way today, a green eared newt. Beating either senseless made the elderly men with the cauldron of spice brew a handsome reward instead of an indulgence.

Near the stables Soranin was addressing the men, and as he saw Porter approach he strode toward him looking like a bull whipped to his last breath.

"Leoric competes today. Against me. He's requested," Soranin said, looping his arm around Porter and coaxing a smile and a wave from deep inside to some young boys who marveled at the gleam of his armor.

"Aye, that's the rub, man. Has he had Bord push it through this year?"

"I've been told he's made sure to keep the cork on his plan until today, but has indeed been shaking Bord's already thoroughly shook bottle for months now."

The men grabbed an arms full each of the wooden swords that the men would use to wail on one another for the following hours from a pile the king made available, and flipped back towards the barracks entrance where the ropes and flags were set up in anticipation of the bout.

"You'd think serving on the end all be all "King's Swan" would be enough for the lad," Porter said.

"He can't stand that we share rank. He cannot stand that a man whom he believes is inferior to him in combat could command a larger force, with much more grace I tell you, and have a stronger kinship with the king." Soranin spoke soft but quick, to avoid any lingering ears as they cut through passages of townsfolk who even in the hot morning ate and drank like they were Bolor the Rotund Rabble Rouser down at Long Drop Down, Trainer's Row's most frequented public house past sun down, when the heat was cut by the moon's rise.

"Today I suppose you'll find who deserves to wear the mop of red hair, no?" Porter joked.

"Porter," Soranin said with the reassuring look that had roused a nation's army of men. "I'll best him. And only in the King's Swan is one allowed to have such a tangle of hair. Damn artistic fools."

◇◇

Soranin and Porter stood, arms crossed like stone monks, and *A Brave Hearted Man's Look on the Bastions of Tellor* pocket book in hand for the second captain, resting out of sight by his side, on the barracks side of the Rough Bout which had gotten under way not long ago.

The tournament went as followed: in each battle there was a newt, or a new recruit as the king and only the king referred to them, and there was either by chance another newt or a man of the king's service. The battles consisting of two newts were the plodding, eternal affairs that tested a man's patience and vocabulary in an attempt to find new and even more destructive ways of calling the young men pathetic, boorish and all together a waste of good time. The two newts would cower with shields raised over head so that with swords lagging behind them, often resting with tips in the brown and rusty earth, they created a shape like an ant hill and would circle around each other until one had the amazing courage to flop their swords over their ant hill in a stupefying arch that would come crashing on the other's hewn shield. The newt who was struck would do his best to retaliate, and at this point it was the beginning of the end, for one man would either muster the strength to polish the other off with a blow that truly was "not SO bad" as Soranin might put it or one would "damn near throw away" his shield and yield as Porter would put it. That's not to say that some of the men didn't have a true "rough bout", it's just to say that most of them were a bit too embarrassed and all together new to this type of thing that they wanted out as soon as possible while looking as cool as possible. Quitting never seemed fair to Porter, but that's why he rarely tried, he thought.

When a man of the king's service was drawn from the round and large barrel stationed atop a podium is when things got quite exciting, what the people turned out in hordes for. The town crier, a plump man who made his maroon doublet's buttons strain to keep in his Hopejule Sweet Bread belly from bursting through, though the feat seemed less and less feasible each year he emceed the event, would pull the names for each match and shout the lucky ducks through a hollowed out piece of wood that did a poor job of amplifying his voice.

The match that Porter and Soranin looked on with glazed eyes and sticky, thirsty lips was one of the better ones. Robert Joyin, a newt from Marryfarm, had been battling in ant hill pose for a good twenty minutes now while Ronald Bodeman, a knight of the King's Sword for fifteen years, pounded and pounded on his shield. To Joyin's credit he had been resisting with a shocking steadfastedness. He made an excellent case for being a human shield in the front line of an indefensible battle.

Bodeman was a stocky man, with a curly, skunk colored beard that dropped to the spot where his neck should have ended, if he had had a neck. His skunk colored hair stood in contrast to his silver knight's armor, and he wielded the wooden play sword with cruel deftness. He tore at Joyin like a dog with a rope, biting and pulling unbroken. Neither Porter nor Soranin knew Bodeman, though he had been serving on the Knight's Sword longer than any other knight, but had heard that his skunk colors only reflected his sulfurous personality.

The crowd cheered, drank, bet and altogether loved every minute of this honorable man of the city devastating the green eared newt. Drinks clashed together and poured down ecstatic throats. Opal slid in and out of hands like a long green snake.

"I yield, please I yield!" Joyin called out, again.

Bodeman noticed a few more people noticing him ignoring the plea, and after giving three more hard hits with every inch of force his arching shoulder swing could give, he dropped his sword and raised both fists over his short but thick frame. The crowd sounded like a stream of jingling gold and roaring beasts in their praise.

"Man, if for my whole life I need to turn out for Rough Bouts on the regular, I think I'll be jealous of the marsh tenders in Khu'Ron." Porter said to Soranin, hoping to gauge his emotions. If indeed he did face Leoric today, he knew his captain would need all the support that Porter could muster.

"I think you ought to consider yourself lucky, Porter. Lucky for every bit of grace Caprica has shown your family," Soranin said with a frown.

"I suppose you're right, though I knew not this was a time to rake me. I thought it was simply the Rough Bout, which did all the day's raking."

"You're right. Damn this bloody upstart Leoric. Until I know whether or not-" Soranin was interrupted by the stretched maroon doublet wearing man with a piece of wood.

"OUT OF THE BARREL WE HAVE," the crier hooted between bites of bread and jam. "AMI TROUT AND PORTER ROSSET".

The crowd nearly fell apart. Porter didn't know why. He was sort of popular, but was no King's Sword.

"Ami Trout, eh? Stay light, Porter." Soranin said as he offered some of his signature drink. Porter chugged a bit, wishing it were something harder with greater release, Soranin laughed at his eagerness, Porter grabbed his flat wooden axe by two hands, in a stupor made his way to the center of the arena while the crowd went on like a horrible wind-up toy.

The grip on the axe was always an empowerment to Porter, consolidated his stresses and focused his confusion into one point, and he knew with a hurling blow he could send all of his problems catapulting into another man, by grievous wound if possible – it often was. Porter unfastened his cloak as his fellow combatant toed into the ring carefully.

Well she's tall, Porter thought, *and not a man.* Porter knew better than to assume any fight would be as simple as reminding his land lord every day that he had indeed already given him his coin, but he had also competed in a Rough Bout many more times than he could count and it always pained him to remember just how talentless these soldiers could be in the first tussles. In their defense it was hard to even qualify many of them as soldiers, he feared, since so many were weed pullers and rock splitters by family trade.

Ami Trout had tanned skin, a dark brown that seemed like burnt butter at first but harder. Khu'Roni native, Porter assumed. Ami had blonde hair growing from her head in six long braids: each one matted and proud. The woman stared at Porter as he was assisted in fastening his armor and shield with eyes that seemed to sympathize for Porter, but that sympathy came from a promise to make the loss go as quickly as possible.

Porter only thought that this woman didn't understand the city's ranks, had confident eyes like a calf before branding and would be asked to get a military regulation haircut. He thought Trout would probably take issue to regulation, be an upstart who refuses a shave.

With ale sloshing in his belly and a bit of muffin in his open hand the crier ringed his bell to allow the match to get under way. His patchy and thick beard had food and a wide, toothy smile in it. Aristocracy eat your heart out.

Porter kept his axe behind him, tip a bit off the dirt, as he moved towards the broad shouldered youth. She must be at least ten years younger than I, Porter thought; I'll get a good exercise in today. The woman moved in toward Porter and he noticed for the first time that she carried neither shield nor sword.

Standing a bit taller so in an attempt to call attention to this, Porter left himself open to the newt's attack before he realized that it was by no error she was unarmed.

With long braids flowing behind her in a golden sail, the soldier darted in to Porter and placed her armored shin in Porter's side, just between breastplate and leg piece. All the air rushed from Porter's lungs and he nearly lost the grip on his weapon. The blonde locks moved back to regain composure and Porter was thankful he was given a moment to do the same. Porter stared at the young woman who only showed a youth's smirk of swagger.

Trout moved in again, but Porter feinted back before swinging his axe towards the young woman. The swift solider ducked and punched into the elbow joint of Porter's armor, again hitting where only chain mail covered his tired and hot flesh. Porter hissed out his breath and attempted to recover quickly, but not before in the same duck the young fighter took Porter out from beneath himself with an arcing ankle level kick. Falling hard on his back Porter clutched onto his weapon and was able to use the broad side of his axe to defend himself from the gatling of punches that rained down. Mustering most if not all of his energy Porter gave the axe a shove towards the copper guise and rolled to his left, stood up.

Ami Trout creaned her back, laughed, said:

"Second captain? This man is my new superior? Let me bow low to you, second captain." She gave a joking and deep bow and pricked her head up to smile at the crowd, who Porter now realized had been cheering for this stranger from the moment their names were picked from that groggy barrel. Porter swung, but of course the young fighter dipped to her left and kicked Porter again. Porter guarded, and then received a blow to his right ear. The crowd gasped and cried out in splendor.

Trout swam like her name sake to follow up her attack. Porter was soon dropped to his knees by a kick in his back, a yellow move Porter thought, and the woman soon sat on top of Porter with her strong arm around his neck. Ami lowered her mouth to Porter's ear as he pawed at the bracer coiled around his throat. Porter smelt the savory Khu'Roni spice on the woman's breath, a smell of salt and autumn leaves rotting slowly on a porch step.

"Yield, I can only hope? For both our sakes, aye?"

Stars and dragons played through his sight, but Porter did not falter.

I did hope to have an exercise today, but not in humility, he thought. The foreigner was strong, Porter could feel it in her grip. *If I win today, she will surely surpass me. It's only a matter of time before folks like me go the way of Reprico in favor of this order of powerful youth. Were we not in my city, in my arena, she would have won already.*

Porter threw his arms over his head and heaved the woman by her arm pits forward, where Ami was forced to roll to safety, delighting the happy betters and drunks to a point of near ecstasy.

The second captain and Rough Bout veteran sauntered in towards the fighter, feinted again, now up with his axe, and as the woman began to duck to his left Porter brought his play weapon down to his right at a sharp angle and with remarkable strength, strength Porter seldom used for anything other than breaking himself down. He thanked the heavens for Rough Bouts that roused his memory and reminded him his love for the two-handed axe. In the moment he nearly broke her beautiful dark leg, he thought on his own axe, Krude, which bore his family name on its hilt. One of his family names. A green dragon stood inlaid in jade between the two silver blades. Pod Rosset spared no expense to prompt others to ask him of his unique interests, as was evident also by Pod's green dragon brooch, flagon and letter head.

The masses of onlookers were hushed, resting in shock. Porter sweat, bent over. He panted and coughed. But Ami Trout cried and sputtered beneath him in the dirt. Porter cocked his ear and could hear just well enough the word he needed to retire. Porter cast aside the wooden axe and turned around to pick up his cape, and the crowd exploded. Porter managed a smile as he heard the young woman yell in a different tongue to a few other newts, and was cheery to see Soranin welcoming him to his old post at the end of the arena.

"Hallo man! I thought you were as good as gone out there," Soranin cheered as he patted Porter on his back.

"Not so rough, would you?" Porter said. Now he felt not

only dirty and hot, but he ached as well. He drank.

"You know of this Ami Trout before I went to get clouted by her?"

Soranin laughed and shifted his position a moment.

"Ami Trout is a brawler, by way of exile from the Bad Troll Trolley. She came in only yesterday, as you can see by those flowing and marvelous braids of hers."

"The Bad Troll Trolley? And I was to go in and just have a go of it? See what fun misadventures she and I could have?" Porter asked, laughing in near contempt.

"It's not me to say who clubs each other around for our amusement," Soranin reminded his old friend. "And beside, you did fine."

"What was she exiled for?"

"She thought Figoror's ways were a bit too old fashioned, that the group was not selective enough, but mostly she exercised her skills upon a travelling shoe-shine from Jobelnon who mistook her for a man."

Porter snorted a laugh, Soranin followed suit. Neither of them had much love for what went for style in the Southern city, but neither of them had pity for those foolish enough to question a stranger's style. Culture can be strange to those uncultured in the ways of culture.

The victor navigated towards the vendors, dragging his left leg and wishing that his armor weighed a good fifteen pounds less. If the treats had goaded him before, they captured all his mental faculties now, not a sliver of resistance within. A cool Agatha's Ale running down the dry canyon of his throat, or perhaps a Malignant Muffin, sounded like a prize worth another beating.

Porter dropped with all his weight to a stool provided by a rotund woman from the Marryfarm Malignant Maladies stand and chewed his treat while he watched his former duelist hobble away towards the barracks. Porter smiled as he unwrapped a second muffin.

Khu'Ron had a rich and extravagant culture. The forest just outside the city's walls was an inspiration to musicians, painters, sculptors and even pastry makers. Marryfarm Malignant Maladies', a good example, had its very own Khu'Wrongly Awful

Sap, which was a sparkling sweet jam many Capricans sought after after Tellor's Respite, a daily hour of praying and fasting.

Khu'Ron was even inspiration to a fighter's guild upon its founding. This guild was none other than Ami Trout's former troop the Bad Troll Trolley. Figoror, by now an artifact, was a teacher and exceptional man who came from Ollette and had named the guild after mispronouncing the knolls he saw to his East. Porter's father preferred the theory that the man had trained with trolls who had been passing through the area, because as we all well knew trolls are a nomadic species and a family of trolls, anywhere from fifty to seventy of them, were known as a trolley, of course.

Figoror had struck the trees at the edge of the forest until his fists were made of bark themselves, folks say, and his fighting group began the premier dojo to train in the hand to hand combat known as Khu'Roni Brawl. Caprican soldiers had once been taught in such battle until it became apparent that too many men were uninterested in joining the army any longer, but the in-fallible King's Sword knew damn near every blow and parry. Leoric knew every blow, parry, feint, and could explain the origin of each move to you in Tellorian tongue or Khu'Roni, Porter thought with a nervous swig of Agatha's Ale.

Which goes to show the power of the rogue disciple Ami Trout.

Porter had sat for too long, drank too much ale and ate too many Malignant treats, and sure, a bit too many farrowberry scones, and decided he had better mosey back to his post of disinterest and general apathy at the end of the make shift arena. He dreaded the thought of leaving his shaded stool, and even eyed the shadowy line where the sun dared not go in desperate sadness; back in the oven. With an oof he stood and thanked his servers, nodding and smiling as he did, but tipping like an impoverished vagrant as he usually did. He brushed some crumbs out of his beard like a jaded old man hosts even older friends - with slight disgust but a minute amount of admiration for their ability to cling on this long.

As he walked back, leg still lurching, Porter was beckoned. Porter was not often beckoned, but he unmistakably did hear a beckoning. The voice rang clearly even in the cacophony that filled the dirt square, and it called his name.

Porter cast his eyes to his left, and nestled between Joan and Joan's Jewels and Long Bern's Bottling was a mess of cloth. It struck Porter like a baby bird fallen from its nest, obviously out of place and chirp chirp chirping for help.

As Porter approached the matted mess it began to unfold and from its origin a face grew. The face seemed to swell and twist, but Porter knew it was the unfolding of a many times swirled robe. Porter thought this character must be burnt to a crisp in all that fabric, and from his initial take on the figure he thought he wasn't far off.

The scent had hit Porter first, to be fair: a vague aroma of fish. Thankfully, fresh fish. Also produce. Unfortunately, rotten produce. There were more smells, some foreign like Khu'Roni spices and some familiar like soiled linen.

The face that had contorted from the middle of the graying and frayed robe had deep pools of purple beneath each blue eye, blue like streaks of light from the sky. A spotted and stubbled beard grew around the chin of the round face, and sweat stuck bangs of thin brown hair were plastered to the wrinkled fore head. A Cheshire grin full of joker teeth spotted with rot held

Porter's attention best; the smile was timeless and warm, inviting Porter in for a drink and a treat, saying I'm sorry and I love you in one fell swoop.

Hands like leather reached out for Porter, rooted fingers curling towards him, "Porter Rosset. Porter Rosset! Porter Rosset." Porter felt sweat on his brow, the heat of the day no longer being the cause of the now chilly liquid.

"I don't think I know you, sir." Porter managed, eyes dancing around him due to discomfort. He never pulled rank or felt in any way superior to his fellow man, but there was an aura to this vagabond that made Porter feel like their interaction ought to be had in private, in a cellar somewhere musty.

"No you don't, no you don't," the man said as he inched, shuffling foot in front of shuffling foot, to plead at Porter's knee, "but enough of that. Current events press us, Porter. Important things brew; seeds of sin are blooming into disarray now, as we speak!" The man had placed a sick hand on Porter's leg, and, though he hated himself for it Porter flinched away.

"I don't follow," Porter spoke in a coo, hoping to calm the man down. His ominous words created a wealth of doubt inside of Porter.

The man stood, and his height impressed Porter. Were it not for an obvious deformation in his spine that caused his head to sprout like a warp in an old tree from his chest and his thin appendages, the man could have the broad shouldered, vast stature of a Caprican. The stranger's humped back had Porter looking up at least an inch.

"Then follow."

The man whirled around, causing his dishelmed and still smelly robes to twirl under Porter's nose, and began to walk with a limp, hand digging firmly on a wooden pole that Porter hadn't seen under his robes, towards the entrance to the bazaar. Tugging up his hood he looked over his shoulder to Porter who hadn't moved a muscle. Sadness washed over the man's face as he saw on Porter's own visage the gaze that Porter was sure the traveler had seen a thousand times: sorry, man, no change today. Or the better go of it next time, eh? Or probably worse the ribbing silence that was the typical response cast down on him wherever he slept or begged.

"I know your name," the man said with a half-smile. "I just fought not three hours ago. The whole arena
knows my name as well as they have got their neighbor's opal and a muffin crammed in their pocket for tomorrow."

"I know your father's name. Podrick."

"He too was a man of Rough Bout fame, and moreover Caprican fame and valor. Mostly fame and valor...besides at your age it's possible you came up with the name first and are sore someone else fancied using it a second time."

"I know of the tattoo on your right breast, and have seen those golden horns rip through the clouds that sink on the Bastions of Tellor."

Porter wasn't sure of a clever response for that one. He was still working on the basic motor functions associated with reattaching his bottom jaw to its top.

◇◇◇

The two men sat where Porter had rallied himself to move from not twenty minutes ago, in the shade under the Marry-farm Malignant Maladies sign which swayed to and fro lightly with the breeze like an old grandfather clock's pendulum. He was, in a way, glad to be back.

Porter looked at the man as he worked on his third sweet of the day. Bits of scone tumbled in his mouth as he squint-ed his eyes at the elder chap, who so far only sat looking thrilled to have gained his audience.

"Were you planning on letting me in on the whole story of sinful garden plants and fairy tales or did you just want a better look at my beard?" Porter said as he leaned back, drank from his flagon.

"Porter Rosset, with the rapier wit and tongue as sharp as griger claw," the man chimed as he slapped his palms on the table. Porter rocked in his stool a bit when the man pole vaulted his upper body across the table. "You don't believe that they're fairy tales any more than I do."

Right to it, no time to waste then! Porter thought as he

wiped food across his face, oil mixing with oil.

"How did you know my father, hm?" Porter asked.

"I had set up a goodes shop in a pleasant, pleasant but dangerous, being-gentrified village, just near the center road on the West edge of the Bastions of Tellor, at the steeple of Mount Torn, when a man who, come to think of it-

"A small village on the West side of the Bastions of Tellor? You mean Ollette? That's on the Eastern edge, man, just the outer brim," Porter said, with great interest. Hearing what he could only assume was a mistake in the man's recounting, but was praying was something like the obscure passages in his texts. Something new to cling to.

"Ollette is lovely, pleasant as well, sure enough, but no this town was...Cleain. Right, Cleain, or was it...? It's funny, I was so busy selling ropes, hooks and pick axes to remember the name of the damn place. HAHA!" The old man guffawed, a half-dozen or so racing their heads to look at him, and then he devolved into a series of snorts as he covered his mouth in embarrassment at his outburst.

"Cleain isn't the name of any city, township, village, or even out post I've ever heard of. I won't be made to look the goat, man," Porter said as he stood to return to his demon hot, though waning in heat as the day simmered, post with his red headed captain.

"OH COME NOW," the man said as he winked and leaned closer to Porter. "No kid of the man I shared drink with would be so quick to take offense simply because he wasn't informed on the world outside his borders. Don't let your ego crash you now. Your father was a bit more enlightened than that, or humble at least. Then again, I knew him on his later travels, or so he made it sound when he spoke of his brown haired beauty and his new born son who waited patiently like a couple of Forever Frogs in a shack outside of Caprica for their adventuring old man to come back home!"

Porter sat down. When the world came to his front step like this he wished he had some of the elixir. It kept him from being so introspective, bleeding the noise of the world away. None of it now, though. Only facing the noise.

"Your father said he had traveled through the Bastions of Tellor only once when he was younger, on a bit of a coming of age of sorts, exploring the land like an elf skids rock - brazenly, and with much vigor. Pod struck me as that type of man," The traveler coughed into his sleeve, body racking, and Porter felt anxiety. He hadn't realized how gripped he was by the story until then, nor that the man had not much longer to live until he saw the bloody mucus in his sleeve when he pulled his arm away from his mouth. "Jeevers Cough. Nothing to do but to put shit in and put shit out until the reckoning, eh? HAHA!"

"I, I suppose you're right. A drink?" Porter spoke in that same coo.

"Please, please! Water would do me fine," As Porter returned with a glass the man continued. "With a bright brown beard and eyes that shone with the same wonder your father struck me like a Lorary of Light out of Khoro'Shceen!"

"Sorry?" Porter hadn't heard this turn of phrase before, but the words sounded thick and strangled, like they came from the thick and strangled accents out of the Southern city of Khu'Ron.

"Oh ho, perhaps on your travels, no? The point being that your father and I sat together and told stories at the Cleain Public House from dusk 'til dawn, and each story was easier to drink to than the last. Your father has a way of riling people up, getting their brains rolling in a way that you need to shove a stick in the spokes to get it to quit when you lay in bed at night. Do you lay up thinking, Porter? As your father caused me to?"

Porter had been doing so since he lived with his mother and father under one small, insignificant yet totally significant roof out of Marryfarm.

"No, no I sleep well most every night."

"Oh, good, second captain, that's good," the man said as he guzzled his glass of water. It splashed around his spotted skin, and when he finished a noise of distinct pleasure ran from his cracked lips, and a golden tooth shone in the dim shade.

"My father truly traveled through those mountains, then?" Porter asked, careful to ask the questions he was curious about, not the noise we often serve each other instead.

"He did, and boy did he. Your father split those mountains in twain with the adventures he set up for himself. It was like every day he knew could be the day that the Mason again stirs and that every day had the same green grass as the days of his memory, to make sure that every day was the ripest fruit on the lowest branch and to use it, damn it, really USE IT," the man pounded his palms again like a boy informed of dessert.

"Please, you'll need to quit that..." Porter began.

"Ortimer. Ortimer Bean."

"Ortimer, you saw green dragons?" Porter's stomach clenched, his chest heavy.

Ortimer smiled a dumb, wise smile as he folded his arms.

"It swooped right up our sleepy town's chimney. I had come out that day, from a bar mind you, and the wind was blowing the Golliper Stalks at the foot of the mountain so that they hummed and buzzed like hollow hornets at the mouth of a cave. Celian Yearning opened into the East on a plain with one twisty and narrow path that seemed to cut your gaze in the middle, and I enjoyed looking at the grasses sway in the wind when I was hung over so that my head felt like a furnace. I'd still give you a thousand opal that it was the same plain your father recounted looking up from that I saw the green dragon on."

Porter felt pins, needles, bee stings, sweat, bites and nips attacking his body. His hands stroked his thighs, waiting.

"Its tail was the only bit that dragged at first, sinking from the clouds like the rudder on a boat, shifting back and forth with indecision and fancy in its sway. I dropped my hood as I tilted my head back to see the bit of belly that descended dip from the clouds up almost a league ahead. In one dropping move the whole thing was there, wind caught in its great green wings. With the great motion I was rushed to my arse as it flew overhead. I thought for sure this big beast was going to crash into the small town's only watch tower, but it pulled up so quickly that I thought it more a sparrow than a drake, and heard a low boulder's tumble of a roar as it curved up into the mountainous sky line."

Ortimer reached over in front of Porter and nabbed the last bit of scone Porter was saving.

"I always feel the bard when I tell that one," he munched with a dazed look on his face.

"I don't believe it," Porter said, no pause given.

"How not? Does it not sound nearly the same as your father's tale? I thought it was uncanny!"

"No one can tell that type of story with such ease, like it didn't matter at all. No matter how artistic you take yourself for. When you speak on it, it was like you hardly cared. Who can justifiably eat a bit of scone after telling that story?"

"I can, dammit! I'm hungry, I'm dying and far more importantly I know you believe me and there are more important things to discuss," Ortimer said as he slammed his palms once again, this time in anguish, the boyishness vacant now.

Porter trapped the angsty hands under his own.

"Say I believe you, what of evil weeds?" Porter thanked his mother, for he knows he inherited no ability of subtlety from his dear old, adventuring, apparently honest, dad.

"Mock an old traveler all you want, Porter, but know that I do speak true. The city of Reprico fell how long ago now?"

"Hundreds of years ago."

"And the citizens of the West have known peace since, eh? A raiding here or a tussle there - that's good."

"Again you speak as though folks lived in some other region of land, but the Roiling Tide came across the sea to-

"Porter enough! Enough coy talk! Don't pretend that you don't already know of the villages, townships, and yes even cities of thriving people in lands just a stone throw from the Bastions of Tellor," Ortimer leaned. "And across the sea."

"I don't know that for certain," Porter spat back. "No one in Caprica believes it, no one in the West at all. Everyone here knows where man came from and where man has gone, and what happened to man when they thought it'd find itself a new home in the earth shaped by Tellor to keep us safe."

"You say 'men' as though they are the only founders, builders and owners of a community," Ortimer smiled. "You truly haven't left this country."

The Rough Bout was smaller now; the day was drawing to a close. The majority of the people had wandered away, lost interest in the stream of newts flailing like children at each other in the arid box of an arena.

"There's a reason for that, yes sir. There's truth behind locked doors and resting in dusty tomes, but perhaps you know that already." Ortimer said as he reclined, folded his arms behind his head to cause his robes to droop around his wrists.

Porter wasn't happy about the implications the man made, their blatant correctness, and was going to ask for another telling of the green dragon yarn before the crier caught his attention again with his thundering voice. The masses funneling towards the gate turned their attentive heads as the fat coordinator spoke the two names to enter the ring. Ortimer, who felt interrupted, which he was, even looked a bit dumbstruck at the sudden silence.

"SORANIN REDBELL AND LEORIC NORRIN, SORANIN REDBELL AND LEORIC NORRIN," the crier exhausted himself to his seat after calling out these momentous names.

A huge noise erupted from the crowds as they channeled themselves back to their seats, or perhaps the ones a bit more tender for viewing that evaded them before, and Porter flashed his eyes to Ortimer.

"I hope what we've discussed is true, Ortimer, because if it is and holds any real significance to you it will need to wait," Porter stood and began to head to his familiar perch at the foot of the ring where Soranin readied himself for combat.

"You'd interrupt talks and tales so important so as to tie your lineage and your country's future for a rough bout showing?" Ortimer asked, beggar's mouth bent in a quizzical frown.

Porter tossed an opal on the table and it rocked, smooth yet tilted.

"That's not all of my lineage...and Soranin is both in his own way," Porter strode away before stopping a minute later, "He's also my superior, and probably my only friend."

Chapter 6

Soranin had just swung a leg over the dilapidated ropes the arena was composed of when Porter arrived at his side.

"You're fighting the bastard?" Porter asked in between breaths. He had sort of jogged the last few steps and was amazed at the ability he had to wind himself with little to no true exercise.

"Do you have a clever notion on how I would be able not to?" Soranin asked. "And besides, it's high time someone spanked the haughty child."

Porter felt a pang of worry ripple through him, and knew that though Soranin had the grace Porter did not possess to act one emotion while experiencing another, he too probably felt that same worry as Soranin waved and smiled to the crowd around him like an actor during his ultimate performance. High in the rafters, shaded by a canopy, Porter knew the king was watching this exercise. Knew what the king's opinion meant to Soranin, and to his name.

Soranin had a practice sword, just as beaten and warped as any of the rest had been, and a shield of the same caliber, in hand. The plate adorning him shone just as it should in the sun.

From the other corner came Leoric Norrin, Captain of the King's Sword. A mat of curly red hair nearly the same color as Soranin's, but a tone lighter, a bit more straw berry blonde, sat on his head and sharp, sharkish features reigned beneath. The man was clean shaven and had a dark hue to his skin that was historically unexpected in Caprican communities; this was changing. His family knew much success in the ranks of the King's Sword, though, so there was no doubt of his origin. Whereas Soranin's huge grin lit up the darkest tavern, Leoric had a smaller, more biting smile which he wore now, in addition to his plate, as he moved to meet his opponent.

Soranin watched Leoric watch him, swinging two wooden swords at his side, then watched him walk straight to Soranin until he could smell him and their chest pieces touched.

"Leoric. You're standing a bit close, lad," Soranin mentioned as Leoric's unkind eyes looked up at the other captain.

"I'm no more lad to you as you are to me, *lad*," Leoric said. He pushed Soranin with the flats of his swords, moving the older captain back a touch. "We've finally come to find who's more suited for the job, no?"

"Your predecessors never felt the need for such cock fighting. We both lead different sorts of folks."

"Yet we are still. Both. Captains. How can that be? You are nothing more than a...a lout, a lackey, a loser, a.."

"A leader?"

"No, I lead, you are lucky to have ever been in the presence of a leader only because of your family name, old man."

"And the Norrin's are no better famed?" Soranin asked. Leoric raised his swords up to his sides as he lowered his head. "We don't need to fight, Leoric. We don't need to embarrass ourselves here in front of these people," Soranin motioned to the largest crowd of the day, roaring and hooting for sport.

Leoric smiled his tiny smile again.

"These people? These people love it! By lord they'd love it if one of us died for pity's sake. They're probably waiting in as much anticipation as I have for so long," Leoric said. Then he lunged.

Soranin's shield blocked the first double bladed strike Leoric made, but was shunted back by the force the younger man produced. It was no secret that though hot headed and brash, as he could be, Leoric exercised and trained harder than nearly any captain of the King's Sword ever had, except Valorous Van who would lay on his back with a Billy Yak firmly gripped by the horns in his hands and press it to the sky fifty times every morning before proceeding to whip each man in the King's Sword in man-dated combat. Then he would eat breakfast. Leoric was second only to Valorous Van.

Leoric grunted as he continued his attack. He leapt up and brought both blades slashing down in an arc, and as Soranin blocked those shots he struck four times more in quick succession. Soranin felt like an old brick wall in comparison to this catapult of a man, and knew what happened when brick walls were met by catapults.

Fearing the same fate, Soranin planted his back foot,

blocked another downward strike from his opponent and gave
Leoric a blow in his middle with his sword. Leoric grunted and
a fire lit in his marble eyes. Soranin feared the fire. The captains
continued their sport.

Leoric struck and struck, Soranin blocking as many as
he could but relying also on will power to keep from failing. Were
Soranin to lose to this rogue he knew the consequences; he would
lose the until now passive rivalry between the two men, he would
lose face in front of his king, and he would lose morale for his
men, his newts, and himself. He bashed Leoric in the nose with his
shield in the sliver of time it took Leoric to raise his swords above
his head. Leoric's nose mangled to the left, the crowd gasped in
one big gulp of air, and Soranin felt the need to throw up at this
immense and unprepared amount of physical exercise that his
favor of brew and age did not enjoy.

Leoric touched his nose, saw red in his hand and, like a
shark to his own blood, charged his opponent with an inspired
fury. Soranin's eyes widened; he had hoped the blow would put the
youth out of the fight. Soranin had known better, but had hoped
all the same. With age and time, hope learns to trump knowledge
so that one can get up for the day..

"You. Are. Incredibly. Boring. Old. Man." Leoric spat as
he continued to strike at Soranin, jabbing over and over like a
snake. As Soranin tired and Leoric grew more enraged at the embarrassment of his protruding nose taking on a new shape, more
of Leoric's attacks connected not with Soranin's shield but with his
shoulders, stomach and kidneys. One nasty and inevitable shot
struck Soranin's head and caused him to sway for a moment. Leoric thought he looked like a dancer at the Gilded Lilly, Khu'Ron's
most esteemed lounge.

Leoric realized it was not the time to compare his
opponent to the beautiful dancers he had the luck to enjoy once
upon a memory, but instead to wrap up the old man and put him
in a home for good.

Leoric yelled as he spun, dipping to his left but then
hitting Soranin hard in his opposite side with both of his wooden
swords. Soranin whoofed with pain, and as he readied his own
attack Leoric began to employ some of the same tactics that Ami

Trout had earlier in the day. Soranin looked fierce as he lunged his blade forward at Leoric, but the younger captain glanced the blow with one of his blades. As Soranin lunged forward, Leoric saw the chance to swing his elbow up and into the captain's chin. Leoric knew it would be the only time he'd get away with such a knavish move, otherwise he would shatter the poor chap's jaw.

Soranin's eyes widened again in disbelief, in shocking pain, feeling his skull rattle from the attack. Leoric then seized the moment to place two hard kicks into Soranin's now soundly bruised side, and Soranin fell to the earth hard. His armor clanged. Leoric panted and felt the sweat in his hair.

Placing both hands beneath him and pushing hard just like it was a push up in training, Soranin attempted to rise, but felt like he would have just as much luck raising a boulder above his head. He lay for a moment, as he could hear Leoric asking him to yield. Come on, yield. The people don't want to see you die; well maybe they do, but let's give you another day in the service of the king, eh?

So cocky, so rude, Soranin thought. He tasted dirt and blood.

"I yield." Soranin said, rolling to his back and releasing his sword from his hand, the sun mocking him from above.

Leoric's tiny smile grew as big as possible as he raised his hands above his head. In that moment it didn't matter to him that he had had the center of his face imploded by the old captain, because finally the people knew what he knew: there was only one real captain in Caprica. The other was simply a political puppet of the king.

Soranin knew some said he was indeed simply a face for the king and not of any true significance, just an artifact. He knew these narratives would become all the more pressing and that his brand new recruits would show him as much respect as one does to a dancer at the Gilded Lilly, that same Khu'Ron's club where dancing well, being encroached upon, made the job feel more important, more tangible and more needed. There wasn't any cashing out.

Nor will there be for the lesser captain.

Chapter 7

Porter watched as the man he loved to share Skell Brew with and looked to for friendship took a blow much worse than any the young man could have delivered from his swords or fists. He drank, glanced to where he had sat before. The table was empty, and he knew his curiosity regarding his father's travels, green dragons and perhaps times far worse to come would not be sated today. His body slumped.

Soranin was helped up by two newts and led towards the barracks. Leoric raised his fists higher and the crowd screamed. The distance between the two then was a gap of age and despair, growing as one figure slumped away and the other swelled in the sun filled glory.

"Soranin-

"There are three more matches today," Soranin said as he managed his way over the rope and to Porter's side. His voice was an embarrassed child's. "I had been keeping track all day, hoping against knowledge our names wouldn't come out. What say we watch the last of it in silence and head home, Porter. We can piece things together with more clarity tomorrow, as I train men and you attend to Bord's list. Like we do."

Soranin's face was bleary and big, thrashed, and his eyes were bowing. Porter nodded, kicked a wooden post. Scratched his arm.

A few organizers asked Leoric to move so the next match could begin, and when he ignored them, blatantly, one dropped a hand on his shoulder, stupidly. Leoric recoiled, shouted at them, but did make his way out of the arena as he tossed his weapons at the feet of his oppressors, in his own time. The men stooped to pick up his tools.

The two army captains spoke of nothing more serious than the declining heat while the six remaining men beat each other over the course of the following hour.

Soranin's cape followed him as he entered the barracks to gather his things before riding home to his wife and two children, and Porter watched the cape disappear into the dark building before turning to face the arena. Nearly everyone had

41

gone. All that remained were some government organizers tidying up, the fast asleep and grotesquely over fed crier who remained on his podium perhaps until the next Rough Bout, and the vendors cleaning up their wares and saddling their goods to depart. Porter thanked the sun for having nearly entirely set, and began to move through the vendors to ask what he could do to help.

Two Billy Yak, brown and white each, with long horns that were half as long as Porter, sat outside the Marryfarm Malignant Maladies booth. The older woman who had been serving him throughout the day had her back to him as she packaged away her goods. To match the Billy Yaks were two boys, one white blonde and the other brunette, who ran to and fro around their mother before she barked at them to please just pack up the last of the Stink Swamp Strudels so that they could leave. Porter looked up at the oblong eye of the nearest Billy Yak and ran his hand through its matted fur. It grumbled and snorted through a hoop pierced nose. The woman spun around and gasped in surprise at the unexpected visitor.

"Oh I'm sorry to startle you, ma'am, I-"

"Porter, right, I heard your friend say your name as he stole a bit of your Dredge Scone," the woman said with a wink.

"Friend may be a bit too, well, friendly a term for that man," Porter said as the woman showed him a sign to be brought down, the same one that had swayed over Porter earlier that day.

"You were no stranger to my stand today, any ways. Here," she tossed Porter a Dredge Scone and he caught it in his free hand. The gray green batter with Burgeon black berries made the unpleasant looking pastry one of the more excellent fares from the shop. The Billy Yaks grunted and mooed behind him. Porter laughed at their impatience.

"Thank you much, ma'am," Porter said as he crammed the sign into the back of the cart saddle designed to sit on a billy yak's back. The two boys now sat in the other billy yak's cart saddle and teased their mother for taking so long.

"You here for much longer tonight? It's been a long day for everyone. You ought to get some sleep," the woman said as she stood on her toes to place a few wrapped paper packages in the cart saddle. She placed a foot in the step cut into the cart saddle she and her boys were riding in and hoisted herself up. She brushed her long brown gray hair out of her eyes and straightened the small pastry-chef hat resembling a blossoming flower on her head, and she straightened those of her children's, too.

Porter looked up at the traveling trio thinking that he could have had not a care in the world today and still not gotten any real sleep tonight. He did have cares, though, and had not a clear mind. Their togetherness, even with the yaks, was so warm and kind that in that moment he wanted nothing more than to saddle up with them and become a husband, a father.

He scratched his arm.

"Eh, today is one of those days for me. I'll be here for a while tonight, unless those old men with the spice brew can move their asses, as good as it may taste," Porter said with a grin. "Excuse my language," as he remembered the boys.

The kids sniggered.

"No problem, they've heard me say worse," the older woman smiled, and Porter smiled back. He had a thought to ask her a pressing question.

"Ma'am, do you know much of a township called Koro'Scheen?"

"Fraid not, it's on the Northern outskirts of Khu'Ron though? I'm not too familiar with the area," she asked in turn as the Billy Yaks lifted heavy hooves and began to shamble towards the entrance gate. Porter walked at their side.

"No, it isn't."

"Is it a township out of Roiling Tide?"

"It is not, no."

"So it's in the eastern region then. You'll need to just tell me next time, Porter," she said with a tired smile.

"Oddly enough it isn't there either," Porter said in a hush.

"Where is it then?" the woman asked. The Billy Yaks began to pick up some remote speed and head through the gate.

"I wish I could tell you!" Porter called as the small troupe rambled their way down the hill and towards the city gates. As cloying a thought as it was, he saw the elderly hot brew men struggling to strap up their horses and almost falling under the weight of their cauldron, and was tugged right back into the present.

He wondered where they came from, too. In a time of uncertainty, with few truths relied upon, what makes sense? Only the togetherness of those three, and the Billy Yaks and the fact those men came at all. And how much Porter's arm itched.

Book II

"Resistance allows possibility. Possibility grants ingenuity a space to breathe. Overlords and fascists will try to suffocate you, so without resistance, we cannot breathe."

Melinda, Archive Patch 3.3.1

Chapter 1

In the midst of a burning village, scoured and ruined, a maiden fights in golden armor not hers and never would be by right against enemies unknown to her. The mace with eleven iron spikes and a leather hilt she clubbed skulls with feels awkward in her grasp, but were she to give it up she would give up any chance of seeing another human being. Long curls of brunette fling back and forth across her grime crusted face which would otherwise be a picture of elegance. Not that it needs be – her worth runs deep in her muscle and beyond what anyone could hope to see with only their eyes. She grits her teeth as she clubs, bashes, destroys.

I will find a Western city, I will persevere. A torched hut crumbles to her right and wood idols burn like angry visages of disgust. On she fights, ever slouching towards expansive, storming mountains.

The mountains acted as a shield for some and as a ceiling to others. The Western city she prays for will not take her, as it is shielded, and in the meantime the earthern monuments keep her from justice. She sees them as the only way out of her predicament, though, and troubles she did not choose.

Bash, goes her mace, into the body of an opponent. Her muscles expand and burst as she yells. Another opponent raises a sleek, blue spear over her and she ducks to the left, then with both her calloused hands she drives the head of the mace into its body and explodes the combatant. It falls, and she drags herself forward

Big black clouds roll ahead. The mountains must be

closer than they seem, she thinks, but they aren't. They are still a shield and a ceiling far away. The path out of the village, however, is just ahead. A dangerous path forward is still a path, and from the ashes any path is a good path.

Huts turn to trees, their ancestors she thinks as she walks forward. Her posture straightens, now that she has crushed her opponents for the time, and she drags the long hilted mace through the mud behind her.

Long grass and fruit bearing bushes crowd her on either side and scratch lightly against her golden plate and she smiles, thinking she has stolen her once oppressor's tools. She wields them for herself, now.

How she came to the east doesn't matter as much as why she goes to the West. How she has changed, and how the world is changing around her. The coming division. The rising tides.

Moon creeps into vision easier now as the fires fade. The blue battalion she eliminated ruined that tribal place, the cultivated culture provided to the world by farmers, lovers and leaders. All of them dead, the visages of disgust branded in the maiden's brain.

Hoots and calls come to her ears now as darkness envelops her shelled body. She lifts the mace and places it along her back, in two loops designed to hold it. Life and joy and shelter, she thinks.

This little region, called Ciur by the folks in the town she comes from, is a crop growing place. Big bushels of skell are hoisted by the brightly painted natives into crates strapped to either side of the Billy Yaks. The land provides a life to the laborers and the laborers love the land and the Billy Yaks love the laborers and when the time comes the natives strap themselves to the beasts and ride them to the mountains where they sell the skell for a fair price to merchants who take it to the West.

And the West doesn't even know where the skell comes from. The thoughtless peasants just buy the stuff. They don't meet the laborers. There isn't enough respect over there. They don't think to ask.

But the maiden isn't thinking much more about that.

She hears the brightly painted natives, now, their cries released into the aether of the nearing foothills echo-making dirt walls. The noises of the cries are not life, joy and shelter, though. She hears warbles and yawps and screams.

She grinds her teeth. Blue spears rise out of the long grass and fruit-bearing bushes on either side, now, and she knows what has happened. What is happening.

The two loops holding her mace will be empty for a while, now. She unsheathes the heavy tool and amplifies her walk to a jog, then to a run and a sprint. The tribal land comes into view. A fire burns in the center of the village, as it is supposed to, and it burns on thatched roofs and in community gardens and on brightly painted bodies, as it is not supposed to. But it does. It burns like a volcanic saber slashed the sleepy place to blackened nothing.

Blue opponents hear her cry as she charges into the clearing. They pause, surprised anyone would interrupt them. They ready themselves, recognizing her again.

They charge, dropping their prey's lifeless bodies. Some continue their pillaging, killing children and punching big holes in the bodies of farmers.

She continues her charge.

Murder ensues.

Tides are rising, storms are churning.

Porter rose a few mornings later and stretched his arms above his head in the mirror, glum by the cracking of his joints but feeling pride in his shoulder muscles still retaining their taut shape. He pondered the purple under his eyes; his sleep had been even more disturbed ever since his interaction with the would-be prophet Ortimer.

Porter hadn't believed his father had really taken any journey, and the old yarn-spinner had made it sound like a one-time ordeal - a coming of age of sorts. He couldn't much believe that one of those trips had occurred after he was born, sitting in his mother's lap in their small shack.

Porter contemplated this strain of thought amongst others as he laced up his tunic; what did Podrick Rosset really do before serving as a second captain of Caprica. Why did he care?

He arranged his armor and began to fasten it. What sent Ortimer all this way and why now? Just to recount this tale of green dragons? What items did he need to discuss with a man whom he had only heard about as an infant? Porter slammed the door and evaded Frogg on his way down the steps and into the familiar ardent sun. Finding the answers to his magmatic questions could lead him down a spiraling, lonely hole he knew he may never retreat from.

He began his walk.

The vendors in Trainer's Row were in good spirit and couldn't discern perturbed-by-thought Porter from either sleep-deprived Porter or entirely-hungover Porter. They were really three in the same today anyways.

Porter maneuvered his way into the general office and met Bord there. With his usual sense of cataclysm, Bord was scrounging up papers left and right from Ula's desk.

"Morning, Bord. How are you this fine, sunny day?" Porter asked as he winked at Ula.

"King Ernhart has five thousand, no, TEN thousand tasks for us to complete today before the chancellor of Jobelnon arrives to discuss zoning issues. Don't get me started on the Forever Frog problems we're facing in the Southern swamps, they just won't move-"

"That's what they tend to do, Bord. Nothing at all. Forever," Ula chimed in.

"Well of course but that makes the problem no more amiable! Porter, here are your tasks, I need you to go collect tax on the businesses, particularly Old Ivan's which has been quite spotty on, can we be crass enough to say, "fork up the dough" as of late, right, and to inspect watch tower regulations on the Southern wall," Bord straightened his thin collection of hairs over his liver spotted scalp and exhaled.

Ula and Porter looked at him, the moment dragging.

"AND Ula you'll need to file all of those zoning papers by tomorrow at midday or else King Ernhart will barge in here and rip my puny head off, I know he will himself," Bord seemed on the brink of folding into his robes under his own anxiety.

"Bord, old chum, we'll survive today, and I bet we'll survive tomorrow," Porter slung his arm under the sage's arm and hoisted him to his feet before following him out the door, regretting not having more of a chance to speak with Ula. He looked over his shoulder, seemed as though she had the same regret painted on her face. The Billy Yak riding trio flashed in his mind.

"Porter, I know you'll do excellent today for King Ernhart and the passion of Tellor," one of Bord's favorite lines to spit at Porter before departing for the day.

"Why thank you, Bord, but I must ask you something."

"What's that, Porter?" Bord watched his papers and straightened his small olive spectacles.

"There are no men outside of the West Lands, correct? Any attempt at a departure, the Bastions of Tellor Revolution, was squelched?"

"Right, Porter, that's true," Bord kept his gaze down still,

"Have you ever heard of a township by the name of Celian Yearning? Or Khuro'Scheen?"

For a moment, only a despicably brief one, Bord dropped his papers. His old spider fingers claimed them again before they dropped any noticeable distance, but Porter noticed all the same.

A pause.

"Porter those names are foreign to me! You have quite the imagination, but no, those must be from some old story or so."

Porter shook his head, disbelief.

"How does the city of Ollette exist? I know it seems a strange question but it is the only township in the mountains. All the others were destroyed by the army, labelled as rebellious insurgents."

Quicker responses now.

"Trading purposes, and they were grandfathered in to the West Lands."

"Meaning they were there before us?"

"No, but they did have a settlement around the same time Reprico was initiated as the first elected body, everyone knows that."

"That didn't stop the Bastions of Tellor revolutionaries from claiming that they had had citizenship there for years. And for that matter why are there books in our own library that speak to the notion that there were men in these areas before the construction of Reprico? *Tools to Explore the West Lands* suggests that-"

"I will not have this conversation again, Rosset!" Bord broke the rhythm of their talk with a bellow he thought the man couldn't produce without assistance from a war horn.

Porter was taken aback, embarrassed by the situation all of the sudden. Bord straightened his hairs and looked ill.

"I'm sorry if our brief and noble history is confusing, Porter. The peoples of this land were decently far flung and we encompassed them all in the christening of the West Lands six hundred and thirty years ago, after the tribal period, but from then on dissenting was strictly forbidden. I suggest reading *From Tide to Mountain: Seven Hundred Years of Man*. It was written by my great grandfather." Bord turned and scurried into the rising sun which hung over the courtyard of the compound. "Tellor craft your light?"

"Right, Bord, of course."

Porter watched in a state of silent amazement as the often fumbling and anxious assistant footed away towards his king. Porter scratched his beard and wondered, turned and began to walk to town. He wondered where Bord obtained his fury for this apparently sensitive subject, he wondered how much more to Bord there was to know, but mostly he wondered what he meant by "again". Porter drank and moseyed on.

Often times he felt that was all he could do. Mosey.

◇◇◇

Caprica had Trainer's Row and the king's compound on the Northern end, but it was a vast city all in all. There was the Open District on the western side, below the hill that the compound sat on and began the Northern District housing the government's crops, livestock and all of the serfs employed to tend the land. The families lived in a small semi-circle of cabins that enclosed some of the more precious crops. Porter didn't know the crops as well as he was supposed to. He went to these poor lodgings for different reasons.

If you followed Boon Street through the middle of town from the head of the quaint peon housing to the east you would find yourself in the midst of upscale apartments, grand buildings standing taller than any other in the city, and bearing an air of Caprican pride and glory not shared by those in Trainer's Row, since they peddled their goods to any and to all. This prestigious area is known by the plain name "the Block," because though there are numerous small neighborhoods and districts with combos of businesses and apartments, none are as well put together with the important glue known as capital like the Block. The Block is the largest piece of the Caprican puzzle.

On any given day one could see countless bright faced children darting in and out of the countless sweet shops and toy stores, tugging like tyrants at their parents' coats, while countless high priority Capricans walked from their homes to their works. Each morning Block natives like Arthur of Agatha's Ale, Crowley Turm, the proprietor of Turm's Tourniquets, a major distributor to the Caprican Health Ward, and Soranin Redbell, of course, would stroll amongst fellow Caprican elite and know they were home. The bell chimed for the Block, it's said.

Quite unlike any of the other quadrants on the South end lies the Strumbard. The Strumbard, with a name coming from

a fat and decrepit bard of legend who strummed a melodious tune
before burning the entire sector to a crisp in his drunken folly, is
a ravaged looking area known primarily, well, entirely, for its bars,
brothels, bestiaries and general bamboozling. The southern end of
Caprica is darker, not only because of how the sun seems to cast a
shadow on the array of charred, misshapen buildings but
also because of the deviants that inhabit the collective assortment
of public houses and hostels. Old Iron Ivan's Boarding House
neighbors Dirk's Dirks which neighbors the Caprican Public House,
and Porter needed to gather taxes from all the three of the fine
establishments in the name of the king, according to his task
sheet, Bord's favorite. Porter was thankful since his morning round
was complete and he was free to finish these errands in his simple
tunic and trousers. No need to broil today.

Porter approached the Strumbard and felt the general
haunt of the wary eyes and the reek of the pools of filth attack his
senses. This is nothing new. He feels kindred because of the itch
on his arm. The sweetness of smoke in his dreams.

Sweat pooled on his brow, he wiped with the back of
his hand and smiled a sick smile at two enormous bald men who
had posted up outside of Caprica's one and only post office. Not
many people sent mail because of the location. They eyed him
with a vacant gaze like Forever Frogs staring across a pond, only
much, much meaner. Porter noticed they were fat, but under their
fat was spring coil muscle which seemed to flex on an unknown
cadence under Usul tiger pelts that they both bore in their twin
appearance.

Porter's boots thudded in the near silence, or it would
be, spare an old woman ranting in the middle of Rein Street about
the husband she lost in Reprico, and he thought that this area of
town could make a nice tourist attraction were the denizens and
shoddy buildings not here. It would lose itself, then, though.

The history of the Southern end was explained in
Strumbard's Many Faces: The Charred City by Hurnan Hurnan,
which also contained a few suspicious lines that Porter had stumbled upon in his earlier readings. Porter thought the mentioning of
the bard, Stewart "Fat Man" Fratelle, who wore rhombus spectacles
of opal to show off all the money he didn't have, as "so large in the

stomach and so tall to perhaps be not a man at all," was notewor-
thy. Moreover, the text also spoke to the conspiracy that he was
not one who fancied pipe tobacco, nor was he a kilnsman, and if
no eyewitnesses could claim that they saw the large fellow spark
any matches to start the epic fire then how in fact did he? Porter
thought all this would make an excellent bit in a museum, but the
grungy area of Caprica was a bit too disheveled with too disheveled a clientele to house such a facility. Better to stick to what it
knew - whores and hounds.

He enjoyed Ivan's, he grinned at the sight. It had been
too long for the second captain. The doors to Old Ivan's were
remnants of the saloon that once stood in the same spot, and the
entire building still held a vibe that spoke to the frontiersman in a
city-going pedestrian stopping through for the night, or week, or
month if one had the opal. Porter stepped into the boarding house
and out of the heat.

The doors opened into a large game room, in many
sorts of the word. Heads of assorted West Lands creatures were
mounted along the walls ranging from a Moltov Wolf Mother
(Big Ivan) to a Usul Tiger (Bigger Ivan) to the enormous black and
yellow Billy Yak head that positioned itself right above the slew
of alcohol behind the bar (Biggest Ivan). Darts, cards, and a game
called Sqwees Rat wherein players bet on a rat as it darted to and
fro on a table trying to determine which hole on the corners of
the table contained a trove of Rushlove cheese, one of the city's
favorite dairy goods, and which had a starved cat with a bit of
cheese tied around its neck, enough to baffle the rodent. Bets flew
in day and night.

This new mouse, dubbed Little Henry by some of the
regulars, has lasted eight rounds.

Porter asked the girl working the bar if she would have
Ivan come downstairs, as it was commonplace for the owner to be
upstairs having some type of inappropriate interaction with one of
the guests. The young girl with startling green eyes said she would
be right back down. Porter sat at the bar and looked back at the
glob of men shouting after Little Henry. He made it past his ninth
round!

Cool whiskey slid down Porter's throat as Ivan came

down the stairs.

If the bald brutish men outside had been large and intimidating, Ivan was death itself in a long brown duster. He squeezed his enormous frame behind the counter and the girl who had been washing out a glass covered her nose and maneuvered away from the bar, finding work elsewhere; Ivan always smelled like a tender combination of a young woman's perfume and Lagoona rum, which smelled something like a beach and a trash repository. The bleary eyed, black mustachioed stack of muscles placed both of his forearms on the table in front of Porter and raised his head.

"Tax man today?" he spoke in a slow, Khu'roni drawl.

"Tax man today," Porter said.

Ivan smiled as his head lulled around his neck; he was drunk, and for a man his size to be this drunk Porter knew he had been drinking straight since last night. People said Ivan was a bit more bear than man, and his big paws swept up another bottle before making any attempt at producing overdue funds. He swigged.

"Your king never gives me a break, you know," Ivan said. "Damn near every night," he said every in three syllables, "a King's Swan comes to my door and says my Sqwees Rat is rigged, and that gambling is illegal, and that housing criminals is illegal."

Ivan quoted illegal and rigged in the air with fingers that looked like blood sausages.

"Those activities are, of course, illegal," Porter replied.

"In Caprica maybe, in Khu'Ron we..."

"You are no longer operating out of Khu'Ron, Ivan. I am sure King Ernhart is just as regretful about this fact as you and me."

Ivan slammed his hands on the table. The bar became quiet. Little Henry froze, and a Rushlove cheese adorned cat darted out of the furthest hole on the table and gobbled up Little Henry in the silence.

"You will not speak with any authority in my hostel. You will not have your taxes," Ivan again quoted in the air, even though Khu'Ron also collected taxes on its establishments, "and according to my sources Caprica-"

Ivan was interrupted.

Porter thought it sad considering the misty, drunk rant
had just begun to peak. Two black haired twins wearing
foreign looking sashes covering their chests only had entered the
downstairs of the hostel, saloon. A blanket covered both of their
lower halves as they stood hip to hip. They beckoned for their
house sized hostel owner to come upstairs and to pay the tax man
already. Ivan frowned and glared at Porter. He pushed a diseased
looking wad of tax forms and a cloth bag of opal and blue towards
him.
     "Have a good afternoon, second captain, and get the
fuck out."
     Porter collected his items and turned for the door,
remarking to himself something about Little Henry's ill begotten
fate.
     "Oh, second captain," Ivan called, halfway up the stairs.
Porter turned.
     "You won't be needing to come here for root anytime
soon."
     "Ivan don't be foolish, man," Porter smiled. "Root isn't at
play here."
     "Enjoy the opal, tax man," Ivan threw up a paw and
marched upstairs.
     Porter itched his arm and pushed through the now gate
keeper's saloon doors on his way out.

The day was less muggy as it trudged on and Porter thought so far it had been a rather lackluster one. Bord and Ivan had, in their own unique ways, given him the dick end of things and he was hoping his interaction at Dirk's Dirks would go smoother. Just a few feet away and in a much smaller building, he embarked on the second leg of his tasks.

A little bell rung as Porter opened the door. It made him think of the morning bell that roused him each morning, which made him reminisce on his hang over, which made him almost barf. Hundreds of glittering blades brought him back to the present, and Dirk was, unlike Ivan, working the front counter of the rare, quaint establishment.

Dirk's Dirks was one of the few well-kept businesses in Strumbard, and were Dirk a little straighter with his taxes and a lot straighter with his shady dealings, he would probably find himself subsidized by King Ernhart in the Block, or at least in Trainer's Row. He keeps things shady on purpose though, the second captain thought.

Porter fingered a few small knives as the short, pasty man in the red vest moved over to him. Dirk Clearsby's great-grandfather had moved to Caprica right after the Fall of Reprico, being one of the few to predict when the government would meet its end (folks knew a colluding political group had laid plans for ruin) and had set up his shop in what was at the time an enterprising location. Again, had he enterprised in actually selling weaponry instead of housing thieves and supplying thugs with deadly items off the books for a bit of extra opal, he would have been one of Caprica's premiere entrepreneurs. Dirk's tufts of gray hair shot out from under his green cap with a short brim like goofy, storybook cannon fire. He lit up when he recognized Porter.

"Taxes today, right? No problem at all. Porter, Porter! How are you any ways?" Dirk said as he rushed back to shuffle some papers into cabinets. Dirk was the type of man who complimented with simple, cliché phrases but seemed to mean them every time.

"Oh I'm hanging in there, Dirk," something about his desperate attempt to shield himself from legal harm made Porter think of him like a Rough Bout newt.

"Drink?"

"It's early isn't it?" Dirk said.

"Hasn't stopped us before, eh Dirk?" Porter and Dirk laughed as Porter screwed off the top of his flask. Dirk brought out two glasses from an ice chest and they shared some brew. Porter thought it was nice they could interact like gentlemen even though they knew their occupations could have Dirk darting around Porter to supply arms to those who would thief and vandalize. Porter had to keep tabs on the shop owner to make sure he didn't supply goods to another Fall of Reprico. He had to make sure the kind old man didn't lead to his demise.

"Much to do today, Porter?" Dirk said as he cleaned up the glasses.

"Not much. Old Bord has got me collecting taxes and investigating some Forever Frogs. Prize stuff." Porter said.

"Your father thought Forever Frogs might be the stupidest creatures in all of the West Lands," Dirk said with a laugh. Dirk knew Pod from when he was a younger man; Pod had collected Dirk's taxes and even arrested him once during an ugly little scrap between Dirk and a travelling knife salesman.

"How well did you know my father?" Porter couldn't seem to help the transparency since his interaction with Ortimer, asking the questions he had been asking himself with different pronouns.

"Your father and I were well acquainted after that shifty vagabond tried to gut me," Dirk said. "And I defended myself and my livelihood in proper."

Dirk straightened his vest over his white buttoned shirt.

"Ha, I've heard your side Dirk," Porter said. "But did you ever hear any from my father? Anything that ever seemed a bit extra-ordinary?"

"Hrm," Dirk chewed his thoughts like a child chewed a bit of gum. "He often went on about green dragons," Porter expected this, "and there was one night when he came in, piss drunk, and went on and on and on about King Ernhart and the captain of his army keeping him down, and oppressing the good men and such."

"Sorry?" Porter asked.

"I really couldn't tell you what he meant, Porter, he was quite inebriated, but it sounded like he was upset at the faculty of his army all the way up to the king. He also broke my lock coming in here, the dang fool. But I do miss him."

Porter placed a hand on his chest, over his tattoo

Podrick had been gone since before Porter entered the army, when Porter was 17-years-old. He had been on a routine visit to Jobelnon, but nobody saw him for nearly a month's time. A couple of young newts said they found his body in a park on a sunny day, cause of death unknown. He left Porter with a career, a collection of unpopular theories and a tattoo. And a shack.

Dirk recovered himself. The two hard drinkers had been allies in their debauchery.

"Did you agree with Pops? About men beyond the Bastions?"

Dirk lost himself again, seemed dumbstruck.

"You can't be serious! Men came here on the Roiling Tide, Porter, come on now. You'd better be off on your errands, rather than chasing rum diaries written by your dad," Dirk had regained his composure.

Porter thought he had seemed alarmed, decided he must have drunk too fast, apologized for his abruptness, excused himself. He considered what Ortimer had said about "men" settling the city-state, tossing it in his mind again and again. Dirk watched the door close and breathed a sigh of relief.

Last on his list, and adjacent, was the Caprican Public House. There was no question the Caprican Public House was the place in town for a drink, a date or a clue. Porter was always struck by the lack of merriment. He knows at night it comes alive with the spirit of adult indulgence, the spirit of people too sour to behave with childlike glee in their day-to-day life who finally let loose and behave like they ought to for the evening. Throw in the usual drunkards and deviants with a dash of broken bones and broken promises and you capture the character of the Caprican Public House.

By night, though. Right now, late afternoon coming on evening, the narrow and long and musky bar was quiet except for the light din of conversation between the some-odd fifteen familiars enjoying fare and drinks. Porter needed to see Olaf Reir, a Caprican native who inherited this place from his father and he from his; the timeless story often recounted in Caprican lore of a family line operating in one post. Privilege begets privilege.

The difference in the CPH was that Caprican royalty offered to place the pub under subsidy and make it "a proper eatery and dispenser of good drink." Said royalty being the first Ernhart king, Dorigin, but the eldest Reir at the time, Olaf the First, denied him, claiming just because he bent the knee didn't mean he would kiss the ass.

Porter asked for Olaf, and the second green eyed server of the day scuttled off to find him, this one being much older and much less a girl. Thine the Bartender seemingly worked day in and day out, and was known for his eyes which matched the delicacies that beset the table: pickled olives. Porter sat and reflected on his stool. It seemed that since his interaction with Ortimer his concerns regarding the questions of his father, his stories and the possible world outside of his own had been injected with a sense of impeding importance, an imperative for the moment. He thought it was possible this was because someone seemed to understand a bit of where he was coming from and could even elaborate. Soranin never could have entertained the notion of underhandedness within the government, and it occurred to Porter then that he had no one else he even would have talked to about it. Perhaps Ula, but he only liked her, he didn't know her. There's a difference.

"Porter!" a voice bellowed as thundering footsteps fell. Thine, already large, was dwarfed by Olaf. Thine was straight, Olaf sloped. Ivan was muscles, Olaf was fat. But Olaf was still bigger than either of the men, and had a giant and sprawling yellow beard to match the nest of yellow hair that tangled from underneath a simple brown cap.

Thick black glasses rested on his small nose and pointed ears. He resembled a giant, or so Porter imagined one, mixed with an elf. The green button shirt, stained by grease and sweat, was hardly seen from beneath his big white apron. Olaf was the head cook and brewmaster at the CPH, as had Olaf before him and

Olaf before him. His malt and yak's yeast sour is a centuries-old regional symbol of pride.

"Olaf, man it is good to see you," Porter said as the men clapped each other on the back.

"And you, son of Podrick. Pork belly? A crepe? Maybe two of each? Har har! You do look thin though!" Olaf was like an elder who almost faints when they hear you haven't had anything to eat yet. Olaf gestured to Thine to bring out some sausages and a crepe. The cook quickly lay three fatty bits of pig into a thin crepe and wrap it around three sausages, wiping the oil off the plate for a particularly neat meal. Porter sighed, knowing he couldn't resist as Olaf smiled like a conniving grandparent and pushed the steaming plate towards him. Porter quite enjoyed collecting taxes from the public house.

"Thanks much, Olaf," Porter said as he cut into the crepe. Little vessels of grease exploded onto the plate.

"I ought to give you more for making you come down here again," Olaf said in turn. "Times have been hard. Ish."

He began to rummage for money in a chest underneath the counter. Thine rubbed his hands and watched Porter eat, and this made Porter quite uncomfortable. Olaf noticed this and shooed Thine to the back, reminding him of tasks that were more important than being "a creepy old hag". Thine hobbled away.

"Aren't they every time I come down, Olaf? One of these times, times ought to be as good as they seem," Porter said with a wink. "I hear business down here is as good as ever!"

"Perhaps the previous umpteen times I have been late on taxes you would be right, Porter, but truly. Caprica feels shallow lately, like...like the peace before a crash. Not so peaceful."

Porter's gut tightened, Olaf noticed his squeamishness.

"Something the matter?" Olaf asked.

"I suppose not, but I have had similar feelings, Olaf. What makes you think so?" Porter dug into his crepe again, careful not to splatter on his shirt.

"Eh, the town has seen less travelers as of late."

"The Rough Bout had quite the turn out."

"The Rough Bout, of course, but a bigger rough bout means a people with a greater blood lust, no?" Olaf smiled, "Perhaps the common folk still come around, but the Strumbard has been dead for weeks. Less people are in and out like they usually are, coming into the neighborhood for a drink or two before heading back to Jobelnon, Ollette or what have you."

"It wouldn't be too odd if you knew," a thick voice called from behind Porter, "what they know. And what I know. And what I tried to tell you, Porter."

Ortimer sat in the shallow light behind Porter, legs crossed, a smile spread wide, rotting teeth decrepit as putrification peeking behind bird thin lips. Porter wasn't sure how he had missed him, but he was undeniably present in his blue and black robes.

"Olaf you'll need to give me a moment. We'll continue later?" Porter said as he took the money Olaf had collected in a pouch for him.

"You come in any time, Porter. I will make you a mountain of eggs, eh?"

Olaf clapped him on the back again and slid into the back kitchen, resuming his yelling at Thine for nearly ruining his meal with Porter.

Porter took a swig of his ale, Agatha's today, and sat down across from Ortimer at a long table crafted to host a feast. It was just the two at the table. Porter missed the enticing smell of his pork sausage crepe now as his olfactory senses had been assaulted by Ortimer's aberrant funk. Moldy cheese, where the little bubbles of fungus have grown too large, Porter thought, or something even worse.

"I thought you had moved on, Ortimer," Porter said. "I'm sorry to have left you at the bout, but when duty "

"Spare me, Second Captain." Ortimer said with a shocking bite. Porter was taken aback, but as soon as the venomous attitude had come, it went. Porter assumed Ortimer had been drinking and decided to give him a free one, considering he had lost track of the traveler after their conversation. "Besides," Ortimer said with a familiar crocodile grin, "where would I have gone? Roiling Tide's fish are belly up, I've come from Jobelnon, and I don't think I would have found you in either of those fine cities."

"Why did you want to find me?"

"We aren't done talking."

"I've heard your stories, Ortimer."

"About your father, yes," Ortimer reclined on the bench, "I want you to know I'm a good man and of the same feather as you, Porter, but I do not mean to swap tales with you like I did with your father. It's because of his stories, leading me to you, that I feel like I can tell you that I've brought a warning."

Porter's suspicious and looming feelings flooded his mind again, and he wanted to reset his life to the morning bell ringing on some other morning when he had not begun to worry and think of things better left untouched by a second captain. Then he remembered that such a day had never truly existed for him. He wanted to blow into oblivion, not thinking of the past or the future. Sunny days in the vines, please. With the haze.

"What warning do you bring, Ortimer?" Porter meant to come off as condescending to the man, remind him that he would not be had for the goat.

"You needn't be so proud, Porter. Let me remind you that I am on your side," Ortimer responded as he swept his hands out in front of him.

"Let's hear it then," Porter said.

He tried his best to remain cool, his heart kicking and his mind clipping. The future and the past together at once.

Ortimer's demeanor thickened like concrete, and Porter could have sworn he felt the temperature drop.

"I believe it is safe to say we both understand that there are peoples beyond the West Lands."

"Ortimer-

"Enough, Porter, let your questions stew for a moment. Now, in the East, past the Bastions of Tellor by a good forty leagues, is the Erchinon Reef. The Reef is not too unlike these West Lands. It is composed of cities, townships, and villages, but where the West Lands deny the existence of anything past its well-kept borders, the Reef men are learned in their knowledge of the world."

"What do you mean?"

"They have cartographers, they have sailors, they've got sciences your people here will perhaps never grasp. Willful ignorance is stifling, since that's the point. Their quest for progress is unrelenting, and has brought them a paradise of culture, wealth and infrastructure. Their soils are not as forgiving as the West Lands' noble pastures, Porter, and they have become lean like their world demanded, trimming the fat of ignorance and peddle pushing from their people."

Porter wished for a distraction to mitigate the onslaught of revelation. Olaf provided: it was four sausages this time, in a crepe a bit crispier, less chewy. Ortimer kept on.

"In their refining of resources and mixing of potions, they began to tinker with the very world they lived upon. They discovered wealths of an energy known as azulana"

"Sorry?" The word sounded slow like a drum beat to Porter and rang in his ears the same.

"Azulana. It is a fuel from the land sourced from the furnaces deep inside which churn and roll to power this world. The Erchinion people have discovered a source of power that grants them strength like they were gods. No sword can break it. No shield defends against it. The power is unbounding and inde-finable," Ortimer said. "Though gods they are not."

Porter was not dumbstruck, a bit of sausage clinging to his beard. Dumbstruck is too simple.

"This recent unearthing was at first another techno-logical marvel for the people of the Reef, beautiful in its divine ways like Atorus' spells or the two-toned Oroki people," Ortimer went on, speaking of notions Porter had not encountered in even the more delirious conspiracies he read in the texts at the library. Porter wondered not for the first time if he was being strung along. But he was, in his layers of shame, an optimist.

"Alas the gluttons of the Erchinon Reef were not finished. They began to toy with the azulana further, arming them-selves with great machines to destroy and to conquer. Average sol-diers gained new skills and abilities from the mana, and the people of the Reef wondered why the weaponizing was necessary. Though the Reef has known battle, it has known it little in the present era," Ortimer began to cough, racking his cloth frame. It stirred Porter from his captivated gaze; he noticed he had eaten all of his crepe. Porter asked for a glass of water for the old storyteller.

Thine brought over a glass and Ortimer drank deep,

wiping blood from his dirty hands onto his dirty robes. Thine stood over Porter's shoulder. Porter sighed at the lackey's remarkable ability to be unpleasant in appearance and behavior at the same time.

"I haven't spoken for this long since I campaigned to allow trolls a seat at the voting table in the town of Gurin! HA HA!" Ortimer had regained some of his familiar character. Porter thought it was sad that it was only in the face of weakness and a painful death Ortimer found a resurgence of joy. Porter smiled and asked Thine to bring them some chips and a bit of mustard dip.

Porter noticed it was getting late and he needed to be on his way. Ortimer had lost his drive to preach once the food had arrived, destroying his basket of fried goods, lathering each bit of potato with the creamy sauce of ground mustard seed. He left traces in his short stubble.

"Ortimer, I'm having a hard time believing all this, as believing a fellow as I am on these fronts, but we do need to continue," Porter was thinking aloud considering Ortimer was nourishing himself and not paying Porter any mind.

"Ortimer. I'm sorry, I do appreciate your time, but I'm going to be on my way now."

"Deny deny deny," Ortimer muttered between bites. "You do a lot of that, don't you?"

"I'm not," Porter began, swallowed. "I'm not sure I know what you mean."

"How much opal went to Frogg this month, and how much went to Ivan?"

The second captain was afraid of the traveler's knowledge. He wanted to escape to his sacred desires, but decided to plunge into this instead of his older habits:

"Then join me on my last errand? I need to take a jaunt over to the watch towers here on the wall to make sure everything is up to snuff. A bit of beauracracy, but not my place to question. Interested?"

Ortimer looked up with a few forlorn fries hanging from his mouth.

"Shmounds gudth," swallows. "Though it is always your place, to question."

Chapter 4

The two men left the pub after being comped the meals
by Olaf. Their boots thudded in time on the dirt, the sun setting
behind a watch tower away to the West.

"So azulana is dangerous?" Porter asked.

"Not by nature, not necessarily, but the eight that control the realms of the Reef decided it was important to pressure
the scientists to harness it as such before anyone else could. They
couldn't know how other humans, or the elves, or tengös would
use it against them."

"Elves? Tengös? Are you joking me, man?"

Ortimer looked at him for a moment, now the dumbstruck one.

"Porter these neighboring mountains of yours are composed almost entirely of non-human peoples. You knew that."

"Ortimer, old man, I didn't. And don't," Porter said with a
shrug and a swig from his flask. The sense of doom was put on ice
whenever Porter drank. He decided that it wasn't a proper reason
to drink more, but he did anyways. That's how he got by when
he was young and his mother's name would float into the Rosset
shed. Porter rounded the corner past the public house and saw
dead ahead the purple door to the entrance of the watch tower.
The watchtowers, as many as there were, sat in a near perfect
circle around the borders of Caprica. Only the Ernhart castle had
proper walls, the city was instead protected by a series of smaller
walls, gates and the omnipresent watch towers.

Each watchtower was built of the same white stone as
the castle, but was much less grand in appearance. The roofs were
topped with a purple shingling and had windows adorned just
below that ran around the entire circumference of the structure.
A watch room sat inside the upper most set of windows, a small
armory and disaster house in the basement for any calls to arms
that may occur, and a winding spiral stair case ran the length of
the tall building. Porter began his ascent up the stairs, with Ortimer
chatting behind him the whole way.

"The use of azulana as a weapon was not the root
of the problem. It was the over consumption, the hoarding and

raping from the land," Ortimer continued. "The azulana is nearly all gone. And many died in the making, in the reaping."

Porter's air of pseudo-drunken confidence was perturbed by this comment.

"Heh, why is that the source of their problem, old man?"

"The people of the Reef are going to have their azulana, they decided, all eight of them who deem themselves the noble rulers and protectors," Ortimer spit on the crude gray steps. "And they have released their azulana-infused army upon their own townships and villages, harvesting all the energy that they could down to the last bit."

The two twilight figures climbed in quiet for a time.

"Their greed is infinite, Porter. They plan to move on the West Lands."

Porter stopped, hand on the door to the inner watch room. The door swung open, Porter teetered.

"Hello sir! Here for inspections I take it?"

A young watchman saluted Porter and did his best to cast a balance of chipper and stalwart. Porter felt sick.

"At ease. Let's see your logs and have a man send me up your inventory list on rations and arms," Porter said, the entire luster from the ale gone. He didn't want to drink any more. He scratched his arm.

"Of course, sir," the man hurried away, eyeing Ortimer's bloody sleeves as he passed down the stairs. He had left his logs on the watchtowers observations for the past three weeks out on a small wooden table facing the most forward window, the one looking down on the road leading to Khu'Ron. The two men sat in silence at the table. Ortimer stared at Porter as he flicked through the logs, attempting to get his mind straight.

The seventh of the month. Four travelers for the audience of the king, sighted from Marryfarm. Containing three jars of Hopejule Jam, eighteen-

"Porter, what do you think?"

The sixteenth of the month. A small family for the audience of the king; sighted from Marryfarm. Containing-

"Porter there is azulana in these lands, under this tower, and they mean to clutch it in their disgusting little paws, they-"

The twentieth of the month. One man from-

"Porter, come now!"

Porter shuttered the papers in his hands. Like Ortimer had slammed his hands at the Rough Bout, Porter was losing it.

"I know you're sick, Ortimer, but we have healers-"

"No, Porter. Their razing of their own lands is coming to an end. There are only a few weeks now until they'll have wrung every last drop from the Reef. They've scoured the coast, the foothills and beneath every home in the now ruined cities they claim in their own empire. Their council will meet soon to finalize the move: the council of eight will plot the sacking of the Bastions of Tellor and the West Lands, and in their zealotry, consume all."

The sun was doing a poor job of lighting the room they sat in. Porter rose and approached a cabinet, and with now shaky hands fumbled through the contents for matches to light a hanging lantern. Porter felt no warmth from the fire as he raised it to the wick, and the light that shone seemed to do little to illuminate the room.

Porter steadied his breath, exhaled, ran a hand through his hair.

"What proof is there?"

"What?" Ortimer said.

Porter sat down again. He was trying his best to remain calm. Playing cool was again his go to tactic.

"Ortimer let's say I am on board with your notion there are men outside of the West Lands-"

"My notion," he harrumphed. "Porter there is no time to play coy, I said. And not just men."

"Let's say it true, then!" Porter raised his voice, "What proof have you got? What proof do you bring of men living in a way so as to bring about the ruin of this...world." Porter adjusted his speech, now discussing lands outside his own. Conspiracy becoming reality invited some conversational awkwardness, he found.

"There's proof enough in the West Lands of the powerful ruining the people's lands in the name of expansion. The Erchinon's cancerous growth is tenfold this greed. Isn't that enough?"

Ortimer looked at Porter straight on, and Porter felt like

he was playing the part that Ortimer expected him to, like a child cast as a tree in a school play. Porter felt about as important as one too.

The stranger removed his hood. Etched into Ortimer's neck was a riven of ink, a dark blue marking. The patterns cut jaggedly in three short lines that met below his left ear, and from there a single, thin line ran along his neck and into his cloak. It seemed to pulsate, the ruinous fluid, in time with Ortimer's somewhat shallow breath. A thing both mechanical and visceral.

"I come from the Erchinon Reef, Porter," Ortimer hacked blood into his sleeve. "And have made my bed with azulana, as have many. To harness it, one takes the energy into one's self, and as the people find a port of energy the azulana has found its conduit. Azulana on its own does nothing but spirals around like a wisp. It takes spirit and soul to hone it, to give it life."

Porter didn't understand, and asked what this meant so far as weaponizing was concerned. It seemed natural, not combative.

"Each person has a way with it – it is an innate ballet. You cannot understand the azulana until you have felt it deep in your body, and if it has not been thick in you like that it cannot make sense."

Porter wanted to know more; Ortimer told him that even now little was known of how azulana worked and what limits it had. The intrinsic collaborations kept evolving.

"Porter these questions are as important as what shoes to wear to a barefoot convention, don't you see?" Porter saw the man didn't mean to spend these precious moments delving into the sciences of the land he left behind.

"You'll need to act. And soon."

The time had slipped away and a young newt came exploding through the door, with the same uneasy mixture of chipperness and stoutness that young soldiers assumed they need to have to interact with an officer:

"Inventories, sir!"

With his mind in fifty strange places, Porter perused the list of rations and stocked arms before muttering how it seemed fine and then handing it back to the lad.

"You don't mean to check yourself, sir?" the boy asked, looking up and down between Porter and the list he had scrutinized for ten minutes before mustering the courage to interrupt his superior and his guest.

"No, I do not, and your logs are just ship shape, lad. This is watchtower seven?"

"Eight, sir," the boy squeaked.

Good, then. Keep up the proper standings," Porter said, patted the boy on his shoulder, and he and Ortimer left. The boy didn't know how their inspection went, but the cool way Second Captain Porter just didn't care about him made him long to be a second captain himself one day.

"What would you have me do, Ortimer? You've rung me like a bell with all this. Tellor, I meant only to collect taxes and inspect a damn tower," Porter said as he half-jogged down the steps. He and Ortimer burst into the street, Ortimer doing his best to match pace.

"Porter...Porter wait!" Ortimer was coughing quick now, like a mad bark, and Porter knew he had lost his manners in his flurry of thoughts.

"I'm sorry, Ortimer," Porter placed a hand on his shoulder. "I'm just a man, you know? It was only until today that I thought, truly, my notions of fantasy were only that." Porter was lying, a bit, and he thought Ortimer knew regardless.

He did.

"Porter you need to stop this ransacking before it begins," Ortimer said. The only light provided for the duo came from the lanterns of the awakening businesses in the Strumbard, which was now a bit more alive with music and the stink of drink. "And I do not mean simply the azulana. Think of your life, of your legacy. Of your father's legacy."

"How?" Porter asked. People began to mingle around the duo, bumping and jostling.

"The council has not yet met to declare the army's movement; there is a gap of time now," Ortimer's voice above the heads of passerbys. "This is why I've come, Porter. I knew there was a man in the West Lands yet who could rally his people. Who could be the ambassador. The bridge. I knew it because of your father."

"That again?" Porter asked.

"Your father was an enlightened man. Men as versed in the world as him pass over the mountains only a few times in a generation of man. I remember him speaking of his son, with the green dragon tattoo on his breast, and I knew that if the fracturing and harvesting of the world were to be stopped it would be stopped by you."

Porter didn't take himself much for a hero. He glanced at his hip flask, but he saw Ortimer's eyes. In between strangers, his were piercing and needy, less a sage and more an expectant student.

"Right, that's a good thought. What should I do, Ortim-er?"

"You'll need to travel to the Erchinon Reef, Porter. Speak with the council now. Infinite growth in a finite place, it can't work. Remind them of this lesson, or find yourself, and the good-intentioned folks of the West Lands, a new home."

"Home," Porter muttered. His sun hat dream, the shack, the rows and rows of his father's plants. There were times when that felt like home, but it was a wide word. It's meaning was out in the mythological abyss that Ortimer told him about, but it was also Caprica. Somewhere in the middle.

"How am I to do this, Ortimer? What would you have me do?" Porter couldn't seem to relay to Ortimer that he possessed, really, no ability to act. At this thought, Porter was sad. His hands slowly fell from their emphatic perch above his head, where he had had them when he was questioning the old man.

"I ask you think of yourself and what you can do, today. What you can do for your certainties, the ones your father spoke of and the ones I come to you to confirm."

Porter was exhausted by this verbal battery on his mind. It only led his hopes and dreams into a sense of urgency, which only lead to a real sense of urgency, which only lead to his current state of insecurity. What he needed was time to think.

"Ortimer, I need to retire. I desperately need to rest. We'll council tomorrow," Porter turned to march up the road to the Dermio Building.

"Porter," Ortimer called from a few paces behind. Porter turned to meet his stoney gaze.

"Remember what I've said. Do not deny your past. Do not deny your future. But do NOT deny your present. Quit going in a middling circle."

"I heard you, man, I heard you," Porter marched. Ortimer watched him go, hoping he would be proven right in his choosing of a vassal to breach the Reef. The old man looked at the stars and counted them one by one as he looked for a cozy looking alley way. The stars favored Ortimer, he thought. The gods, too. One of the eight surely must.

Her body is worn and bloody and ready still. Unreadiness is apathy is death. These lessons have been taught to her by family and by time. She trusts both, though the latter is her experience and she knows truth lies always in her life, body.

The path narrows as it becomes noonday. Enemies are unheard and unseen so she decides to practice breath, bringing herself to the thoughts she chooses. Her mind focuses as her feet carry her forward.

She was born in the year 998, just before the Great Leap, and on that day a starry bird crested the night sky. Her mother had seen it, and had known it was a sort of falcon, great and twig bearing and powerful and poised. It was made of dust and numbers and this made it all the more spiritual, better to be born under. The Great Leap, the turning of millennia to millennia, was going to usher in a vision of tranquility for her people. Her people were not unlike those to the West, she was told.

Fathers being what they often are, it wasn't shocking to the maiden to see her father four times in her life. And four times only; their town had great need of him, she's told. She is told many things, but her experience understands the starry falcon to be more real than these excuses and unkindnesses.

Beyond the upcoming hill she hears the crashing of trees, splitting and timbering. A war machine, she imagines. On and on, because physical or otherwise industrious kinds have assaulted her with war machines for all her years now. And she was born in 998.

The first time she saw her father was her second birthday. He had been fighting in the West Lands, in the foothills, for her people, on the frontline, a hero. He had fought there in years before and is somewhere fighting now. So she's told.

When she was thirteen, he came again. Her mother had been sitting on the porch watching the maiden, still very much a maiden, run to the tree in the yard and back, tree and back, tree and back. He had approached like a boar rooting for truffles, he had come to their home very drunk. He had tossed her a sword and her mother had yelped. Not a scream because she was not surprised.

The maiden had taken the sword in surprise. Her father had stood there, breathing heavy, like a big beast hoping for its prey to twitter. Then he eased, wilted, and asked his daughter to strike it against his own blade, a well-paid for rapier, as if nothing in the world mattered. To strike with ease. She obliged, and they clashed metal for an hour.

Rolling noises plow the earth around her now, tank treads pushing earth into flat space. They are led and formed by the mind of a creative thug. The world rewards these kinds. The maiden does not like them much because they tend to be manipulated by creative kingpins.

When the maiden was eighteen she saw her father again. She was an apprentice in a smithery, working every day to create tools for homemakers and weapons for assassins. He had come into her shop, and she had not known he knew where she worked. He tossed her a blade and she clanged it against his for an hour, two, three, and it became a past time of hers once again.

Fires licked the town where she grew up the fourth time her father made an appearance. Their home with the tree in the yard was ash and logs. The center of town was a white and blue church-like building with a bell and forty or so citizens of Koro'Scheen squirmed and cried in the low light of terror. She was twenty-one; it was just a few months back.

He had come into the town center with his beard blooming and his eyes swarming. The maiden and her mother were alarmed when he approached them. He had told them the enemy was cruel and would not spare them, women or no. He had told them the city had failed and ingenuity had gone awry. He had told them that he was wrong.

Grabbing the maiden's hand, he led her away from her mother and toward the rear of the town center, a storeroom. There wasn't any time, a much worse case than "there's no time," and he couldn't stop himself from locking the door behind him. He was too afraid. The maiden didn't see her mother again. She had been a lovely woman.

Big black curtains covered boxes and paintings and notebooks. They were draped to keep the dust out, and now were dusty reminders of civility, when picnics and bazaars were reality instead of massacre and chaos. But they always co-existed. Just not in the privilege of temperance is that duality examined.

A tall black curtain became her father's focus and he pulled it back to reveal a display case. In the display case was golden plate. It was brilliant and holy and grandiose and enormous, a complete set. A suit of armor made for the titans of war. It had been worn by a paladin, and her father had said she needed to wear it. He had told her that he would wear his chain mail, her this powerful relic, and that they would escape on the old road to the Gorbish Mountains.

A mortar the size and shape of a yule log catapulted through the window, destroying the display case. The maiden became alive and began to dress in the plate, seeing it was far too big for her. A mortar the size and shape of an oak sapling careened into the roof of the town center and knocked the roof down on the huddling citizenry in the other room. After brief yelling and grunting the maiden knew they had died – noises of pain are not creative, often recycled.

She moved to unlock the door, silent still, and her father grabbed her shoulders; he had told her to keep suiting the armor. There wasn't any time. She suited the armor. Heard the noises and winced.

The noises began to near the door, the locked one, and another yule log sized projectile blew through the wall. Wicked villains clawed through the walls now, and her father was screaming. He smelled like fear, too, like shame and a void of hope.

A ball of iron with spikes, held on the end of a stick, probed the hole created by the most recent cannon fire. The maiden placed a protected hand around the exposed stick and pulled it to her, strong, and she heard the head of her attacker slap the exterior wall. The mace was longer than she anticipated, and heavier, yet she is realistic before she is worrisome and knew she needed the thing and she clutched it to her new golden carapace.

Attackers came into the building and killed her father. He died as he lived, unavailable and difficult to pin down. She killed her first that day, and she did it so she could move through the opening and into paradise. It was a black, fuming majesty but coming from a grave hell it isn't hard to craft heaven.

He had been wrong; he was right about that. As she cried a few quick tears and heaved the weapon which she claimed away from her home, the town destroyed and crushed under its own aged structures, now tumbling into trash, she thought of when she was a girl, at thirteen.

Striking steel against steel as though nothing mattered was foolish, naïve, ignorant and lazy. Real strength could not be mustered this way. It was too lackadaisical. Striking steel against steel as if everything mattered was the only way to wield power. When she attacked the invaders this is how she swung, like her freedom swung with her, depended on her. As it depends on everything we do. Nothing is meaningless.

War machines pitching yule log and sapling-sized death are just over the hill and she grits her teeth and goes to meet them. It isn't the life she wanted. She wanted to be a smith. The lords watching her gave her a new identity, one she uses to persevere and to kill.

Porter hadn't turned into work the next day, or the next or the next. The first morning Porter had gone to the Caprica Public House to find Ortimer but couldn't. After an hour of scouring the alleys behind Ivan's, near the watch tower and even ruffling every spare bundle of cloth, which Ortimer seemed to have an uncanny ability to look like when he wasn't moving, Porter gave up and returned to the darkness of his home and mind. It had been three days of pacing his apartment, breaking the home arrest only to watch the sun go down from his floor patio. He drank to feel alive, which is ironic because drinking may as well be bottled death. He questioned himself and his history, identity. The second day Ula was sent from the gate house by Bord to make sure that Porter was alright; this made Porter feel even worse. Even more sunk. His arms itched.

He questioned Ortimer. He glared at his green dragon tattoo. It seemed to taunt him with promise of legitimate fulfillment. It was the third night that really captured Porter's thoughts.

As Porter approached his drawer that contained the all too used wooden cup for which he intended to pour another drink he asked himself when he began to use drinking not as a communicative lubricant or to appreciate a warm moment but as a thick tree trunk to crash his head against. He cried then, sat on the bed, screaming questions against the rear mirror of his forehead. Porter stared at the floor and knew that he couldn't do this much longer. The plan was forming.

He ran it over in his head again: Porter wanted to leave Caprica in search of a quenching of his wanderlust, exploring the past. Porter felt Ortimer's stories were believable judging by Porter's own inward beliefs on the matters discussed, based on his past. Porter had identified a short list in his alcohol infused insomnia of these obstacles:

1. An important post and duties in Caprica he would be noticed absent from.
2. No knowledge of how to get to Erchinon Reef.
3. A deep concern that not a single person in the West Lands

would not brand him a loon, sack him, ridicule him, and if these stories were true then all of them would proceed to be slaughtered in a tyrannical foreign kingdom's quest for plunder. Also no one would go with him, not to mention he had no supplies, provisions, cooking goods...

Porter figured the first two issues could be handled when need be. His post would seem insignificant to the good people of the city when he explained the direness of the scenario, and once he made it to Ollette, which he believed to be the true gate to the world. Apologies to Jobelnon, but for Porter it was also the gate to his ultimate destination. It was the last point that kept the second captain awake for more than seventy hours and kept him quenching not his wanderlust but his vice.

Porter rose like a marble statue cracking out of its skin and put the cup in the top drawer of his cabinet.

What have I got to lose if it is true? Porter hadn't posed this particular question to himself yet, but he liked it. *Really, if blue rune-hungry peoples do come to the West Lands and start tearing things up then what have any of us got to lose? Be in the moment, man, kick Bord in the opals and buy out Malignant Maladies with all the money you would have paid Frogg over the next fifteen years.* He paused, deciding that that wasn't where he intended the strain of thought to go.

Ortimer's parting words came to him for the fiftieth time. Porter knew of no one in the city who could or would aid him, not really, but he did have Soranin. He decided it was worth trying to pierce the veil, to throw caution to the wind and try and rally Soranin to his cause. If he couldn't convince Soranin, then it would be nearly a lost cause. Ho doubted his ability to face any perils on the trek alone, and he wasn't sure he could muster the courage to travel to a distant land scarred and scoured by renegade azulana hoarders with help or without.

Porter blew out his candle. He realized that though he had drunk enough to drown a Roiling Tide marlin, which is funny since it's a fish, he had eaten only a bit of stale bread from a few weeks ago which he uncovered next to his stores of Agatha's Ale. Upon this realization he fell backwards, his body collapsing hard into one of those positions that will really jack your neck up the next morning, and then he fell asleep.

He dreamt about Ortimer, his rotten teeth illuminated like Caprican suns stained blue with the magic in his neck. Ortimer smiled and smiled, his face growing larger as Porter shrunk. Then blood seeped from between his teeth. Ortimer's head began to roll in on itself like a ghastly wheel until only blood poured out like a spout. Ortimer's raucous laugh still stung Porter's mind when he woke the next morning.

Afternoon, but functionally the same.

He thanked Tellor he had slept through the damn morning bell.

Porter realized it was so late he had missed his window to speak with Soranin at the compound - he would need to go to his house in the Block. Porter slapped on his tunic and breeches from a few days ago and hurried out the door. The Caprican sun bore on him as it always did, but today it seemed to amplify the sense of urgent haste that he had been feeling. His conversation with Ortimer had solidified the feeling into an unfortunate reality.

What have you got to lose now, Porter? Porter thought. Perhaps this could be a good thing for him.

Perhaps. Arm itch.

He always felt uncomfortable as the dusty path the Dermio Building was on began to morph into Keane Road, the dusty trail becoming a polished and paved by-way for business and family. Porter was a second captain, but being a bachelor and a bit eccentric with his tastes of literature and coping, he, and the residents of the Block, knew how he stuck out in their home like a criminal who's already confessed.

The wonderful scents did entice him, though, more than anything. They began to hit him as soon as the buildings also transformed into the premier institutes that the Block deserved; smells of farrowberry and Hopejule jam, light honeys with dark black notes, Urgent Usul Tiger pizza pies roasting on a fire, the cries of popping cheese bubbles and thickly salted meats letting their juices run, and even the less-aromatic, visually flooring flower boutiques tickled his fancy with their pleasing arrangements of Reprico's Heart and Delilah Stag being put on the sill for display.

If the Rough Bout distracted Porter from his missions by means
of sensory overload then the Block took Porter's senses hostage,
bound and gagged them, and offered no means of ransom until
touch, taste, sight, aural and olfactory had been all treated to a day
in the Block's finest establishments.

He straightened his gaze away from the flower shops
and pizza carts and the singular Caprican Loans and Bonds Building with its glittering opal doors, with ingots of lesser currencies
like blue and dove, and to the street itself. 888 Keane Road. The
Redbell residence, Porter had to remind himself as women laughing inside a nearby café did nothing to assist him with his focus.

Porter saw the enormous consort of houses at the end
of the merchant area. On his left and on his right the fronts of
stores turned into green lawns, decorated with miniature statues
of kings and queens, horses and cows and Billy Yaks. Well only
one house had a Billy Yak statue, and the thing was enormous and
though Porter had little design skills he thought that particular
statue really threw off the nice aesthetic these folk had otherwise
cultivated.

But who was he to judge? He continued.

The Redbell home wasn't far down from where the
homes began, and it was plain to see which home was Soranin's
even if 888 Keane Road was not laid in gold on the side walk in
front of the place. The house was big. Bigger than Dirk's Dirks, as
large as the Caprican Public House and seeming as large as a
watch tower. The home was painted a cherry red and farrowberry
lay in three pots along the sill of the porch, upon which sat two
rocking chairs with red seat cushions. In between the two chairs
was a table, and on the table was a displayed bottle of Skell.

Upon seeing the table and the nice bottle, passerbys
and visitors, like Porter, would see the enormous red bell of wood
placed above a set of windows on the second story. A Caprican
bell was inlaid upon the larger symbol.

An enormous black hound came bounding from the
back side of the house, braying as a small girl with intense red hair
chased the much more threatening dog.

Now that's the picture of a Block home, Porter thought.
He waved to the girl who had fallen down to catch her breath, the

dog sat by her side until she did so, protecting.

Porter clasped the golden knocker on the door and rapped the door three times, waited, knocked again.

A young lady, not as young as the one in the yard but with the same intense red hair, answered the door. She had a book in one hand, If You Were Meant to Catch Me, a popular young adult's novel about a handsome criminal who seduces their beautiful assailant, and a bit of scone in her mouth. Unknown purple jam sat on the corners of her mouth, her eyes went wide.

"Prowell!" She swallowed. "Oh my, father!"

The girl dashed away.

Porter smiled. He had met the girl at a royal dinner that they had all attended when she was young. She was still young, but they had all been younger then, so it's important.

Soranin was dressed in a tunic and breeches not different than the ones Porter wore; it was common garb for royal men in Caprica to wear a simple white shirt and brown pants when nothing is required of them for the afternoon. Soranin grinned, the grin faded into worry and a bit of a stern fathering look, but back into a grin like an elastic band.

"We need to talk?" Soranin asked as he came to the door.

"Please, on the porch?"

"Did you see my-"

"I did, Soranin."

"Vintage bottle," Soranin beamed. He was so proud, so very in love with it.

The two sat in the rocking chairs and, as per usual in the Block, had a terrific view of the passing by squads of children playing, young couples with their bouncing babes, and even, just to paint the picture, Porter imagined, a travelling pie cart with "pies so good it's a-pie-lling." Porter wasn't a fan of the older pie salesman's wit.

"Bord says you've been AWOL for days," Soranin said. He poured them drinks.

"Bord always was the astute observer. I've had a hard time sleeping," Porter said. "And really, far more important things have come to my attention." Porter decided not to pussy foot around the issue, or mention his recent activities ,to help him get right to the thick of it. He thought he would probably not be poured his drink if he did.

"More important than Bord the Wise's endless task list from hell?" Soranin winked.

"More important than Bord's dastardly list, my post as second captain, your post as captain and perhaps more threatening the entire armed force of Caprica," Porter said.

Soranin set his drink down.

"Alright, what is it?"

Porter inhaled deep. What have you got to lose?

"Some man came to me, and told me crazy things. He also old me a few important things, and a lot of bizarre things," Porter eyed the drink Soranin had poured him, hesitated, then indulged in a small sip of the brew. Spicy.

"He told me of lands beyond the Bastions of Tellor with folks in them, and more than that he spoke of those who mean to bring about ruin to the West Lands."

"That's a bit of a revolutionary story, don't you think?" Soranin asked, a small Leoric-esque smile spreading on his lips.

Porter sighed, knowing it wouldn't be easy to convince Soranin of anything. There was an accepted truth and history and wrenching it around is never a popular pastime. He wanted to convey his point to Soranin, to people who could help him, without being shunned for lunacy. His father taught him one lesson well.

"I know it's a bit ridiculous on the surface, but-"

"Didn't you read *From Tide to Mountain: Seven Hundred Years of Man* when you were a boy, Porter? There are no men, or anything else, over those mountains," Soranin said down his nose, drinking his draught.

"What about Ollette?" Porter asked. "And I said folks."

"It was too old to be moved, and they have excellent soil in those mountains."

"Neither of those statements make a whole lot of sense, Soranin. How could the township be older than Caprica, or Reprico? And the Bastions of Tellor are mountainous, not tillable for Caprican crops by even a third generation Marryfarm farmer,"

Porter retorted, not wanting to play a game of facts with Soranin but, knowing the old codger, it could be his only leverage point.

"Your city's library references Ollette being amongst the first townships settled beyond Roiling Tide by men who set out to the east when the ark first landed."

"So if men never meant to go into the mountains, a subject made clear by our stringent zoning regulations, why did these initial scouts venture there and set up shop, a scouting expedition which was approved by King Huin of Reprico? If Ollette is considered so old as to be grandfathered in, exempted of taxes, and all around an artifact of such why isn't Roiling Tide, the West Lands actual first city, also revered as such?" Porter was becoming a bit excited, and Soranin was eyeing him over his drink. Porter swept his hand through his hair.

The sun sat high over the Block.

"What's this all about, Porter? You take it upon yourself to untangle a well-tangled history, now?" Soranin spoke away from him, looking across his yard. "I ought to be offended."

"The man who I spoke to-"

"A complete stranger."

"Right," Porter said, a bit quieter than normal. "The stranger did raise some interesting points, and spin some yarns," Porter decided to not include Soranin on the fables of his father, since by challenging hundreds of years of accepted knowledge of a cherished land he was already freaking out his respected friend. "But mostly it was the bit about a horde of powerful people assaulting the West Lands. The risk! It'd be irresponsible-"

"Irresponsible? Irresponsible is wasting my damn time," Soranin said, his voice raising like he was giving a speech to the city's new soldiers. "A risk means a possibility of something bad, and since there is no possibility that there are any other folk past the-"

"Soranin, you're a learned man, you must also realize that we at the bare minimum haven't been told everything there is to be told about West Lands history."

Soranin shifted in his seat.

His wife came out, a kind and smart woman, and asked if they would like any cheese and crackers, just brought in from the artisan deli Capricanica down the street. Porter said he was fine, Soranin remained silent. The air between them was uncomfortable, as it had been when Soranin lost to Leoric in that dusty arena.

"We should address Bord with this, if you're serious," Soranin remarked after a while.

"I don't believe the news would fall on kind ears with Bord," Porter said, remembering the uncharacteristic implosion of old Bord not long ago.

"What is your plan, then?"

"I hadn't thought past bringing it to you, oh noble captain," Porter said with a wink.

Soranin relaxed. Smiled. Grinned.

"Alright Porter, look. I don't know about any of this, truly I don't know if you've lost it or what, but if you think it's best to slide past Bord then the only person to slide to would be King Ernhart himself," Soranin said. "I warn, though, now isn't the best of times. It would be best to wait a week or so to-"

"According to my most reputable of sources," Porter interjected. "Time is a luxury we have not been afforded. At all."

Porter explained the Erchinon Reef's council of eight and their, well, counciling. Soranin was silent again, with less awkwardness, more thought.

"What time is it?"

"I'd say halfway into the afternoon, not sure," Porter said.

"We can't half-ass this, Porter," Soranin said.

What have you got to lose? Porter thought.

"Let's see the king," Soranin finished his drink.

Chapter 8

King Kalan Ernhart, fourth ruler in the Ernhart dynasty, whose family started their political career as the first official town criers in Reprico during better days, is known for his charity. The Ernharts as a family are known for their generosity. The Ernharts, it is said, have been the kindest rulers the West Lands have ever seen.

Now, granted, their family may sit the throne and rule the entirety of the West Lands, true, but each city has its own ruler - a minister who answers to the king but rules their city. In Khu'Ron there is Janstel Intop who is known for his fishy odor and for his incredible ability to demonstrate zero care for anything except the finest olives. In Roiling Tide there is Gregor Mousit, a thin and ancient man, who is known for shivering like a rodent and answering citizen's questions with either complaints or more questions. Lastly, ruling in Jobelnon is Frederik Doro who is known as "the hot one" in the West Lands, but has no brains to match his beauty.

In the West Lands King Ernhart is known as the ruler who will listen, who will care and who will tend to your every need as though he were a hotel concierge, "and in his own castle!" it is often said. King Ernhart then spends most of his time travelling the West Lands, or hosting citizens, and spending quality, almost paternal time. This serves as a good memory of how the Ernharts catered to refugees after the Fall of Reprico, circa 736.

King Ernhart is known to till farrowberry in Marryfarm every harvest season, meditate with the monks in the Green District in Jobelnon and even embark on brief fishing voyages from Roiling Tide to pull marlins once every three years. His nobility knows no bounds, and a story even swears he once saw a woman struggling to the front of a crowd to witness his passing through the roads of Jobelnon whereupon he hopped off his horse, assisted her to the front of the crowd, then provided her a horse and gave the unkempt fan a job keeping records in the library in Caprica.

He is, most agree, like Tellor come to live amongst his disciples.

Porter and Soranin reached the front gate and were cleared for entry. Porter thought King Ernhart was an admirable fellow, too. He only interacted with him here and there, but liked him. Soranin did most of the speaking with the king, so his relationship with King Ernhart felt the same as anyone else's. He thought the king had a marvelous smile and that it must be an enormous boon for moments when a common folk looks up to their king as he rides through town. "Golden souls. They got golden souls," Podrick would repeat.

Soranin had a very close relationship with the king and, though he didn't pour on about him, he knew the king was a good man and very much valued their friendship. It was through this, and through his reputation for kindness, that Porter hoped to make a plan of action with his king.

The two companions approached the foot of the Tower of Indecision. The king saw guests in a parley room in a wing of the library, but this was after hours, and it was Soranin. The king and he were close enough for this type of meeting, he confirmed. Soranin assured him it would be fine.

Soranin knocked on the front door, a golden wooden hulk. A young attendant at the door asked what business the men had with King Ernhart. Soranin told the man they had private and pressing news. The attendant was stalwart in his belief that the king would not want to be bothered with the zoning issues he was facing today, but visibly flinched when Soranin reminded the attendant who the hell he was speaking to.

The bell and hammer on the boy's chest darted out of their sight when the two men stepped inside the enormous first level. Porter saw books upon books and much art he would never understand. Soranin on the other hand elbowed Porter at the sight of statues crafted by Ion the Slow, carvings by Derrik the Motley and paintings by Walter the Titled. Walter was a bit avant garde. The men walked up the stairs.

The staircase went on and on, and Porter almost regretted coming. Soranin continued a flow of conversation which Porter was sure was a combination of genuine interest in the impressive building and at the same time an attempt to lighten the burden of this affair, which was good of him since after all it was Porter who pushed him to come. Porter watched the stairs, looking into each sprawling room they arrived in to see more works of culture and rows of windows that looked out upon forever.

The last flight of steps had an inlaid ornate purple rug, and the rug ran up to the door at the end of the stairs and encompassed it. All the stairs prior to this had simply fed into the next observatory like room, but the last room had a plain looking wooden door. A gold knocker was on it, and a simple knob. Soranin exhaled and looked at Porter, rapped the knocker twice.

Porter felt time stretch into a thin crepe.

A man opened the door. The man had tundra sky blue eyes, and a short nose. A beard of salt and pepper and hair to match, both very thick. He was a man's man, and hiding behind his white tunic and brown pants were two black haired boys that proved he was a father as well. A spicy scent rolled down the stairs and out of the room.

The king seemed shocked by the arrival of the men, eyes open wide in alarm, but his presence softened and a wide grin spread on his face. He embraced Soranin and stuck his hand out to Porter.

"Porter Rosset, we haven't spoken in a very long time," the king's voice was soft and warm.

"Yes, your majesty, I apologize for bothering you during what I can only assume is dinner."

"If it's Soranin who brings you here, I am sure it is a worthy cause."

"Actually sire, it is I who needed Soranin ths night."

"Please come in," King Ernhart stepped out of the way, smiling at his sons as they ran off into the eighth floor. Porter marveled at how different this floor was, a well-equipped kitchen, with a well-equipped queen cooking in it, and a stuffed Wool Bear in the den. A crackling fire roasted in front of an Usul tiger pelt, and this floor seemed to have numerous rooms beyond the field of view to boot.

The queen turned and smiled at her guests who were busy undoing their laced shoes. The king was caught in a laughing conversation with Soranin, and Porter smiled back at the queen. Queen Sarah Ernhart, the Apple of Caprica, who had no real duties other than to support her husband and rear her children. She excelled at both, and both were real duties. Porter was struck by how she made Porter feel like a rickety old chair by how alive she seemed to be. It didn't even matter that her midnight black hair and that honey yellow eyes were the most fantastic things Porter had seen on a human being, except perhaps Olaf's beer swollen stomach; it just mattered how much she was there. How much of now she had in her pocket. She invited Porter over.

"You're Porter Rosset, correct?" Her voice was smooth like her eyes. Porter was easily overwhelmed by beauty. He crumpled, and he wished he were king for a day, then.

"Yes, your majesty. Podrick Rosset was my father."

"Porter," she touched his arm as her other hand tossed the leafy greens in a wooden dish. "We're not enjoying pleasantries. Call me Sarah."

"Sarah, that's fine," Porter realized his ineptitude. "What are you making for dinner, then, Sarah?"

Fish sizzled in a pan while she dressed the salad.

"Roiling Tide trout with nuts and a little slaw of greens. It's all from the castle, not the fish of course, but the nuts and the vegetables," her eyes tried to be kind and meet Porter, but she was intent on preparing a meal for her family.

"That sounds divine, Sarah."

"Well you'll have to tell me what it tastes like, not just what it sounds like."

"Oh we can't stay for dinner," Porter said.

"Maybe you can't, but I surely can, if Sarah is cooking that is! Not this old foagie!" Soranin hollered from the den. The king laughed, as did Sarah, both of them in the nicest not-too loud but thought it was the funniest thing they'd ever heard or so they'll make you think kind of way. Golden souls indeed.

Porter moved to the den to see that everyone but him understood it was now time for food. Porter didn't complain; he could smell Hopejule jam in the kitchen. That citrus, bright smell like flowers bred with just-baked cookies slays Porter each time. He hoped dessert was on the menu.

Porter and Soranin sat next to each other with one black haired youth on his left, and the remaining three Ernharts across from them. Sarah set the table; the silverware was goldware in reality, each one bearing the bell and hammer on its end. Porter and Soranin bit into their fish, smiled at their plates, and plowed on. The king smiled; a tight man but one of tact, a thin smile..

"Mother, this food is delicious," the boy on Porter's left said.

"Thank you, mother," the boy on the king's right echoed.

"Thank you, boys. There's milk from Marryfarm in the fridge for dessert," Sarah said, stopping her fork a moment away from her lips. "Chocolate."

"What interests have you got, Porter?" The king asked.

"Oh, nothing to remark on, sire. I read, er, I enjoy reading."

"Oh, reading is to knowledge as eating is to health, no?"

"Certainly, no doubt." Soranin interjected.

It was quiet for a moment.

"So," the king continued. "What brings you both here tonight?"

Porter gulped too loud, not due to the general trope of uncomfort, but due to a too big piece of trout. Soranin took point.

"Porter has had some strange news from a traveler."

"Oh?" The king was cutting his salad; Sarah was smiling at Porter. She had kissing lips. Porter felt like he was twelve-years-old.

"It was a man from the east," Porter said.

"Oh, Jobelnon?" the king said in turn.

"No, he claimed he was from the Erchinon Reef."

"Sorry?" The king's eyes remained fixed on his food; he was struggling with spearing a nut on his fork.

"The man claimed that he came from the other side of the mountains, a place called the Erchinon Reef. He said it is as large as the West Lands, it's own thriving land," Porter tried to explain the best he could beneath his self-imposed pressure.

The two boys made faces at each other. The king chewed.

"There isn't anything but the Bastions of Tellor," The king said with a smile after a pause. He looked at the two men with his smile displayed, then helped himself to more trout.

"I said the same thing, sir," Soranin said. "Porter seemed rather convinced though, and I thought if it were a pressing issue he'd better see you and be done with it."

"Why not speak with Bord first? You know how he titters about any new task to burden himself with," the king joked.

"The topic certainly struck a nerve with Bord," Porter said. "He said I was daft and to read-

"*From Tide to Mountain: Seven Hundred Years of Man.* Written by his great-grandfather," the king said.

"Right, of course a good text, but not the only speaking on the history of the West Lands," Porter said, striking the untapped resource of confidence. Sans alcohol it became harder to mine.

He lifted his fork as he kept on.

"*The Bastions of Tellor Mountains: A Complete Text* actually has some information on tall men who assisted some youth from the Bastions of Tellor revolutionaries during the government's culling of those peoples."

"Tall men? Have you read *Kings and Keeps* by James Roilin?" Sarah interjected.

"Right. Tall men could mean anything," Soranin said as he ate his fish, looking to and from the broad window to his left. "The trout is great, Sarah."

"I've read all the history texts our library has to offer," Porter reminded. "I'm saying some had more to say than others."

"By their merit, they had some nonsensical stories provided by little boys, the sons of a foolish group of rogues?" the king had a small smile as he spoke. Soranin and Sarah laughed. Porter felt uncomfortable, fidgeting his toes in the decrepit ends of his boots.

"We can't count this vagabond's story as definite truth, sire, but it may be well to send a party to Ollette, perhaps," Soranin spoke through a mouth of roasted plumb beets, grown by the peasants on the West side of the city and brought each day to the steps of the Tower of Indecision. Sarah used these plumb beets as often as she could, because she believed local ingredients tend to make good locals. It was a local campaign of hers.

"I'm saying I believe there is more than-" Porter began, feeling the need to cut the fat out of their conversation, but the king raised his hand.

"Sarah would you take Marrik and Jeren to the periscope? The sun will be going down soon and I know they wanted to show you where each township was," he ruffled his older son's hair. "And maybe this one can finally spot a village or two, eh?"

"I pointed out Vian last time! AND Welleron," the older boy's voice warbled like a bird caught by a cat.

"In the middle of dinner, Kalan?" Sarah asked, looking across the nice smelling spread.

"Sarah," the king looked intense, softened, smiled. Sarah offered a weak smile and asked her children to join her on the balcony.

The door closed in a hush. The three men sat in silence, Soranin helping himself to another serving of seasoned fish. Steam rose from a bowl of mashed potatoes.

"Soranin, how long have we known one another - like this I mean," Kalan Ernhart asked. Each word seemed pointed.

"My lord I've been a captain for-"

"No, Soranin, since we've been close. Perhaps the first time you came over for dinner. When we first shared drinks together," the man drank his frothy brew.

"At least fourteen years, sire."

"Did I give you the impression somewhere along the road that you were welcome to drop by my home whenever it suited your interest?" The king's smile was gone, replaced with a thin, stretched look of scorn. His eyes were as pointed as his words, shooting at Soranin who sat with food caught turning in his mouth.

The captain swallowed in the wake. Porter was aware of a change in atmosphere, a pressurized thing. The king's silverware sat in his clenched fists upright like soldiers in his army.

"My lord?" Soranin asked.

"You're right, let me rephrase," the king stood, his chair making a ruckus as it shot back into the kitchen. "When did I give you the impression you were welcome to come to my home, hell the Tower of Indecision at all, entirely on your own frolic and to bring this peon of a second captain, whereupon you would both hope to spout entire heresy at my dinner table and into the young ears of my sons?"

Porter looked to Soranin, to the impressive and imposing statue of their king, and back again. Soranin was incredulous.

"Sire, I thought it would be best to put this matter to
rest and to-"

"Be," the king interrupted, shouting. "Quiet, Redbell. You
have only made yourself out to be the goat yet again. I thought
Leoric's handiwork would have silenced your niceties in my presence for a bit but I see that you are too proud even for that."

Soranin's eyes were ghosts, and he was as white as
one. He rose. He sat down again. Ernhart kept his pointed gaze on
him until he was sure the captain would be of no more trouble. He
swiveled his leer to Porter.

"When did you see this 'traveler'?" It was a question,
but it felt like an accusation. Porter thought it could have been just
a harsh inquiry. It wasn't until King Ernhart barked his question
again, knocked over his glass, that Porter understood it was an
interrogation.

"This last week, sire," Porter moused out his answer with
much less bravado than he had hoped.

"Why have you brought this to Soranin's attention?"

"I was told to go to the East to dissuade the men who
rule there from attacking our lands," Porter felt like he was in
school again, being reprimanded and yanked at the ear to tell the
truth.

"What makes you think you're a big enough man to
fly in the face of hundreds of years of history, and in front of my
family?"

"I didn't mean to harm anyone. Nor the proud history of
this city and the West Lands. I was hoping only for your clarity on
this issue."

"You believe there is more than the Bastions of Tellor
then?" The king crossed his arms. Smiled a thin facade.

"I-I do sir. Sire. I mean. I've always had my thoughts, my
father's thoughts, but-"

"Your father was a loon."

"Excuse me, my liege?" Porter boiled, angry and confused.

"Your father ruled under my father, and my father gave your raving old dad his position mostly out of amusement," the king began walking around his kitchen, drawing curtains on his family gazing out of their telescope. "He was drunk at least half the time, and would never shut the hell up about the wild things he'd seen over the mountains. It was a good thing he was drunk, too, or else people might have actually believed him."

Porter gripped the bottom of the table like he gripped his axe. Soranin sat in silence. His fish had gotten cold. The king's eyes were much less kind than they'd been, and he was employing his tact with none of the familiar warmth Porter had seen him use for his Capricans.

"My father knew how to keep your father's stories so ridiculous to the public they would never believer him - he just gave your father access to spirits during the day, and night. Podrick Rosset was oiled with sly drinks by his comrades day in and day out, and was extended invites by the Caprican Public House near every night. This was no accident. King Kalan Ernhart the third, my dad, and Captain Sero Redbell, Soranin's dad, played your dad's vices like orchestra."

The king paused his tirade and an enormous grin broke out of his face. He laughed.

"Look at us! Shadows of our fathers, the next generation! Making the same. Damn. Mistakes." The king walked around the table and smashed the untouched drink from in front of Porter away.

Porter stood, so did Soranin, both unsure of what the unstable man they called their sovereign ruler would do next.

"Your dad was a broken fool and so are you!" The king spat his words into Porter's face. "IF I NEEDED TO I'D DO THE SAME THING MY FATHER DID AND SLANDER YOUR NAME IN THIS TOWN. DO YOU UNDERSTAND? DRAG YOU THROUGH THE MUD!"

At these words the bearded man gestured for Porter's head and mimed, dragging it through floating mud in the air. He smiled an angry, primitive smile that showed his teeth like a challenging ape.

"I'd say it would drive your wife away too, Porter, but clearly you haven't got the stones for one of those. Does all the

alcohol make you limp, and quick? Maybe that's why your mom
left your dad, eh?" The king dropped this fit of assault and walked
back to his seat, sat down and took a drink as he slicked his hair
back.

Porter shook.

"Your father was a bloody drunk, and a fool," Porter was
ready to pummel this most esteemed man, "but as foolish as he
was he was damn smart. Like father like son, eh Porter? Except you
smoke the root yourself, not quite as smart as dad, hm?"

The king swirled his drink at the second captain. Porter
stood tense. Then the king seemed to think of something else
and reclined in his chair. He sighed like all the breath in him was
leaving for good, a universe of possible plots exhaling.

"I won't ruin your reputation, Rosset. Nor you, Soranin.
It seems as though the other reigning captain did so well enough,
any ways."

Soranin looked away, entirely regretting having left his
home at all today. It was his day off, after all.

"I won't, yet. Sit down."

The men eased into their seats, shoulders crunched
back. The king repositioned himself and faced them both. Then he
clapped three times, giving each one both power and time

"There's an Erchinon Reef, sure," Porter forgot about the
character change, the hateful words. Now he was piqued. Even
Soranin looked back to his lord. "The Ernharts knew as soon as
they were elected to power there would be no more rioting and
revolting in the West Lands, no. Reprico fell because of "progres-
sive thinkers" like yourself, Porter. No, my great great-grandfather
set into motion the Ernhart's most glittering act; a slow altering,
generation by generation, of the way we remembered this land."

"Do you know how Reprico fell? I doubt it, maybe not
Porter but at least you, wasteful old man," Kalan said as he gestured
toward Soranin. "Redbell, Tellor knows if your siblings had clam-
bered to the womb before you I may have been given someone
more capable to work with."

Neither Soranin nor Porter could muster the strength
to interrupt this tyrant during his hateful spewing, or perhaps they
both hoped their king would change moods just as quick as when

his family left the room.

"There had been the royal family in Reprico, the Aladashes, and they ruled for two generations. Reprico was a city of white brick, like Caprica, but grander. A prosperous vision of Tellor's work. So gorgeous, his inspiration was felt even in the sidewalks. So gorgeous that men from the Erchinon Reef were inspired to come study, live in the city. A group of policy changers formed, men who sought change in this land like they had back home, and it was these people who became Group F," the king drank. "Group F is the group who revolutionized the people. They destroyed the city."

Porter had read it was a greedy political coup, and through their misdoings the people rose up against them. In the conflict between rulers and rulees the city was destroyed, and the people elected the Ernharts and Caprica as a democratic city-state to rule. Porter was completely unaware of any Group F.

"It's no mistake that no history texts speak of Group F," the king spoke like he had peeped inside Porter's head. "Because mentioning an unruly group creates an unruly group. When Dorigin Ernhart was aiding people out of the city he would lead Group F members to a separate camp, a camp for foreigners. It was unbeknownst to them that they were being led to a separate camp, see."

The sun had gone down, but, due to the king's barking and shouting, his family knew to stay at the periscope.

"My great-great-grandfather beheaded each member of this group, except for when the baskets became heavy, then they would feed the trouble makers to the tigers. Their eastern ideas, like mechanizing and community-shared ruling, existed only in their heads," the king tapped his temple as he spoke. "So it made sense to remove those heads. Collective ownership and no gerry-mandering into zones. Tiger food."

Soranin looked sick. Porter was sick, choked it down.

"Was Caprica not elected by the people to lead, then?" Soranin asked. Porter noticed he had finished his flagon of Skell Brew.

Golden soul glared at him.

"It was, Soranin, and it's true Khu'ron, Jobelnon and Roil-

ing Tide have their ministers, sure. But Caprica has the people's hearts. Caprica has the king. And Caprica has the army, the war machines and the money," the king smiled his new smile. "Besides, democracy is only as democratic as money says it is, no? Dorigin Ernhart was not foolish, as his more patriotic running
mates proved, and did not leave the election to people's votes. The numbers were swept right under the rug, just as were a bounty of other undesired tid bits. How many proxy voters my family enlisted, for example. No one will ever know if Caprica was meant to rule or not. But who am I to boast."

The king seemed to Porter like a maverick flame of his former self, one who could stab Porter through the neck or pass him the mashed potatoes depending on his fancy. An intelligent but capricious power.

"As soon as Caprica was raised to Reprico's former glory, the movements began. The men from the east could never implant their notions in our West Lands again, right? No king coming to power wants to think, 'Maybe I'll get assassinated and my city sacked like that Repricoan fool.' No, a king demands control. Seizes it. But how to best address the concern?"

"The notion was simple; there are no East Lands, no Erchinon Reef, no Group F. There is nothing but dry, dangerous lands in the mountains. There is only bark in the Ennabon forest," the king polished off his drink.

"Bord's grandfather came up with it during a dinner in this room. Better dinner guests, eh?"

The king slapped Soranin's arm to prove his depressing point. Soranin recoiled, frightened. Ruination runs as thick as blood. He was learning.

"The West Lands. That is what you've got. Sweet farmers. And bright eyed bakers. And salty fishermen. Good, Tellor-loving folk. It didn't take long with the systematic omitting of any books saying otherwise, the publishing of government periodicals, the institutionalizing in school and the defamation of anyone speaking against the crown."

"When you've got all the power, all the money, and all the reason it isn't hard to make a truth into a lunacy; it just takes time."

The king looked at Porter for a response to his mono-loguing. Porter was quiet like one of Ivan's doomed mice, trapped and confused. Porter thought he could bash in the king's brain with the salad fork and proceed to beat his body into something that resembled the mashed potatoes. He decided against it.

"Why did so many have to die?" Porter asked.

"Some remnants of Group F had to go, no? My grand-father's men bet how many foreigners would be in their midst as they destroyed the pitiful shacks they called homes. It's funny, there weren't any. Only West Lands folk, though they had had help from Ollette and from the elves," the king leaned in his chair. "But the bodies were only folk from Jobelnon and some small nearby villages," Kalan poured himself another drink. "Almost all women and children. What does this say about their dedication to the West Lands when they were already populating East? Treasonous."

"You're a beast," Soranin muttered.

"As I said, a king can gain control from domination, sure, and must, but deceit is easier. I mean, you have no idea how the people love the Ernharts, when all along I do my best to make sure they achieve nothing. And if they do achieve - you'll like this Soranin I think - I profit. Maybe some recompense, but what if these folk had enough money to do what my family did one day, eh? No good there, not at all. Reaching and striving only to get better under my thumb. The system begets the system, and they swallow it like Skell."

The king rose and went to an ice chest in the corner of the kitchen. He came back with a bottle of chocolate milk. Porter recognized it from Marryfarm. Even in the midst of this decon-struction of reality, there was time to appreciate the delicious treats the West Lands could produce, apparently.

"I thought we would need something sweet to counter all this sour, eh?" Kalan Ernhart grinned and poured three tall glasses of cream, drank from his. Some cream in his mustache.

"So we continue. Tell me what this traveler said."

"He said there are seven days until the councilmen of Erchinon Reef-

"A council. Tellor, the absurdity," Kalan said. "Leadership is not joint. I, for example, don't think Soranin has been useful to me even one time. Would you disagree, Redbell?"

Soranin's old eyes were alive with fury. He opened his mouth to fight back.

"Drink your milk, Soranin. It would be a waste of time if we found need to adjourn early for your hanging."

Porter remembered the attendant. Soranin did too, he drank his chocolate milk.

"The Reef hopes to move across the mountains and ransack the West Lands, as they have their own land. For azulana."

"Azulana, eh? One of the rumors coming across those fucking mountains when my great grandfather took the throne. Near everyone who still spoke of the East Lands existence were dead or disappeared, and thank Tellor for it. It sounded like something to marvel at, though. No sense in taking the risk, thought dear old great-grandpap, when he was well on his way to financial domination. Our people don't even care. Best part."

The king shook his head, not able to believe the genius of Caprican hegemony.

"So," he snapped back. "They're looking for a war?"

Porter remembered Ortimer's description of azulana. He wondered if Ortimer had ever tasted that thick power he described.

"I don't believe it would be much of a fight. Azulana gives them strength we could never hope to combat. It dwarfs us. We'd be spanked. Slaughter, I'm told."

The king's smile broke and drooped, tired.

"You sound so certain of the traveler's story."

"I can't question it further. An over-analysis could spell our demise," Porter forced himself to speak. "Only seven days."

"Look at you!" The king wiped the chocolate milk out of his mustache. The room was silent for a long time. Porter and Soranin were not eager to fill the void.

"Meet me in the public room of the library tomorrow. We're done for the night. If you speak of what transpired here tonight to anyone, you'll both find yourselves wishing that I was more the defamer like my father and less the beheader like my great-great -grandfather."

Book III

"Give up your light.
Give up the ocean and the jungle and the ancient way you believe
and understand the moment.
It is time to surrender to the life beyond this one."

Daloshen to his justiciers, speech from the pinnacle during year
312

Chapter 1

Frost etched its way along Pansen's korekwood bow. In
the snowy hole he had dug on the side of the mountain, Pansen
had a moment to admire the craftsmanship of his weapon.
Korekwood was harder than most metals, and a Korek tree left
undisturbed would grow as high as the clouds. That's why Pansen's
people often called them Blue Rakers, since they grew higher in
his village than anywhere else in the world. Pansen was sure of it.
I mean, have you SEEN the korekwood there?

Pansen smiled for a second. The wind whipped it away
like a lash would, and the journeyman returned to the mountain,
the nostalgic thoughts of youth and scaling trees with his sister,
praying their father wouldn't come home to find them shirking
their practices, all robbed by ice.

The wind yowled again, and Pansen ripped the length
of rope tightening his parka's hood down, bringing the janniken
fur to crowd his face in warmth. Pansen's short black hair itched
against the inside of his jacket, and he remembered the janniken
his father had killed to make them all jackets.

Why was he so nostalgic, he wondered? It's this place,
this quest, he decided. Leagues and leagues from the closest
semblance of true pride, pride in the family and community and
ancestry and heart they shared. He thought that heart was on his
old desk in the back room, next to his lantern.

Sun dappled each snowflake as it raced around Pansen's head, invading his hovel. With hands housed in janniken mittens he strung his bow into place across his back, and shoved himself up, forward up the mountain. He loosed a knotted accessory hanging from his pack. Inside were three balls of crushed nuts, herbs and leaves. The three of them together was called Eenthine, and to other cultures it may be considered gross to eat this food. To him it was the only warmth on the mountain, his grandmother's cooking and sweet days with friends in the market.

The janniken had been larger than Pansen's father, a few times as big. If Pansen's father was the size of any other member of the village, the janniken was like ten of him. Marbled libs and pouches under its eyes, a fine purple that surely was tropical royalty struck Pansen's memory now, along with the three segmented arms dragging on the ground, kicking up dirt. In between each finger sprouted short stubs of claw like knuckles. The jannikens had tongues which they lolled like lunatics, and this one's tongue was forked like a reptile. Its fur was a gorgeous storm, black and swollen.

Between the primal force of the janniken and Pansen's father was only a spear topped by Starbark, the sharpest stone for miles around the village. A sense of necessity, too, crowded the space. Pansen's father needed food for the poor farming season, to protect their village from the continued destruction wrought by the unruly beast, and to clothe his children. The janniken needed to kill the man, desperate like a refugee.

The janniken swung its mighty arms and the village gasped, huddled behind Pansen's father, who danced backwards to avoid the boulderous fists. The huge monkey's screech made it sound like it had just had a leg cut off. This call is the way the janniken lets its prey know the janniken will spill its blood today.

Gruffing, spitting, mashing its teeth, the janniken slammed its fists again towards Pansen's father, who had once been the village's acquestier. Like any hero or noble traveler from any village, the acquestier was ambassador, was protector, was father, and was understood to be the eventual ruler of the village. The village was called Third Maple, and it was established in the year 250. An old reminder of the beauty of land and of personhood.

Pansen's father barked at the janniken, a claim of defiance, a call to leave or die. The two did their work at the edge of the village, and a throng had assembled behind Pansen's father, with Pansen nearest to the front. Every little boy needs to see his father at work.

The janniken hollered its wail again, proving its weight through its too long and clawed arms as they swung at Pansen's father again. The older man jumped again, forward now, and landed on the long appendages. The warrior lodged his Starbark spear into the crook of the beast's second elbow, and gooey blood that was nearly as purple as the pouches under the janniken's eyes began to spurt out like the gasket on a war machine springing oil. A third howl rang from the janniken, and this time it sounded like it had chosen to die instead of leave.

Teeth gritting and biceps tingling from exhaustion, Pansen's father drove the point further into the monkey's arm, then gripped tight as the janniken attempted to dislodge both the weapon and the assailant by flinging its arm back and forth. Pansen felt like his father was a man who had caught his foot in the stirrup of a donkey, and the thing had taken to a gallop with its would-be rider dragging behind, no control of the silly contortions his body now performed. Pansen's father felt like this, yet drove the spear deeper.

Starbark painted purple plunged through the bottom of the janniken's arm, and the monkey again screamed, this time softer and much sadder. The janniken punched Pansen's father off of its now obsolete arm, and gnawed at the stuck spear it wore like a piercing in an attempt to remove the death sentence. Feeble.

Pansen's father proved he was fine, though his shirt was torn through the middle, as he stood and walked towards the janniken. Whimpering and yawping, the defeated beast was too distracted to notice Pansen's father draw a farming sickle from his belt. The sickle was used to cut Grain Flower, the plant Third Hill uses for its export and for its comfort. Many of the other Basin villages know this tool, for they rely on it for meals. Grain Flower stalks are coarse and unforgiving, which means the sickles have to be razor and biting.

Pansen's father almost sluggishly, or at least apathetical-
ly, climbed onto the janniken's back. The beast was ferocious, and
as intelligent as a newborn child, the bullish ones like this forked
tongued one especially infantile, and all it was able to do was
flicker its eyes towards the man once or twice.

The Grain Flower sickle parted the skin underneath the
thick, black fur on the janniken's throat like a comb to hair. The
janniken's ultimate call was the meekest yet, and seemed to be
accepting, rejection vacant in place of finality.

Sans chatter, the crowd dispersed, and Pansen's father
and elder sister began to lay the janniken out for skinning. An
exciting and integral custom in the tribe. Pansen's mother went to
fetch the tanning kit, and Pansen himself went to retrieve the salt
to preserve the meat.

The story replayed in Pansen's mind often, and came to
a close today as he chewed janniken jerky he had brought from
home. Not the same one, of course, just some other, new, young
bull who had taken it upon itself to challenge Third Hill for territory.

Winter existed always in these mountains, Pansen
thought, or if not always in these mountains, always for Third Hill's
acquestier.

Chapter 2

Porter rose early, and was glad that he hadn't had the chance to drink at the king's home. He was not glad that he had gone to the king's home at all, for it had provided him no aid in his journey and might bring about much worse. Porter didn't know what time to go to the public room, neither he nor Soranin had the courage to ask. Emasculation came heavy to the leaders of armies. They both had shuffled out of the room, not speaking on the walk to the gate before they parted ways for the evening. Soranin had put his hand on Porter's shoulder before leaving for the Block, but they couldn't quite make eye contact. There was an aching in both of them that did not need the other's confirmation.

Dressing in his simple clothes again, Porter sighed as he stepped down the side of the Dermio building. Frogg didn't show up, he considered it a good omen. Hell, if Porter did die today he would only be remiss if Hunter Frogg showed up to the beheading. Otherwise, he'd be alright.

With this thought ricocheting in his head Porter decided to focus again on the inspiring What have you got to lose? bit. He swooped through Trainer's Row and purchased himself a farrowberry scone before heading to the library. It felt like the sort of day that required a scone, the kind promising to be as haggard and unfortunate as possible. Scones are the world's brilliant grandmas packing you a bag lunch, he thought. Porter fancied himself quite the poetic genius as crumbs bounced off his chest, feeling lifted.

Porter opened the door to the gate house. Ula was sitting at the desk, and Bord stood to her left. Ula smiled and waved. Bord eyed Porter like a mother bear protecting its young. Considering Bord had no tasks on his list, Porter assumed that judgment day had indeed come. Bord received his task list from King Kalan himself each day, so he must know about last night. The thought of his patronage designing the maniacal system Capricans suffer from made Porter shutter. This handed down estate of deceit was deadly, and Porter smiled a scared smile as he backed out the door. No one had spoken during his interlude into the gate house. Porter regretted now having purchased only one scone.

The library was a sprawling building, located across the

courtyard from the Tower of Indecision, on top of the hill looking over the barracks and the training yard. It was of white brick with large banners of hammers and bells adorning the walls. Porter stepped inside and saw the familiar sight of firm wooden floors and high wooden ceilings, interlaced with brilliant sky lights shining down upon the divine items filed just so in enormous cases: books. Porter was as thankful now as ever that Caprica had such a store of texts, though he was less thankful to wonder how many of them were doctored to create the society that the king had described as "easily manipulated". When he thought of the drunks in the Strumbard, or even the too proud denizens of the Block, he felt like the king had a good understanding of his subjects. Not that any of it was by accident, though.

The library had multiple facilities; like the gate house, over time the archive had become a multi-functioning asset to a government which preferred to have most of its important buildings within the royal complex, or as some called it "the Castle". Porter thought it could be a sort of castle, but castles require the king to be a sort of royalty. Now Porter could only see a mongering politician when he saw Ernhart.

Town folk had access to the popular castle public room, making it the most-used piece of the compound. The public room lay at the end of a hall that lay at the end of the library. The public room almost looked like a church chapel, and could be except for a semi-ornate throne of maroon-stained wood in the center rear. Considering all the pews, which were meant for the public to sit in while they waited to be seen by the king, some may even take it for granted that the throne was indeed a holy relic. Porter was sure King Ernhart would have said there isn't really any difference.

As he walked toward the back of the fantastic building, walking being often his only solace from his depressed life and his anxious mind, as he waved and nodded to attendants who asked him to stow his flask time and time before, he couldn't help stew over the king he once held so much praise for. The corrupted and interconnected façade he was beginning to see unravel kept re-running like bad small talk.

How could the royal family have betrayed the trust and admiration of so many? The people of the West Lands were simple, but it was in this quality Porter saw the best of them. They wanted nothing more than to mind their homes and families, to find fulfill-ment in their trades and to have those little things like the wafting scents of honey roasted bread baked by someone's neighbor to mean something. Doing things they love every day with the ones they love – here or there, this is the prophecy of satisfaction.

It was then it struck Porter that perhaps the collusion to restrain these folk from leaving the West Lands was not as menac-ing as he had been thinking. Would they have left in great throngs had powerful moguls not manipulated them? What would change with a veil lifted?

That's the whole point, he thought. *What kinds of lives, what sort of achievements, would these people make if they had the true knowledge of their world? If they could take their families elsewhere and engage in new pursuits that the poweful moguls hadn't quashed by military violence?*

Porter realized he, or anyone else for that matter, could ever have known what might change, or if they would have left in great throngs because the Caprican government took the oppor-tunity like light from an open room, halting chance while lining their pockets. Porter also realized that some of him was starting to hate the King Ernharts and the Bords of Caprica, these tyrants and connivers.

With all this unearthing and revelation, Porter wanted to take a ride through the hills, to get a chance to decompress all these assaults on the life of basic, sticky day-to-day monotony he had grown accustomed to. After all, it was theories until now.

Now he was opening the door to the public room, and he had no idea what lay ahead. Less basic, sticky day-to-day monotony he thought.

Porter was not surprised by the intensity of the men in the room. The king sat in his throne, and Soranin sat in the pew closest to the throne on the left side of the room. What was surprising was seeing Leoric, in full armor, standing on the king's left.

"Go on in then."

Porter had been standing in the door, and almost shat his pants when he heard the command and felt a hand in the

small of his back. Before the door slammed behind him, Porter had
wheeled around to see Ronald Bodeman, the skunk knight, also
adorned in full armor and with a grin that hurt Porter. For a public
room, Porter got the feeling this was a very private event.

The king wore his full royal regalia, not the simple
clothes from last night's dinner. A long maroon cloak with Wooly
Bear fur lining was hung over the back of his seat, and he wore
a gorgeous silver doublet. Fine black slacks with silver boots. A
maroon and silver crown, with the smallest and most impressive
bell and hammer engraved at the forefront, completed the lord
costume which he wore.

"Running a bit on the late side, Porter," the king spoke
as he motioned for the second captain to proceed down the gap
between the pews.

"Sorry, I didn't know what time to-"

"And how was your farrowberry scone?" The king asked.

Porter said nothing, and this seemed to placate Kalan.

"I won't waste time," the kindness from the king was
vacant again. "That was last night's spirit. Today we'll speak with
haste, honestly."

The king leaned forward, placed a hand on his knee,
exhaled:

"I see this predicament coming at a convenient time,
for me, and have decided what would be the best outcome, for me.
As you have probably heard, there have been zoning issues.
This, thankfully, has always been a vague enough description to
satisfy the curious drums of people, but if they were to really chew
on it they'd realize zoning issues between villages and townships,
all of which I own, would occupy little to none of my time. It is
with the city of Ollette that these issues have come into play. The
explanation of Ollette being grandfathered into the West Lands is
one of the weaker theories created by the Caprican government
to explain the going ons in the West Lands, but it seems to satisfy
your average West Lander who has got nothing else on his mind
but patriotism and Billy Yak manure."

Soranin sat deflated. Porter imagined if these hours
had been hard on him, Soranin's hours must have been a thrashed
mess of isolation and horror.

"In reality, Ollette is the closest township, though they may not call it as such, to the West Lands we do not claim control over. There was a small military force deployed to scout the area, to capture it if it were simple enough. The natural defenses of the region, a difficult new challenge for an army used to flat grounds and plains, proved to be enough resistance to come up with something else. An uneasy allyship lies between the entirety of the West Lands and the bustling, awful marriage of urban and rural that is Ollette.

"The mayor of Ollette, something or another Apple I believe is his name, is oft troubled by our gradual encroachments on his city. Keeping the egg-headed man happy is an enormous amount of strife for me."

It was then the king reached his hand towards Leoric who produced a thin leather skin with fanned-out ragged documents. Leoric's tiny smile shot at Soranin. Soranin's eyes were shot to the ground.

"Before last night, a really exquisite dining experience I must add, my plan was to send a small envoy of men to go on a patrol," the king emphasized the untruth of this word. "A patrol which would deliver these documents. Documents that state, once and for all, where Ollette meets the West Lands. More importantly, it contains a hefty financial promise if this proves to be my last interaction with the fruity mayor."

"This leads to you two men and your fates. Soranin, man, tough business to be wrapped up in."

Soranin scowled at Porter, the two rolled their eyes like teenagers, then returned his gaze to the wooden floor. The king wore an elite smile in appreciation of his once favored captain.

"I can't say if this traveler's story is true. The beauty of things as they are now is that it doesn't matter; I'm in need of an errand run. Here's how I see it: I will provide the two of you with provisions for your journey. Food, equipment and the small group intended for Ollette in the first place. Enough to get you to the strange place."

Porter's heart thumped in his chest; it was beginning to happen. His leaving the West Lands was unfolding. His arm scratched but it faded and was icy but most of all he sensed truth to his excitement, beyond the apathetic joy he already paid for.

"You will meet with the mayor in Ollette and see this matter settled. It will take a certain amount of time, time out of your time-constrained task. This is not of my concern."

Even if it spells demise for your kingdom, of course, Porter thought, his hands balled in fists at his side.

"I again have my doubts that there is a time constraint at all, and it, again, doesn't matter to me. If there is indeed an ambassador necessary to cross the world, I'm glad it is you, Porter," the king smiled. Porter was happy if not confused. "I'm glad this generation's loud mouth theorist has outted himself directly to the government, and now I have both key and lock to disarm you."

Porter relaxed his hands. Remained confused.

"If you should succeed in this task, the two of you will return to your posts and the West Lands will continue to thrive. All is well."

The king rose.

"If you succeed and then decide to share your story with anyone, then you will both be sacked, slandered and maybe hung for treason. Bord can come up with something clever I'm sure."

Porter felt sweat on the back of his neck. Leoric's glare made him feel like a rodent in a python's grasp.

"If you should fail or die, well that does me fine, too! It's a win-win-win; since you two know the raw, unaltered history of the West Lands, you can't just be left with it, and in this plan the government is protected. Things are not bucked. At best, you avert a cataclysmic catastrophe. At worst you are wiped away before you make a noise above the din of comfortability which we maintain for Capricans so they don't buck things themselves," the king wiped his hands like he kneaded dough, patting flour from his hands. The matter was done.

"And what if we fail, and the crisis is real? You seem to deny the significance of this pilgrimage," Soranin spoke, his words flailing about the room, a desperate bargain being made between himself and the corrupt royalty.

"Brave captain, I only condone this trek because I don't want foreigners in my lands. I'm quite confident in Caprica's forces alone, not to mention the militia at arms, plus our smattering of tribal warriors, could repel this azulana powered assault," the king bared his teeth in that primal grin. "I just want these damn papers sent to Ollette."

King Kalan laughed fast like the pop of champagne from a bottle, stopped on a note. "Besides, when you leave the West Lands, I will deploy the majority of my forces to Jobelnon, and a large force to station at the townships of Tunsworth and Whee-tab. As our most Easterly and Northerly municipalities I know they are the best lines of defense, if this "invasion" proves to be real and your excellent skills of persuasion fail us. I'm even sending men to the village of Vian to begin training a proper militia there as well; your leaving, and the deployment of the troops will all be called "The Fall of Fantastic Footmen." So as not to alarm the people, we're masking all of these movements as a 'remember your soldiers, aren't they swell,' public relations event," The king sat down again. "No one will know there's anything amiss, and all the pieces in play are mine."

The king seemed to be expecting the proverbial pat on the back for his brilliance, but was met with silence. Once Leoric clued in, though, he delivered a literal pat on the pack and a word of encouragement.

"Thank you, Leoric. Now, what will you two require of your good king? Besides this satchel that is," the king stuck his bundle out at Porter, he took it like a peasant to bread. "I've assem-bled a group of four soldiers, plus Leoric."

"No. I will not ride with him," Soranin spoke with power, which surprised the king. He only laughed again.

"I don't care if you ride him or he rides you or however it's done, but he is going, there's no doubt. I trust you fairly well Soranin, as archaic and obsolete as you may be, but I don't trust the son of a drunk not to conspire with these Reefmen and lead the attack himself. Leoric will keep careful eyes your entire jour-ney to the East Lands."

Leoric's mocking look slipped away and an uncomfort-able look of dismay took its place on his tan face.

"My liege, you said I was to ride with them to Ollette only, I-"

"Why does he know about any of this, any ways?! You decide to bring him up to speed for laughs is that it?" Soranin interrupted the men. They glared.

"All of the King's Sword know the truth; who else do you think cleans up the unwashed intellectuals, like Pod and Porter?" The king said it like one explains two and two indeed did make four.

Porter felt abused. He didn't want to think any more about the glimmering face of Caprica and what it had actually taken all this time to keep it squeaky clean.

"Sire, who will lead the King's Sword in my stead?"

"If everything goes according to plan, you men won't be gone long. Bodeman will take point if it's necessary."

"Bodeman fights well, sire, but his tactics are-"

"Leoric," Kalan was done with two-way interaction. "Keep this up and you'll be replaced by the time you've set out the East Gate. Do you understand?" King Ernhart boomed. The king grabbed the young man's chin and spoke within a few inches of his face, "I hope you enjoy traveling, Captain Leoric. You can lie under the stars around the fire, or you can lie in a freshly dug grave around the bodies of an unmarked crypt."

There was a hanging silence. Then the men began to disperse.

"Tellor craft your light, men," Kalan cheered form his throne.

Chapter 3

Grass ripped by wind pulled around Hariah. The mail dripping from his headpiece clinked softly as he stood up. Kneeling on top of Tin Bin Hill wasn't new for the journeyman. Tin Bin Hill had its name from as early as the Meinhah culturalists could record, almost as early as 101. The Meinhah don't allow much, and what they do stays in the analogs of history.

Hariah rose and smoothed out his aiit. The aiit is irreplaceable wear for those of Meinhah lineage. It is a kilt and a skirt, a dress and a cloak. Bestowed at birth, Hariah's has the patterns of swirling sand and sun, set upon a crimson back. Underneath his aiit he wears light chain and a simple brown tunic, with tall black boots which are stylish for workman's shoes. A feathered hat, really a leather cap with a single red but now tan plume, sits on the lone man's head, and a tight yellow beard completes his dusty, foreign look. Hariah realized that "a look" can be as important as a man's reputation; it can grant him armistice just by being as reputable as his name in troubling times.

The youngish man kept these parts of his culture. He knew them and loved them and wished they weren't the last things he had.

Tin Bin Hill is not a traditional Meinhah name; in fact, it was not named by the Meinhah at all. Before the Mason arrived and drew the masses, during the Setting as it has been recorded by the historists, Tin Bin Hill was simply the hill many young Meinhah would travel to for dances and parties, without their parents knowing. It gave perfect sight across the land: the rust city of Khu'Ron to the Northeast, the famished Carskren desert and all the way to where gold meets emerald at the line of the Ennabon Forrest. Of course, youngsters of the Meinhah could see their tribe, too, so they would dance on Tin Bin Hill for hours and days and weeks. Hariah had taken his first love here, first with a party then just the two of them, and she had died here, too.

Once Mason Men came, though, they renamed the hill after its odd shape and relativity to the goliath, brutalizing the niceness of the place. Occidentalizing hurts all and leaves no room for tradition. Only greed and parasitism in the name of joking and relations.

The end of Hariah's polearm drew small circles in the Yikatee, meaning "grass which is tall and immortal" in Meinhah. It is impossible to cut the Yikatee grass, and though it's neat for show, it makes harvesting in crops infested by Yikatee grass a frustrating experience for any young cropper. Hariah had once been a cropper, before becoming "Hariah the Pariah", exiled journeyman of Meinhah.

The Mason scourged the Meinhah, who were already a spiritual and tribal people. It took them to a place of frenzied affections for an idol they did not understand. Hariah wished he himself had never seen the obelisk resting in almost the center of his home, and cursed the totem in its likeness which he carried with him day in and day out. The idol's eyes radiated green, and the best he could do was stuff it in his pocket.

He rose, thinking he would again try to save his people from themselves.

And from what the Mason had done.

The king told the men to bring Bord an inventory list by the end of the afternoon so proper provisions could be assembled. He had taken his leave of the three men in the courtyard amongst the decorative shrubbery, and the three men stood there still. The tension was thicker than five-week old cottage cheese.

Leoric looked up and, though he looked sullen a moment before, a competitive strength was in his eyes. His dark skin was strong and frightening in its power.

"I'll make sure neither of you bring any harm to this beautiful city," Leoric spoke with bravado, but it felt like he was speaking to reassure himself of his temporary station in life.

"I would never, I would never," Soranin spoke like a widow, but readied himself, "I'll trust you to mock up this list for Bord?" the red bearded man exhaled as he asked, and began to move away from the group. "Be sure to put thick rope on the list. And Skell Brew." Soranin's glum form walked through the gate and veered towards the Block.

Leoric sneered.

"I'm sorry he's a part of this. He'd do better to stay here, flowing newts in and out, and attending to his myriad of familial problems."

"I think you're probably right," Porter began walking towards the Dermio building, for the last time in what would be a long time.

◇◇

Porter sat in his apartment at the small desk across from his bed facing the stone wall. He wished now, once he realized that he would leave tomorrow morning, that he had put a picture or something decorative on the wall above the desk because now, and most days, he was looking at granite, and granite isn't very inspiring.

It didn't take long to draft up what he thought they'd need, and what he knew they already had:

1. Five fresh faced newts and their horses

2.   One uppity King's Swan prick, his horse
3.   Food for seven; breads, vegetables, MEAT. Food
need last at least one week.
4.   Armaments for men. Three officers have weapons, newts need be supplied with sword and shield,
perhaps pike or halberd, standard stuff
5.   Water!!!
6.   300 opal, for problems of a civilized sort
7.   Ropes, pick axes, general mountaineering equipment
8.   Skell Brew - morale

      Porter wasn't sure, in the slightest, if his list was suitable for this type of venture. He didn't know what type of venture they were embarking on, so how could he hope to know what to bring on it? He knew he would bring his armor, his axe and his horse. Nothing else, he told himself.

      A dusty leather journal, given to him by his father a long forgotten holiday ago, sat in his desk drawer. Once he had written down dreams in it, another time he'd kept a diary. Grabbing it and stuffing it in a knapsack, he thought now he'd fancy himself a secret cartographer. Then he felt the rope around his neck at the thought of King Ernhart discovering his map making.

      Porter hoped Bord would have the insight and fastidiousness to collect anything he had neglected to scrawl down, though he doubted Bord would know anymore what would go on this list than he, and set out to deliver it. The death-like husk of a landlord awaited him outside.

      "Rosset. Your rent is late," Frogg always had the ability to be annoying and repetitive but still haunting and terrifying at the same time; the type of annoying playmate who if you decided to tease about their ridiculousness would flash into attack mode in an instant.

      "Frogg I assure you it isn't, but-

      "I mean for the time you'll be away," Frogg's long fingers rapped against each other in front of his shallow chest. "An old long haired man from the government brought me post saying you'll be participating in this "Fantastic Footman" pride parade, and that I should collect any debts or future payments now."

Bord, ever the wise care taker, thought Porter.

"Well what will it run me, Frogg? I won't be gone more than a week, really."

"The government man said different, he said who can say. I'll take two months' rent now, so 500 opal," his insect hand smelled like a corpse when he stuck it under Porter's nose.

"500 opal? Are you daft, man? I hardly have that much money to my name. I'm not paid for four more days!"

Frogg only looked peeved and impatient. Porter sighed and rooted around his wallet for any money. He hoped the king would be good on allowing them some government funds on their journey, because he realized now he had only ten opal left. To buy a farrowberry scone alone would now deplete a good three quarters his sum.

Disheartened and poor, Porter went to the gate house. The sun was setting in the sky, and he was thankful most of today seemed to give him a chance to rest. Porter thought again on how revolutionary these last few weeks had been. Green dragons, men in the East, a government conspiracy, and to top it off, he was now to embark into the unknown to stave off a military operation by some possibly pretend, addicted fiends. No, no more slow, sticky sun-spent days in Caprica for who knew how long.

He smiled. No care in the world, in his body, for one breath.

Bord was nowhere to be seen. Only one Ula sitting behind the desk checking the ledger for goings and leavings into the complex for the day.

"Hey, Ula," Porter noticed her eyes light up when he called her name. She had teeth which looked like they could be a Khu'Roni Sand Mammoth's tusks, long and stained. But it was Ula he had thought of time and time any ways; nobody else looked at him with eyes of sugar and cream, care and anticipation.

"Oh, hi Porter! I heard you and Soranin are leading some men east for the "Fantastic Footman" festivals, huh?" Ula stood up and straightened out her dress. Porter realized he knew almost nothing about Ula, only her name and her profession and her more undeniable features.

She's beautiful, in a Caprican sort of way, he thought. *A sweet and unselfishly affectionate kind of person.*

Porter realized he was thinking instead of speaking, a habit he sometimes fell into by nature of his peddling mind. Even now Ula was looking at him, her smile turned into a look of discomfort, due to Porter's lack of...

"Oh right, yes! We, heh, are taking a small troop to Olette. Just promotional stuff, you know," Porter handed over his list, folded up to hide its true nature. "Give this to Bord, would you?"

Ula took the sheet of paper and smiled again.

"No problem at all."

Porter smiled and turned to leave.

"Hey, Ula?"

"What's that, Porter?"

Porter walked back to the desk and placed his hands on the table.

"When I get back, would you want to take a walk some time? Maybe we'd have dinner? The Caprican Public House has some fantastic crepes."

Ula's eyes looked like treasure chests.

"Oh, yes! There are some really nice places in the Block, too."

"Sounds like a plan, then. See you around, Ula," Porter left the Gate House, and was surprised he wasn't the slightest bit drunk for that ageless ritual. It was uncharacteristic of him. The thought of enjoying a sausage and cheese crepe and Ula's company together just seemed too good of a coming home joy.

Porter, thinking of being drunk, wished Frogg hadn't robbed him of his small fund, but decided it was some intervention as he walked towards the barracks. A huge banner for "The Fantastic Footmen: What Would YOU Do for Your City-State?" was being tacked up over head of the gate house. The two newts pinning it up saluted him and grinned. Porter shook his head.

The barracks was vast, large enough to house fresh faced recruits for training inside the city and storing government arms en masse. Situated at the rear of the dusty training field, adjacent to the stables, the barracks was not beautiful. With a low hanging roof and too wide doors, the building was awkward, but did its job fine. The building had been a story taller, but during the Second Roaring Thunder of 745 a streak of lightning had cleared one story of the building in an instant, and the building pancaked upon itself. Ever since, whenever a storm is brewing in the West Lands, the barracks tells the citizens by creaking and groaning for a week before. Porter stepped into the dilapidated building and was hit by the smells of some fifty-odd sweaty and dusty men, and his ears were no less harangued by the calls of gambles lost and fights found.

The entrance hall ran straight back to the armory, with dorm room doors cutting up each side. Porter steeled himself and began walking, doing his best to ignore every newt who wanted to ask him one of the few general questions:

How am I doing, sir? *Probably trash awful, but considering we've never interacted before how would I know?*

Wowee, are you the second captain? *You saw me on my horse on the day Soranin roused you all with his speech, right? Same guy, yup!*

When are we going to war, sir!? I'm ready for anything! And was top in my dueling class back in Gelor and boy my mom was sure mad when I...

I don't care, I don't care, really I don't care. Give me a drink please. Tellor help me.

Porter had made it almost to the armory at the end of the hall when a well-toned arm shot in front of him, stopping him in front of one of the open dorm rooms.

"What are you up to, second captain? A little Fantastic Footman preparations with us lowly types?"

"Ami Trout, how are you?"

The Khu'Roni native stepped out in front of Porter, hips filling the hallway.

"Shining, sir," she stooped her head so as to be side to side with Porter's, whispering in his ear. "They say I'll have your job when your mission fails."

Porter hadn't seen this coming, was still processing seeing Trout at all. But really hadn't seen this coming.

"My mission to rouse some rural support in Vian, eh? It's high priority stuff, dangerous work, that's for sure. I believe you're misguided as to the nature of this festivity, Ami," Porter whispered in a semi-desperate breath, feeling much less confident than he had while picturing crepes and Ula.

"The nature of your mission? To council with the men from the east, no?"

"How do you-"

"Some of us more gifted in the militaristic arts make quick friends in the Sword, and aren't so thick as to think it's worth raising hell about."

Porter placed his hand on Ami's shoulder and pushed her back, because though the Khu'Roni spices smelt fantastic, Porter wasn't so keen on having the woman's bare chest this close to his shoulder for the rest of their interaction. At this distance, she could grab him and take him down in a flash.

"Well we won't be gone long, and I won't lose my post."

"If you say so, Capitan. But just in case, I wanted you to rest easy knowing your duties would be going to someone of much higher caliber," Ami smiled, and in the dark hall Porter was sure that Ami Trout was just as sinister as the azulana abusers in the east, Ivan in the Strumbard and even his own king. That was too bad; Porter had thought she was just an asshole.

"Excuse me, Trout, but as your superior officer I'll order you to return to your quarters and get out of my way."

Ami stepped aside, saluted, then Porter kept on. He was thankful again to be leaving these old stomping grounds, even if what lay ahead were grounds only to be stomped in. Not as poetic as he would have liked, he frowned and kept walking.

The armory was ever guarded by two of the soldiers staying in the barracks, and as one began to ask him how he was doing, at standing and minding a door, Porter had the men step aside for his entry. Ami's comments rattled him. He did not want to run sound board for a foolish boy, another foolish boy besides his ego.

The armory was expansive and opulent, with every weapon in Caprica being stored here. In fact, the great majority of weapons in all the West Lands called the barracks home. The Caprican government isn't keen on weapons in the proletariat hands. This was an Ernhart initiative, which made more sense after

Porter's dinner with the fascist. No bearing arms allowed.

If the first half of the barracks smelt sweaty and a bit dusty, the remainder was its opposite. A sprawling garage of rusting catapults and moldy war carriages; rows upon rows of spider web ridden swords, axes and shields with grown rot on their silvery faces. At the back, right by the crossbows, was an enormous blue safe.

The blue safe was used by each Caprican combatant, reserved for those in the government but some of the better-connected Capricans had finagled its use as well. It was for storing prized weapons, heirloom stuff. Porter hadn't been here in some time; if he found battle at all these days it was with training weapons like at the Rough Bout. He had forgotten how gorgeous these artifacts could be.

As Porter opened the heavy metal door he saw Soranin's army grade blade and shield, Striker and Block. Soranin wasn't a creative writer – this was clear from his neighborhood being the namesake of the latter piece of equipment. They were a one handed sword gilded with red jewels and a light, round shield with a matching red emblem in the center.

Porter saw also the king's signature warhammer, Kingmaker, and his long shield with a maroon bell painted on the front, inlaid with golden runes. It felt significant and impressive like a big warhorse.

Leoric's two Khu'Roni short swords, Porter was glad to not know their titles, were hanging from the top near some more of the like. Each was a bronze and golden hue, and each curved like Khu'Roni scimitars. Bodeman's trident sat near the back; Bodeman was a Roiling Tide native, and could gut a man as well as he could a marlin. One scoped crossbow in the lot: Sir Ire of the King's Swan fancied himself Jobelnon's finest marksman.

Krude had fallen under some of the less decorative and important weapons, and Porter thought it fair considering his family name was not as revered as he had once thought. Ego, ego, ego. He lifted it, the axe, not his ego

The Rossets had come upon this axe from Porter's grandfather, Lorne Porter, winning it in a game of Sqwees Rat from "the biggest troll I'd ever seen, but he was an excellent chair caner."

The two handed axe had a black shaft, and the head of the axe was the same black. In the head were veins of red, crawling out and growing as they approached the razor edges of the weapon. Porter thought Krude was perhaps the best thing the Rosset's ever owned, and though Kettlestep was a fine horse, and since the shack outside the city was, well, a shack, he thought it undisputed truth.

Porter took up his axe, and as he began to close the blue safe he noticed what looked like a huge piece of opal. It had the same dark purple as most opal used for currency, but instead of only one color there was a vast array of colors decorating the stone. Red, orange, blue, green, and three brilliant strokes of silver painted the lump. It was also larger than an average piece of opal. With shame and itching in mind Porter snatched it, placed it in the knapsack around his shoulder, right next to his leather journal. He locked up the blue safe; he didn't want to be caught thieving before his not-too honorable departure from the city, which he was a high ranking official of, he called home.

Reality adrift produced a need for control.

Chapter 5

Heavy. The armor felt so heavy.

The four-foot mace dragged through the dirt, making a jagged riven in its wake. Blue and red spots off set the iron head of the mace. Plated hands gripped it tighter than the maiden clung to her sliver of hope, the meager chance her dead feet would take her to a haven, a refuge from the onslaught she faced each day.

Since Ayun she hadn't slept for more than a few hours a day, and those were days she considered herself lucky. Tonight she hoped, as she did each night, that she would be blessed and sleep enough to feel refreshed when she woke up, not just groggy and discombobulated. Moreover, she hoped she wouldn't be woken up to the awful gurgling yawps of her assailants, the horrible screaming of their predatory cry.

The sun was setting behind Old Yit and she knew soon she would need a remote sense of shelter; the empty plain she had been walking through would not suffice. Not far up ahead she saw a rise in the ground, and tall trees began a small grove, a forest. The maiden felt some joy in its sight, but had no energy or desire to smile.

Fire crackled and spit, and the maiden wished she could be more inconspicuous in how she rested. If only squor meat cooked itself, she thought, as a few of the tiny creatures scurried up a tree just out of sight. The darkness of the woods brought the critters to her beacon of light, only to see her roasting one of their kin. Their chittering and squealing carried on like a chorus, and the maiden thought she saw, even heard, a few grigers lumbering around further into the thicket, hollering and laughing. Some called them Cat Apes, some called them Royaltigres, but they were grigers to her. Minute differences are still differences, and matter, after all.

The blue danced in her field of vision only for a moment, but she saw it, oh yes she saw. It had blurred across the path she had blazed for herself on her way to her campsite. Her prayers had gone unheard, it seemed. Again.

Then it struck. An enormous bashing force slammed the maiden in her back as she sat in front of her fire. She threw herself to the side of her primitive oven, and she lunged for the mace which she had stood against a tree. Though she never took off her borrowed armor, she had not kept her weapon at arm's reach. She slipped up – she was so tired.

The baleel erected itself to full height, a creature the maiden hadn't seen outside a textbook. It swayed to and fro, oily body glittering in the fire's light, and in general fashion it dropped its pink lipped jaw and raised its pink fins behind its head; aiming for death.

The creature shot its gaping mouth, fangs forward, toward the maiden. She rolled, grabbed her mace in the dodge. With a grunt she swung it over her head and down on the body of the thing. It shrieked and rolled itself, towards the maiden and around her leg. Its powerful, singular muscles began constricting around her legs, and she felt them contorting, regardless of plate, into unnatural, rooted shapes.

Sporting its familiar, legendary grin, the baleel brought its head behind the maiden's back and over her shoulder, readying to deliver its poison through her eye and neck. The maiden was thankful the beast was not as intelligent as it was exotic and beautiful.

The maiden stuck her mace out forwards, head in, then back into the serpent's body. The abyssal mouth snapped shut. From this leverage point, she head-butted the baleel and pushed it off her legs, easier now considering how shaken up the baleel had become in the previous twenty seconds.

Pole vaulting forwards on her mace, the maiden then spun around. The baleel looked at her in a knowing way the maiden wasn't aware a beast of the wild could look. She would have felt sympathy, but spit-roasted baleel sounded delicious. That, and she was pissed for being assaulted pre-squor kebab. Hunger driving emotions.

A battered and stunned baleel, laying in a pool of layered thickness, and a lunging woman in a battle cast suit were frozen in time, a shaded duality in the dark din of the forest. Time resumed. The next things to happen were the maiden landing, the baleel's head caving in under the weight of a spiked, iron ball.

The maiden panted. Heaved, but was thankful that

some of her squor seemed salvageable and that she had a new
supply of food to pick at for days to come. She sat herself against
the hardness of a tree, and let the fire bathe her. She was thankful
also that the blue blur proved not to be her trailing adversaries,
but a malicious ward of the wild instead.

   Chanting and yelling startled the maiden. The body of
the baleel was only absent life for what felt like the blink of an
eye. Her moment of respite completed, the maiden hauled her
mace over her shoulder and stood. The trees broke with a
screaming wave and death was on its heel. The gnarled world kept
trespassing on her makeshift domicile. For the woman, it seemed
that her body was always unsafe. Invasion driving retaliation.

Chapter 6

The morning bell rung, but Porter had been up for hours. He hadn't really slept. With confidence stored in his colorful stone, he had swung by Dirk's for a loan. Then he had purchased himself a Hopejule jam, for toast on the road, and a bottle of Agatha's Ale, for relief on the road. The jam made it into his knapsack, but he had drunk the entire bottle before making it to his apartment. He then stopped in the Strumbard, purchased the wight he needed, went home. He wanted to feel that sun, have those dreams, even in the beautiful new places he knew he would see.

When he did make it up the stairs of the Dermio building he realized Kettlestep needed fetching, so he slipped into the night to prepare his faithful steed for the next morning's trip.

After scaling the Gate House fence and sneaking through the courtyard, he ran full force through the unprotected brown training area. In his inebriation, he assumed there would be men posted to guard his horse, but the only real danger came when Porter began throwing up and, unbeknownst to him, a newt who was already spooked by the stories of the creaking barracks almost roused his comrades to help him drive off the intruder. Lucky for everyone involved, the boy went back to sleep when the puking ceased.

Kettlestep was sleeping, but Porter assured his groggy mount that it was important to not waste any time in the morning by coming down to the stables. In the most horrible way possible, Porter rode his horse to the Dermio building. How he strapped a saddle on Kettlestep is bewildering, Tellor be praised, then he rode the horse through the back entrance of the stable, past the peasant homes, and up to the North end. He tied the horse off at the foot of his apartment's steps.

Porter then packed his few pairs of extra breeches, pants and shirts into a saddle bag that he slung onto his horse. Most of the real packing would be done in the morning, he thought, and upon the thought he realized the folly of his ways and wondered how he got so drunk. He breathed heavily, vacuuming for air. After peeing as much as possible, he began to drink water like a man salvaged from the Carskren Desert. This is a place just South of the Bastions of Tellor and just east of the Ennabon Forrest, for reference.

He spent the night being an alcoholic. The night invaded him and with the drink being so strong in him his voice was loud and perspiring in its unnecessary carrying on, all night, alone. He spent the night dabbling in his addictions and his thoughts only prepared for another night when he would be one again. Thoughts of his father. Thoughts of his mother. Thoughts of his childhood friends and the games they would play in their sleepy afternoons and how he couldn't understand how the blurriness of his life was so foggy he couldn't even enjoy life like he did when he was eight. Just stimulants now.

After only a few short hours Soranin was banging on his door, calling his name over and over. Porter crashed onto his floor then flung open the door.

"Why is your horse tied downstairs?"

"Good morning to you too, captain."

"You're drunk."

"That happens."

"Tellor, craft your light. Come on, then," Soranin was in full armor. It took Porter only a moment to follow his swishing cape around the corner in similar garb.

"I'm, er, sorry about this," Porter felt embarrassed by his sloppy behavior.

"It's alright Porter," Soranin turned and smiled, putting his hand on Porter's shoulder. "You couldn't have known what would happen, and to be honest I'm glad you came to me. After much prayer and discussion with my wife it feels like this is the best thing to do, whether it is a real threat or not. You're still a good man."

"I meant I'm sorry you had to see my blood shot eyes and my vomit stained saddle."

Soranin's mouth drew tight. With his hand on Porter's shoulder there was a definite sadness shared. An uncomfortable but familiar space between them.

"But thank you. I'll need your support in these days to come," Porter smiled, and Soranin's grin flowered.

"We've got Skell Brew for support."

Porter didn't want any more to drink. Never again.

"Would you help me scrub off this saddle? Kettlestep deserves better."

Chapter 7

	The two army officials rode into the courtyard where a procession was already under way. Men were sitting on horseback, most Porter didn't know, with government peons stuffing food, knives, flint and tinder and other miscellaneous stuffs into their saddle bags. Leoric, the king and Bord were the only familiar faces, and none of them were happy to see Porter. His loss of Bord was sad; Bord had always been like a weird, freaky uncle to him.

	The Caprican sun was blaring into Porter's purple blotted eyes; he thought it must be literally right after dawn. Why did rich people take this sort of thing literally? It seemed like some kind of disconnect was going on.

	The workers came over to Porter and Soranin and began muttering the contents of their bags out loud as they crammed more in. The only items that Porter was conscious of having were his near blank journal, the beautiful stone he had acquired, Krude slung across his back, three pocket sized texts, You, Me, and the Tree: Farming in the West Lands, Heavy Waters, a text on Roiling Tide's expansive water borne history, and Jobelnon and Outliers: Cities East of Caprica, his Hopejule jam, not for sharing, and his spare clothes. So long as these hustling and bustling stooges of the king didn't touch his jam he was fine with them loading him up with any manner of items.

	Leoric was speaking with the king, a tiny space between mouth and ear, and the king did not seem pleased. Leoric's face was tight, screwed up like a sour plum was rioting in his mouth. The king's was just displeased, and he walked away from the captain in not too long at all. Everything seemed in order.

	The men took a formation of Leoric at the head, two of the newts riding behind him, Porter and Soranin behind them, and the three remaining soldiers bringing up the rear. The horses all stamped like they would sprint to the end of the yard as Bord double and triple checked all that the workers had done. The old man nodded to his king who then proceeded to the front of the group as the gate was brought up. The king's crown sparkled in the sun, and he was eating from a handful of farrowberries he had picked off of a nearby bush.

Porter clenched his stomach, waiting for whatever the king's final words would be, sending him on toward fate.

"The Fantastic Footmen is Caprica's way of saying thank you to the countless soldiers that..."

Once Porter realized that the king wasn't going to be speaking in any way about why they actually were leaving the city, he decided to swallow the disappointment with new thoughts. Easier to do sometimes than others to change cerebral lanes.

He thought about old Ortimer, where his final resting place had been. With all the blood he had been spitting up, he was sure he had died, with no one to call friend or family in the city, but nobody in any gutters or alleys. He hoped the mysterious bundle of rags had left the city to die amongst the yaks and the angry beasts of the plains of the West Lands.

""The ride to Ollette is but a two-day ride; you'll get there by dusk tomorrow," the king was concluding his rallying speech. "My most beloved officers, my dearest confidants, represent our armed men like you were representing Caprica, bell and hammer flying proud. Like you were riding into the land with me in your troop. Pray to Tellor daily, fast, and you shall be safe under his bell."

Fuck you, Porter thought managing to make his disrespectful spitting look as though he had simply accrued too much spittle in his mouth. Bord glared at him regardless. Soranin seemed to have his old air of composure about him once more. Leoric looked constipated again.

The eight men spurred their horses on when it became clear that the most-esteemed king was done. The eight horses trotted across the courtyard and picked up speed as they meandered down the hill and toward the Eastern Gate. Porter noticed the Fantastic Footmen banner had been pinned up during their preparation, and the entire city seemed to have gotten on board right away.

"Those chaps working on the banner must have spread the word, look at this crowd," Soranin spoke under breath as the horses began to weave through a hoard of townsfolk. Alive with nationalist pride, people swarmed the vendors lining Trainer's Row who had somehow already devised sales like "Soldier Sundaes –

Frozen Cream at Discount Price" and "Footmen Pay Less: BUY OUR YAK WOOL". Porter thought it was a pleasant notion, but could tell that Soranin shared in his sadness.

The people they rode for had that thick veil pulled over their faces. The fun, story-like conspiracies Porter always believed in, a poem compared to the true conspiracy, dominating the entire land they lived in, was a harsh truth. Kettlestep dodged stepping on a child dressed in an adult's too large helmet, but with a cheering smile on his face and "On you soldiers!" jumping from his lips.

The city looked small behind the troop. Porter hadn't left the city in some time. The last time he had gone outside the wall for anything other than a routine check on crack development in the otherwise flawless brick was to collect Forever Frogg carcasses and pay out the trappers who had slain them near Gelor.

Porter craned his head around toward the Northern entrance, and sighed as he saw the small shack he and his family once called home. Newer shacks had taken hold of the area around it, but he had some silent pride in the idea that no other family had moved into the one room bungalow. The last and only place he had known his mother.

Kettlestep butted heads with Nin'tei, joshing as friends rekindling, and Porter thought about his mother. Porter thought his father's drinking may have pushed her from the nest. He now knew his father was a drunk of a drinker. When he drank, it must have left his mother to take care of their child, and Podrick, too, some nights. Dad had never cleaned up his act, proper, but had become as good as a father as any man who thinks they can raise a human being can be, which is not ever as good as the natural way a woman can.

Porter unbuckled his knap sack for a bit of Hopejule jam on thin bread.

"Let's keep the horses at an alternating trot every few hours," Leoric called from the front, "so as to make a better pace to Ollette. I want to impress King Ernhart with the speed we make."

"Bugger the king," Soranin said into his flagon.

"Be honest, now," Porter said with a smile.

"I don't mean it, damn. I don't know what I think," Soranin said. Porter realized he had spoken to his most trusted,

only friend, as little as ever since their dinner at the Tower of
Indecision.

"Are you out of sorts, man?" Porter asked.

"I still am loyal to the king, of course, but I can't seem to
reason why he feels he needs to," Soranin dropped his voice, "lie
to all his people. An enlightened population could lead to so much
more for all of us."

"There's your problem; all of us, not just the Ernharts.
He means to keep the people as an unknowing, contented lot who
couldn't unseat him and his oligarchy if they rallied every pick
axe, pitch fork and potato in all of the West Lands. His wealth and
station grows while Caprican consciousness shrinks."

"He can't really mean it. I don't believe it," Soranin's
hands tightened on his reins. A look like the captain of the army
had just eaten a Khu'Roni Erroneous Pepper was etched on his
face, and had chased it with more fire.

Porter decided now might not be the best time for
conversation. The road ahead was long, and if that seems poetic
it shouldn't: the road from Caprica to Ollette was a straight,
hoof beaten, long road. The trip took about two and a half days
on horse, and though Capricans took it to collect taxes in Gelor
Porter had never gone past that laboring place. The road spoke
a disquieting unpleasantness. Porter felt that it too yearned to be
elsewhere, that too many hooves had trodden this ambling path
for nothing good.

The eight horses, with silent men upon their backs,
had come far enough now that the city could be said to be "in the
distance." The din of cheering voices long faded, the sun high.
The travelers settled into the concept of riding horses all day;
something one does not forget, but when one hasn't had the joy
of doing so in a while, it can rouse unfortunate memories of being
saddle sore. This was Porter's thought, any ways, as he unfastened
his bag and reached in for a bit more Hopejule jam.

His eyes darted to the saddle bag prepared by one of
the workers earlier in the morning as he unscrewed the lid to his
treat; what goods had the king's men packed on to him and his
steed?

Porter glanced at Soranin, feeling dumb and unprepared. The red head's eyes were soldiering forwards, and the other men of the troop seemed to be doing the same. He never understood the seriousness some took upon themselves when performing tasks for their kingdom. Let's not flatter ourselves, fellows, Porter would think. Heroes we are not, only slaves to whatever master we've picked, consciously or otherwise.

The thought raw in his mind, he untied one of the bags: cloth, rope, a brown paper package, and Porter spotted it: a brownish bottle of ale. Porter wasn't sure what ale it was, but knew he didn't care. His plated hand screamed for it, stretching and contorting towards it.

This is not my master. Porter recoiled, fastened his bag, and smiled a nervous smile toward a not-looking Soranin. Silence pervaded again.

"So what's the plan, then?" one newt called from behind Porter.

"Yeah, what's the plan? We ought to know," another newt called from the rear. Porter realized the two must be eager to impress, or do something besides ride horses across the beautiful country side as their first military escapade.

"You ought to know?" Leoric said, a jarring strength of rage bracing his words. "You OUGHT to be quiet. You OUGHT to speak when spoken to, and you OUGHT to figure out a way to appear drastically more intelligent than you truly are."

Leoric allowed the men behind him to take point as he sauntered his horse next to the horses of the men who had chirped up, much to their remorse. Soranin sighed.

"We only want to know how best to help, sir," one of them said.

"You've got my attention now, and want me to regale you with what you can do? I'd like you to regale me," Leoric looked amused. "Tell me something about Diandre's Road I don't know about."

"Sorry?" the other one of the two asked.

"What do you mean sorry? Tell me something about Diandre's Road I said."

"What's a Dianders Road?"

"Don't you know anything about Diandre's Road? Dee-

ann-dree, by the way. . It's the road we're on – the interchange
from the Bastions to Roiling. I learned all about it during my
studies and training in Khu'Ron."

There was a pause as everyone continued to not want
to talk to Leoric. This didn't daunt him.

"Diandre Muckshoot was the first successful smuggler
during the first years after the settling of Roiling Tide, the sinking
of the Heavy Bay. In the year 121, I believe, Muckshoot saw policy to
sanction exploration east. He saw businesses opening, trade posts
really, and observed the opportunity to privatize the bringing of
goods across the country side. A good campaign, but of course
greed took hold of Muckshoot, as it does many a would be fine
entrepreneur."

One of the young soldiers had quit paying attention,
had never really begun, and in response Leoric paused his story,
grabbed the soldier by his arm and jerked him about on his horse:

"Am I boring you, newt?"

"Sir, no, I only-"

"Your privilege to observe the gorgeous hills quietly
has passed you by like a punished child and supper, so pay attention!" Leoric tossed his arm away in disgust and continued. Porter
couldn't help but smile.

"Muckshoot began to travel with enormous stores of
alcohol. Again, not an issue, but it became clear he was selling the
alcohol to distributors who sold it at abusive prices to developing
townships and their young school children. The gentry noticed
this but paid it no mind. Muckshoot took this as a nod of approval,
and began to move so much alcohol back and forth that his path
began to form, physically, in the land - Diandre's Road."

"Muckshoot would have been able to operate this
business of his more or less indefinitely, but again greed tainted
him as he decided to add ellerwight to his stockade of goods from
the east.

The sent-along newts did pay attention now. The army
captains tuned in as well. Their horses sauntered along.

"Soon school children were appearing in class completely dazed, acting like flies caught in molasses, or simply not
appearing at all. Ellerwight was branded illegal, school children

were ridded of the stuff and Muckshoot was arrested and hung."

"What's that got to do with our ride, then?" Porter asked.

"Bandits and smugglers, Muckshoot's alleged descendants, still frequent this road as much as they did, that's what! Dangerous folk lurk in every corner," Leoric warned.

The troop of men looked around them: completely open meadows that ran into gentle hills as far as the eye could see, except tfor he approaching sight of Gelor, still far to the east.

"Which corners do you speak of, Leoric? To our left or the one just ahead?" Soranin asked, pandering disinterest in his voice.

"That's enough out of you, captain," Leoric said, dragging the last word. "And certainly enough out of the both of you. Now assume rank and be silent, if you can."

And with that, Leoric stopped talking and got back in line.

Chapter 8

Gelor was pleasant, which was perhaps the best way to
think about it. And the only way to think about it.

Porter wished he wasn't so cynical, but it did seem
like a township of little value to him. The land sloped down like
a chute, Diandre's Road following, to the entrance of the brown
and green township. Not every township dressed itself as nicely
as Gelor, though the humble township of Lurse owned the light
blue and pink seascape aesthetic it was going for, and it was still
not dressed very well. A time-taken wooden sign hung from two
pleading pieces of rope over their heads as the road entered the
township: "Gelor: It Gets No Better, Fell-or!" A vote to re-commis-
sion a city welcome sign to replace the clearly void of actual effort
sign had been vetoed by the mayor numerous times since the
township was settled. The mayor liked word play.

Green roofs with brown bodies made up most buildings in Gelor. Green hats and brown vests for nearly every man,
and green bonnets with brown dresses for the women. Overalls,
brown, with green buttons for the kids.

Gelor produced a hardy amount of Caprica's garments
and cloth, due perhaps to Diandre's travels, and it was proud.
Porter realized there was a sewing company or a retail store on
every block. A mustachioed man in his green, chic pointed hat
smiled and waved at Porter. He returned the gesture, regardless of
his fashion-induced cringe.

"How long does it take to travel through?" Porter asked.
The overbearing style of the township made him uncomfortable,
like each person was only a doll replica of the real people who
had once lived here.

"A bit, considering we need to give the horses a chance
to rest and eat before the final leg to where we camp for the eve,"
Soranin responded. Leoric gave a quick nod from the front, having
listened in.

Porter groaned, ran a hand through his hair and beard.
The sun was going down, he supposed, but Tellor did he want to
leave Gelor already. Perhaps it was because he knew his father had
once lived here. Following Dad felt strange, why he felt strange

most days.

"I'm only glad we aren't staying here for the night," Soranin continued, as the group slowed in search of a general store.

"You too, eh?" Porter asked.

"Something feels...incomplete, fraudulent. It's odd, I remember Gelor favorably," Soranin swigged his Skell, and when they did arrive at "Gelor's Grandest General", he explained to the soldiers it was important that they bought plenty of feed because they wouldn't shop again until Ollette.

The captain and second captain waited outside the general store, leaning on the tie posts of the horses, as the soldiers and remaining captain purchased the goods. The townsfolk continued to bustle, Porter continued to feel on edge. Someone touched his arm.

She was blonde, with long long curls running down well past her shoulders. Her smile was big, but she showed no teeth and Porter thought it was adorable. The girl was a sight for saddle-sore eyes, and her body, in a green camisole, appealed to the twelve-year-old in him.

"Er, hello," Porter said, wondering why he tended to pride himself on wit, but then any time he interacted with women it became instant tragedy..

"Hello, you're not from Gelor are you?" The girl wasn't asking like your average, polite stranger might. She asked like she was afraid, or at least curious because of what she knew. More than Porter.

"I'm not, my father lived here for a bit, but no, I- "

"We're just seeing about our Dad's old house, a quick jaunt really," Soranin cut in. A woman, long brown curls, had joined him on his opposite side, but it didn't seem to be as pleasant for him as it was for Porter.

The two women and Soranin were staring at Porter. Porter realized he had spent too much time thinking again and that even now-

"AREN'T we just stopping through, Porter?" Soranin asked.

"Right. Seeing Dad's old stomping grounds."

"What was your father's name?" The blonde girl asked

with a smile.

"Podrick Rosset."

"That's one long first name," she smiled, her eyes shackled to his. Porter saw future in her face.

The girl opened her mouth to speak again when the four soldiers were ejected as one big blob out of the rickety general store door, and already behind them Leoric ranted on about the feed costing as much money as all the white brick in Caprica's walls.

"That's us. Thanks, then," Soranin said as he straightened to join the fellow footmen.

"Hold on now. Why don't you all stay in Gelor with us?"

"We're camping, just for the fun of it actually," Soranin responded to the brunette who had laid a hand on his shoulder. He shifted from foot to foot.

Leoric took notice of the four's conversation:

"For the fun of it? We're to spread the word of "Fantastic Footman" in the name of the king, not enjoy sweets around a bonfire, you dolt."

Soranin dragged his hand across face, buzzing his lips as the girls smiled.

"Soldiers?! You have to stay in town! We have empty rooms down at the Fancy!" The blonde smiled as she pulled Porter her way. Porter smiled and shrugged, Soranin shook his head, Leoric puffed his chest past Soranin and the four half-confused, half-thoroughly confused soldiers lead the horses in tow.

The Fancy was a circular, sort of cake shaped building down the road, in nearly the center of town. The sun had gone down, and it was apparent that with its setting the peoples of Gelor streamed to the edificial pastry-like oasis. The girls, sporting grins like it truly was a building made of cake, slammed open the doors and the inn exploded.

Men, women, and even children adorned in their green and brown uniforms cheered and greeted the men. Leoric beamed, understanding finally that he was indeed correct in just how fantastic he supposed he was all these years. More women appeared, leading Leoric and the four soldiers to the immaculate looking bar, while Porter and Soranin were led by their escorts to a simple but long table.

Soranin and Porter glanced around, Soranin with anxiety and Porter with a trouble-be-gone glee, and they began to absorb the Fancy. The bartender was an enormous, joyous looking man with a baby clean face and a spotted bow tie, brown and green linen wreaths hung over the stair wells bedecking the grand entrance hall. Women were dancing on tables and men were hooting them on, then they would swap.

The blonde woman asked Porter if he wanted a drink.

"Of course I do, but I-"

A tall stout of booze slammed in front of the astonished Porter, and a beguiling blonde stared him down from across the table from whence it came. Porter couldn't deny her, nor did he want to, so he chugged the roasty ale. Another slid into its spot. Porter repeated the process.

Soranin began to unwind. The wary Captain decided this was the Gelor he remembered. Leoric was "captivating" his entourage of four men who had become his personal auditory slaves, catering to both his stories and his fits of anger. The bartender smiled and laughed along as Leoric regaled his audience with the tale of his griger brawling training session in Khu'Ron.

"It really did have arms the size of an ape and the head of a cat, and I'll tell you it wasn't those Khu'Roni spices going to my head either, though those were of course delicious and of course in every bowl of rice," the petite smile Leoric often bore spread from the brim of his mug as very drunk Gelorans and much too sober soldiers listened and laughed.

Porter's head was swimming. The blonde woman was tugging on his armor, asking him to take it off.

"Should be fine," Porter meant to ask Soranin, but he was having a conversation with the brunette any ways. "Jest where's tha room?"

"Come on," she led him upstairs. The Fancy felt like Ivan's, Porter decided, because once reaching the second floor the building led to dormitories. The duo strolled the hall towards the end, holding hands, passing numerous empty rooms along the way. Porter's drunken mind noticed their emptiness, and as they entered a room at the farthest throw of the room he went to kiss the blonde girl. She stayed his lips with a finger, and asked him to remove his armor. He did, and she helped.

"Tellor be praised," Porter whispered.

They kissed, amongst other tangling.

Down stairs the soldiers had finally gotten as drunk as they could. It helped to endure Leoric's now huge, uproar story of bedding three Khu'Roni dancers at once. Soranin sat at the long table, middling his drink but enjoying the taste of it nonetheless.

The night wound on, and Porter fell asleep in the crook of the girl's arm, enjoying the warmth of a slender body for the first time in three years. A grin plastered on his face, he enjoyed a dreamless sleep. The moon was glaring at the Fancy before all the men who had left from Caprica had finally had their take of ale and, after the baby faced bar tender had whipped them up, fish fries with scones before being led to their rooms.

"Hey man," Soranin leaned in to one of the faceless soldier's ears. His name was Duncan Day and, unlike the other newts, he was only a year or so younger than Soranin; Duncan just hadn't made much of himself back in Marryfarm selling sweaters made of Billy Yak fur so he'd enlisted, "weren't we going ta keep on tonight? Camp out a waysz past Gelor?"

Duncan's eyes bleared, and his big black mustache drooped and ruffled in response. Soranin was a bit bleary himself, and shrugged off his nagging voices. Leoric was still rambling on, some story of fishing for Scorn Trout in the Yalei River and how "it was the biggest fish I've seen, plenty sure," but late or not they all found a room. They were helped out of their armor, but Soranin handled it himself seeing as he was only pretty drunk.

They slept. The Fancy's lights went out upstairs, and in the grand hall, but the kitchen light beat on.

Chapter 9

"Frogg I've got your opal right here!" Porter called, a gray color about his face. The morning bell did not ring, so far as Porter could hear, but a ray of sun had beamed through his window. "It's right..."

Porter sat up. He didn't even have his tunic on any more, he noticed. The hungover traveler rested his hand against his face, combed his beard, and observed his room the best he could. There was a wardrobe in the corner, and a chair and a vanity case. Brown and green, the lot. Porter rose and attempted to shake off his stupor. He approached the window and slid his greasy fingers through green and brown curtains. Outside Gelor did not seem to bear the same appeal it did the day before.

People were bustling to and fro, still in green and brown garb, but they were not greeting and waving anymore. They moved without speaking and without glee. Porter spotted a child no older than nine with a far more grizzled look than he had ever seen on Bodeman the skunk knight back in Caprica.

Porter was grateful to find his pants and he slipped them on, reflecting on last night. He ranked events in his mind from least suspicious and or memorable to most: they had been invited to stay at an inn instead of leaving Gelor, Porter had made this decision for the whole party, there was some type of festivity taking place at the Fancy. Immediately their group had been swept up in its delight and hilarity, Porter had gotten drunk off of two tall stouts of ale, maybe more. He cursed under his breath, tying his breeches and slipping on his boots, which he was also thankful to have located.

The blonde woman, who Porter had either never learned the name of or had obliterated with liquor, had invited him to stay in this room with her. Porter paused. Is that how it had gone? No, she wanted his armor off specifically, but that did lead to the most memorable and or important event of the evening: Porter had had sex for the first time in three years. Porter laughed.

Porter's shirt was hanging on the wardrobe knob, and he proceeded to sling it on. To his surprise the wardrobe it was resting upon had no armor. This was an unforeseen and major issue for Porter. The groggy soldier had needed his shining plate to be resting in wait for him, but found only a sense of despair and embarrassment in the empty closet.

There was an anxious noise, a timid cacophony, resonating from outside Porter's door. He eeked his head into the hall, saw all the doors to the rooms were open, and he heard the chatter was coming from downstairs.

The floor felt hard and unkempt with splintery wood under Porter's bare feet. It occurred to him that he was only in his billowy shirt and shorts. Porter didn't mind. The bleary-eyed traveler was confident that downstairs he'd find all his companions, probably eating eggs and porridge, his new once-lover touting his recently polished plate armor. Maybe even goodwill gifts from the innkeeper for the brave adventurers as they departed.

Chapter 10

　　She knew she was being followed by him. It's never as surprising as they like to think, being pursued, because if it wasn't surprising they would have to realize pursuing women is not new or unique. They're predators like anything else in those moments.

　　The trees had been thick and her hunch was confirmed by the noise of pine being snapped. It had been only a hunch in the openness of plains but became a fact once the forest revealed him. The thickness, the togetherness of the woods was a comfort to her. He was ruining it.

　　A clearing opened and sun light became presence. A pond, a small lake really, relaxed to her left with a big reflection of a snowy mountain painting its still surface. Old Yit was visible now, though way off. The first mountain, the base being an hour's walk from her if she went North instead of West, was called Dog's Eye. The summit looked like one of those blue dog eyes that are remarkable because dogs have dark colored eyes, like black and brown.

　　Being pursued never bothered her before. But being pursued day after day by increasing amounts of strangers, and by violence, was growing old. As old as it may be and as much as she clung to a change in that old system, she lived in the day and she continued.

Book IV

Chapter 1

Porter was sad, surprised, at how fully wrong his assumption had been. Usually he was only sort of wrong. In this case, he was fully wrong.

Porter's companions were nowhere in sight. Well, Duncan Day was there. Duncan Day was on all fours like a hog, his mustache and belly hanging beneath him, with a large brown sack on his back. The newt was clearly suffering under its weight, though it seemed like someone had been thoughtful and placed a small dish of water below his head. Duncan had no ability to reach it without disrupting the sack, it appeared, but it appeared thoughtful any ways.

The most rotund and round character Porter had ever seen sat to the right of Duncan Day in a chair laughably small for him. The person had a skin like charred log, black with orange cracked patches, but the skin could be seen only where heavy amber feathers did not prop out like an aviary in a chaotic dream. On his head was a tiny red, velveteen crown with two obelisks protruding from the top like red and green dominoes. Opaque, milky white eyes like tea dishes pinned either side of a long beak, stained hard with time. A man's face was seen there, but through expression and habit. Though humanoid, it was only those famil-iarities that gave humanness. The visage was nightmarish.

To match the crown of hot red was a cape and vest of similar hue, but the esteemed-looking anthropomorph's pants were a grass green, and Porter thought that the person seemed like the ruler of a simple farm now. This person, however, still did not seem like a person at all.

Surrounding this enigmatic giant were three more feathered beings, less round, more muscular, with the same obfuscating, pallid eyes. They had furry hoods and dashing green clothes covering their abhorrable bodies. Porter began to assume gender, foolishly, because of size and shape and clothing. Next to the bigger ones were slimmer bodied, heavy green dresses. Cheer hung on the lips, beaks, on all of them.

Porter was a bit taken aback. He had not a single idea on the spectrum of these folk. He was overwhelmed then that the stories of these wild people beyond the West Lands must be true! How wonderful and terrifying to be introduced to something so novel and unreal.

They paid him no mind. The bizarre looking men and women, folk, were preoccupied with flirting and drinking a particularly brown ale, and the possible leader was running his eyes over a lengthy scroll. Duncan Day really wasn't in a position to notice Porter.

Porter felt it was an even more unpleasant experience that he would have to be the one to have to disturb this scene. Awkwardly, with all the gusto he could muster, Porter cleared his throat.

Fourteen dishes of eyes set closely to beaks struck Porter like a switch.

"Good morning," Porter said.

"You're right," one of the feathery ones replied. This one had a thick caterpillar-like mustache resting over his beak, looking almost like mud to cut glare, and a spiky black beard. "We've got much to celebrate, spread, you're right."

"Oh?" Porter did his best to remain cordial. He took a seat in a tired brown chair. The whole foyer of the inn, where they had feasted the night before, seemed devoid of any joy this morning. The sun poured in from high windows like orange juice into a glass.

"Yes, man. Last night we began the wedding preparations, yes man!" That one's partner laughed as they nuzzled their head in the mustachioed companion's neck.

"That's terrific. You're getting married!" Porter said with a forced grin. The whereabouts of his companions, besides the clearly subjugated Duncan Day, were still unknown to Porter, and burning in his mind.

"No, my daughter is to be married," The globular, prestigious one, who sported the red crown, stood, casting his lengthy sheet of paper aside. It flittered slowly on to Duncan Day's back, and this extra weight seemed to be like a boulder sliding into place for the steeped man. "No."

"Sorry?"

"It is my daughter who is getting married, it is," the enormous one strode towards Porter, closing the small distance, and began to size up Porter with his anchorless eyes. "Bunera! Come out, Bunera."

At the sound of the bellowing voice an eighth black and orange and feathered person strode from a room behind the bar that Porter had not known about before. The newcomer was small, at least Porter assumed by the large breasts and rotating hips, and sported a similar green band and long skirt, both were pleated and seemed to have been crafted in Gelor. This last one had less tarnished skin, white and black, like a sandy volcano pre-burst.

The smallest and newest took a seat by Porter, and gripped his hand. The hand was long with feathers and had thin, strong fingers, and underneath the nesty thing was a loving kidness. Porter had not been touched this way in years.

Porter thought of Ula. Then didn't.

The groggy soldier also remembered the woman from last night.

"Bunera," Porter collected himself as the being laughed. "Did you bring me here last night? From outside the general store? Your hair is, er, I-less blonde-"

"Bunera picked her king, Bunera picked," the largest bird-person said as he began to pace behind Porter, continuing to examine him as though Porter were to be his breakfast. The next item for consummation.

"I don't think I understand," Porter said, gripping the one called Bunera's hand in as platonic a way as he could manage.

"Ah, yes you are a man. So confused, so easily beguiled, never sure of anything in the vast narrowness of his existence, ah," the pacing continued. "These are the dangers of taking a man to wed, these are."

Bunera took pleasure in getting a chance to explain things herself, so as to prove her father wrong. The excited girl managed only to prove him right.

"I was smitten with you when I saw you standing by your valiant steed and friends yesterday. I convinced my sister to let me meet you, we were just walking and - never mind, I'm going on. I didn't want to startle you with my true appearance, and you seemed to be so smitten with my human form, I was smitten," Bunera laughed and squeezed Porter's hand again. The bearded man was confused still, and couldn't find any reason to stop the girl now. Porter could hardly find a reason to leave Gelor at all at the moment. His concepts of what attraction and beauty and arousal were within the Caprican paradigm were changing, growing.

A basilisk stare reined on the laughing lovers from behind Porter, sported by the father of Bunera, prompting Porter to move the conversation along.

"Your human form?" Porter asked. The stories Pod told him had never mentioned bird skinned shape changers, but Porter may have ignored those stories or burned them away with drink.

"My tengö skin may have frightened your uneducated mind, so I simply painted myself a human, my tengö," Bunera said it like a kind teacher, though her repeating the words "my tengö" felt forced, not habitual. The excitement squeezed his hand the hardest after she spoke those words.

The joy of the moment seemed to have slid away. Now Porter felt like he had been dropped deep in enemy lines, but the enemies wanted him there. For the moment.

"And you're getting married now? That's...terrific," Porter noticed he said that before.

"We're getting married now. It is tengö way, we're getting," Bunera's eyes squinted when she smiled. This person had the ability to morph to her surroundings – incredible. He could not explain it physically, but

Porter thought she was gorgeous.

Porter also had an adult Billy Yak lodged in his throat. "A drink, my love, a drink?" The girl asked. She placed
her hand on Porter's chest as he wheezed, and she motioned
to one of the other tengös to fetch some water. Porter sipped it, breathing through his nose, and composed himself.

"I, I had no idea..." Porter said in a sputter. The glass of water in his right hand and the soft pink hand in his left were tethering him to the room, to reality. If this was reality, at all. Tengös in Gelor, he thought. Alright, Ortimer, alright.

"Of course you did not, of course," blurted the biggest one seated across from Porter and Bunera, in front of the six other tengös who had been finishing their drinks and listening to the proverbial origin story of the new couple. "Bunera, this is why it is best to marry another tengö. Capitol Llih has many fine suitors, ones with estates and prestige," he slid one feathery, enormous mitt across the table and rested his hand on his daughter's free hand, "Can you not see what you do to our kingdom with this decision, Bunera this?"

Royalty. Tengö royalty.

"What brings you to Gelor?" Porter interrupted. "If I can, er, ask."

"It was merely a family holiday at first, to visit Diandre's Road, but the lovely garments of Gelor have kept us here much longer than anticipated, it was merely," one of the tengö men said. He seemed eldest, and had the eldest woman with him. If either were the genders Porter understood. Both had large muscles that seemed to meld with their clothing, as large muscles seem to do. King Vonnidine mashed his fingers like his hands were sparring, crowing.

"Bunera was coming of age, so we decided to move out the rest of the family and have a wedding here, in the new tengö city of Honor, Bunera was coming," the muscular tengö maybe woman said.

Porter's face was a tomato after she ended her sentence, and Porter believed the king tengö took note.

"Look here, human Porter. The Vonnidines have ruled Capitol LLih and the entirety of the tengö nation proudly and kindly for nearly eight hundred encathion, and I will not have you muss that up. Especially now that you and Bunera have begun the marriage ceremony, look here," he rose and looked back to his list.

"Heh, I, don't understand-"

"Do you continue to not understand or do you simply take pleasure from aggravating the king, do you continue?" the last tengö man shouted. This one was smallest, with a pointed goatee that was a vibrant green, and his wife had an earthier green coloring to her hair. "Princess Bunera took you to make love last night, in the sentinel outpost castle of King Vonnidine, lord elder of the Tengö Nation, and so this afternoon the wedding will be held in the castle's courtyard. The entire Vonnidine family will be in attendance, so they will need put their chores to task tomorrow, Princess Bunera took."

"We have learned to knit and sew beautifully from their prisoners, we have learned," the green haired woman smiled.

Porter realized why the citizens of Gelor had been so curt now. It was uncharacteristic of Westland folk to treat soldiers as such, but for peoples of a different land, nation, it may not be strange at all.

"Bunera and I did not make love," Porter decided it was time to find his party. "Where are my compatriots?" Porter glanced at Duncan Day, who was doing a remarkable job of being a coffee table.

"You did indeed make love, do not deny it, and your allies are all a part of the dowry, you did indeed," King Vonnidine seemed content to ignore Porter's protest. Perhaps he expected no better from a paltry human.

"How can you be sure?" Porter asked.

"Bunera's skin is feathery, cracked and orange. As a tengö mother to be, Bunera must wear this badge until she weds." Porter looked at her. Her skin was no less feathery, orange and cracked than anyone else in the rooms, except for he and Duncan Day. He began to protest.

"Tengös can tell the difference. We know her body and we know the way it has changed," the most muscular Vonnidine prince said, fast and hard.

Bunera blushed, sort of, then scooted closer to Porter.

Porter rooted his hand through his beard, hoping to pull it off,
damming his stupid lust. Admiring Bunera's power in taking him
for her own.

"What dowry?" Porter asked, as he scooted away from
the bird woman who he could not express himself about anymore.

The king laughed, and on cue his family followed suit.

"You assume someone as lowborn as yourself would
get my daughter purely from, what, some conceived notion of
vanity and confidence? From a lord I would take land. From an
ambassador I would demand a treaty, and from a ruler I'd require
riches that would put your shiny stones to shame. You offer nothing except the promise of resource rich lands. Our vacation has
proved a most fruitful conquest of a land being squandered on
simple natives, and you also provided some sort of treaty to the
mayor of Ollette that the tengös will now claim, and most fruitful
of all are the slaves you brought in tow, you assume someone
as lowborn as yourself," the king was on one. Bunera stood and
went to his side, patting his forehead with a bit of cloth that she
produced from a nearby table.

"Slaves?! Those men are better warriors than I, and better men than you!" Porter said, realizing as he said it that of course
they weren't men, were they. Or were they? Who was he to say, to
know?

"Better at being men, sure. We're thankful tengös are
better than men, better at being. We operate in grays and fogs you
call dangerous and couldn't understand on your smartest day,"
the first tengö man said. All the tengös began to laugh. The foyer
seemed extra big.

"You'll understand after the wedding. You will have new
need of your former companions, for laundry and landscaping
I suppose, you'll understand!" The muscular tengö canned his
laughter until the end of his quip. An uproar of laughter bounced
around the building again, and this time even Bunera laughed a
bit.

"My sons are right, Westlander," the king said. "Once
you are blue skinned you will think much clearer. It is only a
shame you will retain some of your more primal human thought
patterns. The incredible egoism and the restrictive, binary views,

and of course the lack of proper dowry…"

"Oh father, please!" Bunera skipped behind Porter and laid her arms around his neck like a lasso, knotting them under his chest.

"Porter and I love each other, and you did not shame the politician from the Reef when he had little to give along for Lysa, oh father please," Bunera looked pouty at the black haired tengö who was the companion of the first tengö prince.

"Eastern men are different, you know this. It of course did not hurt to have our lands spared from the ravaging as the foundation for a dowry, Eastern men," the prince fired as he gripped his wife. King Vonnidine nodded.

"You're going to turn me into a tengö," Porter hadn't stayed caught up in the conversation.

"Aunt Finora does the incantations like a gorgeous machine, Aunt Finora," King Vonnidine continued to read over his list. "Has anyone seen her? She will need to be ready by mid-sun rotation because I have here that the roast/toast/boast will proceed at late-sun rotate."

"I believe she said this morning that she was going to see how the human feed was holding up in the factory. The grain-sliding mechanism for the trough was jamming, I believe she said," the green goateed prince said as he chewed a fingernail.

Porter realized just what the scenario in Gelor had become: a merry vacation for tengö monarchs which had resulted in the imprisonment of an entire town. And with a marriage for the youngest daughter, their taking of Gelor would become a permanent affair. The gluttonous king's staking of more of the West Lands as a honeymoon would not be far off.

"You mentioned a ravaging?" Porter asked.

"Enough talk, enough talk," the king waved his sausage hand. "You need to ready yourself for the ceremony. Bunera needs do the same, so please return to your room. Your garb has been readied for you, you need to."

Porter raised his hand in protest, but saw the tengös were not interested in his opinion. Duncan Day shook his head at Porter from his tabled form. The groom to be lowered his hand and instead smiled, nodded and returned to his room, wondering

just how many prisoners were in that factory, and how well guarded it would be against a lone, confused drunkard.

King Vonnidine watched Porter walk back up the stairs
and smiled. The king waved his mustachioed son over.

"Is the ellerwight moved?"

"It is with the prisoners. We are ready to end the
façade."

"That's fine, that's fine."

Chapter 2

Community spaces were radical in Third Maple Hill. They had to be because the world doesn't have enough to give everyone everything they want. It's got enough to give everyone enough, and that's enough.

The members of the village knew this precept and they treated it with respect, working hard in the dirt by morning and drinking earthy drinks at night, things fermented long hours and days and brought to warmly kept homes in the dark. The way they worked together and looked after the land was as inspiring as it was revolutionary. The cities wanted to be as efficient and sustainable in their practice as Third Maple Hill. But the urbanites never asked them how it was done, so of course they never did it as well.

Traders would come and buy their goods, goods like korekwood, Grain Flower and skell, and the traders would sell them at their outposts and on their travels to merchants who worked for municipalities, the same types of places which tried un-successfully to be like Third Maple Hill. In this practice, members of the Third Maple Hill community barely ever spoke to non-community members. Only a few of them had any skills in bartering, then, because in their home it was so natural to give each other goods with only a smile and a nod as payment.

Pansen was a barterer, and it was therefore seen as important for him to gain these skills. His learning, apprenticing, training and traveling were all understood to be foundations of his future as acquestier. Bringing home these new skills was under-stood to be the only reason to gain them in the first place

But all the preparing, all the explicitly focusing of his time, of his life, gave Pansen anxiety at times. Not at this precise moment, not on the side of this mountain, but he reflects to a time when he felt the powerful anxiety.

His hands were plunged into soil, strangling the roots of some vegetables, and it was for the last time that day. Dropping the last bit of produce in his bin, he lifted it over his head and walked toward the cart, pulled by dlower. He threw the goods in the back and hopped on the back of the dlower. Only one pulled the cart, because it wasn't a big cart. It was full of gourds. The dlower turned into a yellow chrysanthemum at night, so it was, of course, a yellow dlower.

After riding to the edge of town, Pansen waited. The expanse of Third Maple Hill was covered in land used to its utmost. Of the land, nearly all was cultivatable. It required for its workers to be creative, though, and to listen to the dirt when it was exhausted. Once it was used up, they reimagined it into something different, like the site of a hut or bathhouse.

A slinky, snaky man came up to him on the back of a yak. He had a spotty beard and an oily pony tail. His lips were fishy and his eyes were big, spacious things. He smiled and seemed somehow kind. His yak let Pansen know that he was coming from the West Lands. He did not understand that obfuscated place.

Pansen waved at him and slid off of his mount. He went to the man as he slid off of his own.

"Hello," Pansen said.

"Hallo," the man said. "You're Pansen, then?"

"That's right, I am."

"I'm Duker Date. New to this route, working for Derek?"

"I know Derek, yes. it's good to meet you," Pansen said.

Duker seemed to wait for Pansen to go on. He didn't. Duker continued.

"Still got the Lemoniny? A bushel?"

"Yes, that's right," Pansen said.

"Could we take a look?"

"Yes."

"Now?"

"Yes," Pansen said. They walked to the back of the cart and Pansen undid the latch, letting a small bed unfold and a few of the big gourds slide into a new position.

"Wow, I've never seen so many at one time," Duker said. The Lemoninies were thick and hard, and their pale yellow did not do justice to the sweet, candied insides. "I remember being a kid, me and my friends would sit just outside the market sharing as big a one we could steal with one big spoon. Then when I went home I'd see my mom baking a pie with one she had bought that was somehow even bigger."

Duker turned to Pansen.

"It must be so hard to get these up, out of the ground I mean," Duker said. He began to pull stones out of a pouch.

"It isn't hard," Pansen said, taking some gourds in his arms.

"How not?"

"We all work together. It doesn't feel hard that way, even if it is. The food is for all of us, as is the money we take for selling it, and so we all are rewarded for all of our effort."

Duker dropped his gourds in the knapsacks hanging on the yak's sides.

"You mean the workers aren't paid? They're working for fun or something?"

"There is joy, of course," Pansen said. "But that's not why they're working. The money is for all of us, workers first, even. It's just that they can't use money in Third Maple Hill, so they kind of collect it."

"Collect it?! Like save it you mean?"

"Think of it like you collect paintings, for show."

"Man, what?

"If we ever spend money, when we paid for a kiln last year, we ask everyone if they'd like to spend the money like that. If we do, we do."

Duker shook his head.

"Your society sounds nice. That's not how we do things in the West Lands."

Only a few lemoniny remained. The sun was beginning to go down, the mountains closer than they would be in the West Lands but just as impressive, as real.

"Well enjoy it out here. It sure is beautiful. That slow way of life, beautiful."

"Thank you," Pansen said, moving one last lemoniny.

"Zoning has been getting unkempt, really," Duker said, to himself it seemed. He began to count out the payment.

"Hm, I don't know much about that," Pansen said.

"Olette is trying to spread. Nothing new it seems, though from the sounds of it so are the tengo," Duker said. "Big swells in the world. Folks are taking what they can, from whomever they can, while they can, yeah?"

"We are doing fine with what we have," Pansen nodded. "We aren't concerned with this expansion you describe."

"Oh," Duker looked at Pansen with care now, "I didn't mean you all should expand. I meant you all should be careful of those who would take your land, you know," he lifted a fruit. "The lemoniny and stuff. They'll be knocking on your door in not too long, man."

Pansen was momentarily frozen by this. His mind went from meditating to puzzle making.

Duker placed the money in Pansen's working palm.

"I'll see you again," Duker said. "I do everything okay here?"

"Um, yes," Pansen muttered. "Business as usual, right? Ha."

Duker waved a hand, licking his lips. He rode away. Pansen realized then, like other times, his duties. What he will need to do to defend his community, his family and his livelihood. The lemoniny, the dlowers, the ancestors who have paved the way for his being here now. He thought about these things and others as he rode back toward town, foreign municipality coin in tow.

The roots are already being uprooted, the times already changing, the soil already shifting. His father takes care of these decisions now, but after the blizzard on the mountain, and the ritual slaying that Pansen must offer, this will be his burden.

Retain the orthodox ways, the beauty and the need of love, and be vigilant against this impending expansion.

Chapter 3

The sun was zenithing in the afternoon. The tengö cabal found a spot in the town where the light would be perfect for Porter and Bunera to wed, just outside Porter's window. The bearded groom to be knew time was short, and had formulated a new plan. A plan where he would stay a bachelor, and, if he could, liberate some folks, to boot.

When Porter had attempted to put his plan into action earlier, he had found the door being presided over by the most muscular of King Vonnidine's tengö princes. Jury still out on their gender. Their gender, however, still not affecting their ability to physically intimidate Porter. The prince claimed to only want to know how he could assist the second captain prepare for the wedding.

Porter figured this may be true, considering how the ceremonial tengö groom garb was baffling. It was so foreign, Porter had considered asking the prince for help, but decided it would only give the guard a story to tell over the reception's numerous toasts. If, that is, Porter's plan failed.

The strange thing about the clothing was the length. The robe Porter was to wear made him look like an ancient magus, or an old wizard head of state. Both of these stereotypes in Porter's mind had long sleeves and their robes gave them the appearance of a slug, dragging themselves along the ground. There was also a hat, which also managed to be too long. It was not a pointed cap like an ancient magi or an old wizard may have worn, but instead had almost a Khu'Roni sultan like appearance because of the bloated shape of the red and white hat. The difference was that the hat lay backward over his head and possessed enough excess cloth to fall to the middle of his back, looking a bit like a washed ashore jellyfish.

The only other unfortunate things with his matrimonial garb were the trinkets and artifacts. There were many. Five golden rhombuses hung heavy on five looped chains that drooped from the jellyfish head dress. It took careful threading to implant each one. The crosses ascended in size, culminating with the ultimate cross in the middle, which held a terrific red stone at the diamond's intersection. This last one left an imprint on Porter's forehead.

Porter almost asked for assistance with the last piece, a fine gold and crimson scepter. The hues matched those on the robe and hat, but there was something unfamiliar about it. Perching on the end of the staff was a red stone, tengö crimson, and numerous flexible wires hanging off like dead arms. There were three of them, and they had pointed ends on the end of each.

They were tiny assassins, long and dangerous. All three pieces of garb were beautiful and different and Porter didn't belong in them, they were not his. The implanting of culture was strange to even a Caprican, who throughout history was the one who did the robbing of culture from others.

Porter felt uncomfortable with the ornamental rod, and decided to just tie the three ropes around his wrist. He heaved up the window in his room. Outside his door, the most muscular tengö prince noticed the noise, and decided the human was only being his basic human self, and couldn't care less about his sister's wedding. When his next meal would be coming was of much more interest.

It was windy in Gelor. The garment township's green flags welcomed the wind by bending with it from the point of numerous buildings, and Porter could see them all from his window, almost the highest point for miles.

The actual highest point was the second floor of the cake shaped inn. Porter lifted himself out his window, began scaling the wall. Pointed weather vanes, topped with more green flags, spun around the soldier as he gathered his bearings on the lonesome roof.

Drink would have been nice for this, Porter thought, and then he thought of his night time vomiting exploits the night before his departure.

Leaving the thought behind, Porter scouted the township. Homes, farm buildings in the distance, numerous shops in the foreground, and what Porter knew was the Vonnidine family strolling the town dotted here and there. Enough of a family to raze the town, and enough to have captured it, which is not hard with deceit. Then Porter saw it, the garment factory.

Though it was not the only location to produce cloth-ing, it was the largest. And inside were the hundreds of Gelorans, West Landers and Porter's companions. Except for poor Duncan Day.

The long robes kept Porter well incapacitated as he tried to move about. The basic plan had been to scale down the side of the building, but since the basic plan also required Porter to blend in with the Vonnidine tengös, Porter needed to keep his costume well and alive.

Blending in with tengös in Gelor. Assaulting, Porter thought. Is this what we did to Khu'Ron's tree strikers and Roiling Tide's fisherfolk? he wondered.

Lifting his robes as best he could, and being mindful and quite anxious about his elongated head piece, Porter crept across the roof towards the back of the building. Gelor's only scone shop happened to be here, attached to the back of the cake shaped building. "The Scone Ge-store" it was called. Gelorans were cursed with an awful sense of humor, Porter found.

The bearded second captain took his robes and rod to the ledge, and placed his feet against the back wall of "The Scone Ge-store". The red robes were caught under his feet, and this proved to help muffle his feet, as well, unfortunately, as to reduce his traction. Because of the soft steps, the plump Vonnidines inside the shop heard nothing over the clacking of their beaks, already blue from the scones. Then Porter began to walk his hands over the ledge and slowly slid his way to the earth below. The crimson cloth was a bit battered, otherwise Porter was able to straighten the hat and to place his rod under his hand like a cane. He took to the streets.

Tengös were easier to identify now because as they understood Porter would be married later in the day, they were inclined to applaud him. The would-be Gelorans smiled, chattered at him about the great King Vonnidine and the regent city Capital Llih, the gorgeous Bunera and the holy Aunt Finora. Their eyes were alive with tradition, but Porter was disturbed by the human skins they had not yet to depart from. Porter wanted to see their bird faces, not the faces of the souls trapped in the enormous building at the edge of town, the faces these invaders had stolen.

The building was not difficult to find once Porter had passed enough shape changing possible future in-laws. Brown, sodden, tired and indeed on the edge of town; the precipice of Gelor and the continuation of Diandre's Road. Porter was jealous of Diandre, then. The smuggler and folklore legend prescribed only to his own desires and whims as he curried products to and fro, stopping only to make money or see something he thought was fantastic. The second captain was aware that he was but a tool of a king who was as genuine as a straw man. Kalan and Diandre did not seem too different, servicing themselves first and damn the repercussions.

Cloudy, poorly constructed poetic thoughts will get me nowhere, and quick, Porter thought to himself as the shadow of the factory enveloped him. A smell of sharp gas hit Porter and snaked into his nose. The soldier shook with disgust, and his thoughts flashed to his allies inside. An enormous tengö stood outside, and watched Porter have his thoughts and olfactory senses assaulted before chiming in:

"Shouldn't you be preparing for the wedding, shouldn't you be?" The tengö guard asked. The veins stood out against his muscular arms, the chain mail doing no job of concealing the guard's strong body.

"Heh, erm, fellow," Porter chuckled, straightened his hat and planted his scepter, "I'll need to examine my...dowry."

Giggling came from behind the barn style doors that led into the factory, and the guard and Porter followed the fun noises as they moved along the wall out of sight until they came behind another door, smaller and with an unlit lantern hanging above it. A gorgeous, short haired and small busted tengö came out, teasing the other, following, tengö, who wore chain and also had muscular arms. The bigger one pinching the giggler, giggler asking him to stop, both giggling, and they both had volcanic skin and ashen feathers which Porter couldn't tell was any different than their everyday complexion but to them meant passion and romance and possibility.

The smaller lover, squawked, slapped the bigger one, ran off, half a glide, and the bigger tengö sidled into position next to Porter's recent associate. The tengös patted each other with their wings, grinning the whole time that they clacked and chattered. Porter did not understand their aberrant customs, and took this time to move towards the door. The two big guards continued to commune.

The odor of dye and oil was like heat in a furnace to Porter. The ceilings were high, yet the stench was an unavoidable irritant, and it stung Porter's eyes causing them to water and to run. On Porter's left was a ledger with workers names and their current pay on a small desk, and then a series of desks around him and in a U-shaped pattern around the entire building. He couldn't believe people would work in these conditions or for such a low pay. His privileged understanding kept flexing: maybe rural Gelorans had no choice? Being bred for high ranking military work didn't provide much space for this reflection.

Near Porter and across the front wall were two sets of stairs leading to a bottom floor where spinning wheels, big drum like vats, and printing presses, with some other gizmos only a laborer could identify, dotted around semi-sporadically like seasonings spilt on the table. There were too many to clean up and to tend to. There was one set of windows, which Porter had seen from the outside, but they were too high, they could not be opened and they did little to brighten the working area. Porter thought that working here would be a hellish experience for any sane person. Possibly for insane ones as well.

Sane folk currently found themselves bound to the assortment of machines, tied at their wrists with chords of rope and heavy cloth. Green, of course, like moss. Chronically defeated visages mingled amongst portraits of anger and pity, but most people were sleeping. Resting, since working in this plant was a different devil.

The four tengö guards on deck weren't watching them closely, but Porter assumed they must be close enough to give Leoric that look of despair. The proud First Captain Soranin snoozed against a spinning wheel. The soldiers travelling with Porter were spread out amongst men, women and children from Gelor, who wore only their breeches. The soldiers, and knight also wore only their breeches, which were once-white long johns and loose shirts.

Porter wanted to be sneaky, his plan from the get go,
but in the tepid silence of the factory, the icons on his forehead
jingled against each other, and his rod, which was inescapable,
clanked like a beggar's cup: frequent, unstoppable.
The rescuer began to move, wincing at every clanging step, down
the stairs, when a large feathered hand plopped on his shoulder.
Under those feathers were talons, and they gripped Porter like a
vice.

A meek chuckle escaped Porter as the other hand
clopped him in the head and sent his ceremonial garb flying to the
ground. The fifth, unseen guard spoke about what a shame it was
the wedding had to start with such a mess, how he was tired and
hungry and on break and as he began to call for his friends who
would have aided him in a heartbeat, Porter swung his leg in an
arc and dropped the large thug on his back.

The other four paid no mind to the muffled thud they
heard, and returned to their conversation regarding the Tengö and
Oilero war of 100. Oileros were inherently evil, all tengös knew,
and the gang thought that King Vonnidine ought to get some
courage for once and bash the plight once and for all. Build a wall,
or something, they tweeted to each other.

Porter stood, mussing his hair back with his hand, and
getting his robes all in order. The garbed man wished to Tellor
they had left him his breeches. A covert mission just could not be
performed in this ridiculous royal regalia.

The guard rose. Whether it was his just having had sex
or his just being plain brash that caused the guard to decide this
uppity human could be swatted without his friends was never
made clear, but Porter felt lucky nonetheless.

The guard swung his mitt in a hook, and Porter would
have dodged if it wasn't for his rod going taught against the floor
and keeping Porter in an upright fashion when he meant to dip. He
was clouted again.

The guard hopped over Porter's leg as he swung it this
time, and a quick roll kept Porter from being human jelly on the
garment factory floor. The soldier would have been alright to set
up his next attack except his robe was caught under his assailant's
fist. Porter grunted and ripped himself free, tearing the red and

gold robe in the rear, giving him an uncomfortable looking crescent shaped hole that revealed his butt.

Puffing and wheezing, Porter readied himself for a new round of combat, and the guard smiled, gazing at Porter's tengö get up. Porter did the same, and decided this outfit could be used in a new fashion.

Pun intended. Porter gave himself a smile. The tengö was confused. Then lunged.

When Porter was a newt he had been schooled first in stick combat, or Denny as West Landers call it. Denny Stork was a traveler in the Westlands like Diandre, but Denny was a teacher and a fighter. The Stork could outperform Khu'Roni Brawlers, Roiling Tide netmen and even Caprica's best knights, and with only a staff made of a foreign type of wood. Magiculture: Studies of Rare Earth called it korekwood. This is a book on Bord's banned book list, so Porter only ever associated it with the hazy and fascinating stories of his youth.

The Stork taught the knights and the army how to fight, and win, with only a stick. Caprican masters of kendo are still nowhere as strong as the Stork, and they had to teach their new soldiers Denny upon learning. The tengö ceremonial rod, with the three pointy ropes that were tied around his wrist, became his korekwood staff for this battle.

The tengö struck at Porter's muddled head again and Porter brought his golden staff to catch his hand, and turned it. This maneuver brought the tengö off of his back foot and tilting forwards and Porter struck him in the back of the neck with the staff. Then again in the back of his knee when he continued his descent, and finished by propelling the now airborne back foot even further forward. The large guard crunched into the bottom steps, nose first, and left a pretty pile of goo around his down-turned face.

Tengös deep in their lack of interest in what they are tasked with are at really no more or less observant than humans who suffer from the same bane, so Porter was not even that lucky that the remaining guards didn't notice the rod wielding soldier on his mission.

With the agility of a battered and exhausted person, not

very agile, Porter snuck behind vats of noxious dyes and gigantic garment constructs to the back of the store house. This is where he rested with only the moment on his mind for a moment, catching up with his walloped head and his lack of breath. Then a series of snaking maneuvers toward where he started from, but through the middle of the warehouse now instead of the side. Shushing confused and sleepy children, assuring the parents of those children in a whisper, and alerting with his raised eyebrows the few soldiers scattered amongst the throngs took Porter to Soranin who still slept, hands tied above his head.

Unlike Leoric, who surely spoke up or came off as a threat and was therefore nestled under a sewing table in nothing but his breeches, Soranin seemed to be left to lounge, shirtless. The man had an impressive spread of fiery chest hair. Porter whispered his name, whispered, then slapped his unkempt face.

"Mragh," Soranin's eyes flittered and then fluttered and then sprang open. "What are you wearing, Porter?"

"Never mind it, man!" The two had a vibrant and loud interaction, while still whispering.

"Right, well, thank you. Untie me?"

The subordinate captain released his superior by running the   spiky parts of his rod against the piece of chord, slow as he could while still cutting, keeping Soranin enslaved.

Grinning, Soranin made to rise. Porter stayed him with his hand.

"There are still four guards," Porter said through tight-pressed lips.

"Four? I imagined one, sure, but for an espionage mission I am disappointed. You were trained better."

Yes, Caprican standards are sublime, Porter thought. "Have you seen my outfit?"

"Ah, well, let's do it then."

"With a bit of tact? Release Leoric?"

Soranin pondered the thought, chewing on it with squinted eyes.

"Tact," he said as he rose, slow as yeast, "but let's remind Leoric why I am first captain of the Caprican army."

He extended Porter his hand.

His friend took it. Then one man in only a pair of breeches and one man dressed like a tengö groom initiated their strike.

"Gorat, you cannot pretend soda is not good, Gorat you cannot," an enormous tengö with a tiny sport of cropped yellow hair said in a drawling tongue to his smaller compatriot across the table. The smaller compatriot had a black mustache and his feet up on the table.

"'Soda is not good.' Yinir, your speech is like a child's. Soda can be good and it can be bad, it is just strange is all. The tingling on the beak, that soda is good," Gorat responded. The tinier one was clicking his finger nails, and turned his head to seek approval from the set of twins who rested against the nearest piece of machinery to the small clearing.

"Right y'all, right?"

Both fellows had long, straight blonde hair with long beaks. Their beady eyes directed to Gorat and they responded together:

"Yinir is simpler, and that does not make him any poorer, Yinir is."

Gorat harrumphed and folded his arms, sitting up in his chair, and as he readied to talk a spool of thick green chord the size of a baby pig struck him in the back of his head, and he fell out of his chair.

Porter was glad this panned out; most of their assault depended on landing such a throw to get a heavy first strike. He grinned, and his success allowed Soranin to strike. Porter nodded to Soranin from his perch, which happened to be the machine the twins leaned on.

Yinir began to rise, and from behind him leapt up Soranin. Yinir struggled like a ferocious beast, but underneath all of Soranin's arm rests well packed shoulders and enormous biceps. A bear hug around the neck is not welcome to any, even a goliath simpleton like Yinir the tengö.

Two beaked faces peered up in disgust at Porter who watched the wrestling like a kid at the melee. In as comedic a fashion as one can conjure, Porter looked down and met his enemies' gaze, and then, holding his breath, Porter spread his arms and crashed down on the pretentious tengös.

Punches and kicks and some biting followed for all.

The giant and crew-cut tengö was losing air, but couldn't seem to shake Soranin. The red haired hunter had locked his arms by holding his wrists under the chin of his prey, and his grip was strong.

The Fabio-looking tengös were thin and had short arms and couldn't reach the dirks on their belts. Porter saw their struggle and most of their wrestling seemed to be Porter holding the young tengös' arms by their sides and keeping them there.

Then the giant and crew cut tengö, with his last tangible breath, hurked Soranin off his back with a mighty buck. Soranin's looped arms stayed, so he flew forward over the mighty alien and onto the table, back first, and feet landing hard on the head of Gorat, who had just begun to regain consciousness.

Next the duo of tengös flipped Porter over, and they held him down. The meager light in the store house shone on their knives. The blades were poised above the jellyfish hat wearing soldier, and he could only dodge the strikes by flailing his head back and forth. He was grateful young men think of the head shot to claim as their own, since at any moment they could have plunged the blades into his chest.

Soranin raised his head and made eye contact with Yinir and they understood one would live and one would die. Soranin grit his teeth and with all the dexterity he could muster rolled off the table, missing Yinir's closed fists plummeting down and breaking the table in two, and cocked his legs beneath him, with his hands in a push up position. Then he shot himself in a tackle around the giant's middle. Yinir whoofed out his last breath, and Soranin fumbled for a piece of broken table and drove it plenty of the way through Yinir's neck. It occurred to Soranin that their pale eyes got dimmer still when life's light left them, expand- ing just an ounce in their lifelessness.

Porter had failed, and for this he was going to die. The rod he was going to use to beat the two guards into submission was trapped under his ass, and all the loose fitting clothing seemed to tangle him up in his struggle even more. His ear was cut, and he had been shaved around the edges of his beard.

A bruising and aching Soranin rose and continued. There indeed was a reason Soranin was first captain, and it was not just because of his family's nepotistic politicking. Being bred for success is a sublime gift, but it needs be used right or else in its inaction it is used for harm, against the self and the potential. The passion in the usage is greater still, and without it the gift rots like a stump. Soranin is father and husband, and he is also soldier, and most days he works with a passion subdued. This day, it rose and overflowed like a sleeping giant.

The table had split and left chunks of wood the size of short swords, and Soranin knew short swords. Walking so as to keep a composure and aim, the shirtless hero grabbed a splintery piece of table and approached the scene of Porter's scrap.

The two tengös took notice of Soranin, but not before the First Captain had gripped the bit of wood so that his fingers hurt and his arms felt like a loaded catapult and he struck the left most tengö so hard that his skull splintered like the table and the jolted head flew into his brothers' head, and they both fell off of Porter. Porter, looking like a bleeding avant garde painter in his strange garb, scrambled towards the broken table and watched, his chest body rattling.

The fractured-skull bearing tengö lay concussed, but his brother rose, adrenaline jolting him alive. Soranin yelled and struck the hand holding the blade with a bit of Porter's blood on it, breaking two fingers, shattering talons. The tengö yelled, and in his dismay buckled over clutching his hand, and, once Soranin struck him on the back of his head, was then silent.

Four tengös lay, two dead and two unconscious. Soranin looked savage.

"Thank you," Porter said as he panted and held his long hat in his hand. The storehouse felt quieter even though the people who had been quiet now laughed and cried out. "I lost, I guess."

"Thank you for coming to our aid, Porter. And worry not, these tengös will pay for what they've done to the people of Gelor. Capital Llih will never capitalize these lands, not if the bell of Caprica still rings."

"You two are foolish cocks, foolish cocks, for not letting

me free to beat upon these invading cretins!" Leoric screeched amongst hooting and hollering of graciousness and crying tears of thankfulness. Some of these folk had been here for weeks.

Soranin smiled.

"Embarrassed?" he called.

Silence.

"I'll let him loose. You grab the other soldiers?" Porter asked.

"Is that an order?" Soranin asked as he plodded away.

"Close enough," Porter smiled and put on his hat. "Get a shirt, you animal."

Chapter 4

Oet Oetsun, son of Oet Oetsun, was as pleasant as a Meinhah could be. Tall and well built, a shock of curly black hair and curly black beard to match, he spent most days alone, which was strange only because he loved company. This meant he was always friendly when Hariah arrived.

Hariah sat in the shop with Oet. They didn't have much to say to each other except the blatant. The stony hugeness between them.

"So," Oet fumbled. "Your life going alright?"

"What?" Hariah pulled his stool in further toward the bar.

"I mean is everything going well, not being allowed to... go in and all," Oet leaned against the back wall. "Do you want, eh, something to drink?"

"Spream?" Hariah asked for the caffeinated beverage, thick and sweet, that was customary for valley going men of age to drink. Customs seemed out of place. "And you know, not really."

Oet took a gray, well-shaped cup and poured the regional goodness, smelling of how persimmon might to us visitors, right to the brim. Hariah decided to keep things conceptual – it was always conflict otherwise.

"It's a dilemma," he began. "Am I not setting my intentions well? It seems like every day I want my dreams to be reality. To be easier to accomplish even though I know that would make them all the less, it still is a difficult process you know. Not having them."

Oet raised an eyebrow.

"That sounds obvious. What I mean is look at your shop. You've got customers you like, right?"

"Surely."

"You go out with your friends, in the community?"

"Yes I do, we go dancing and we paint at the gallery when we want to."

"Well that's terrific but it just seems like I don't have anything in the mean time. My goals are," he paused, avoiding the pot stirring. "Well, you know my goals."

Oet shrugged, gulped his spream.

"You don't see the day to day of your life. The day to day is important you know."

Hariah finished his spream, feeling a small kick in his brain.

"What do you mean?"

"Well, what did you do yesterday?"

"I got up in the morning and I had slept under a tree, amongst that sharp grass, and the moon was still in the sky strangely enough," Hariah said. He didn't speak to anyone except Oet. "It was nice to see it when I went to sleep and when I woke up, a nice circle.

"Um, I found some eggs in a bird's nest and started a fire to cook them on. It was good, and I spent most of the morning eating them, there were at least six or so, and drinking some spream I saved from my last visit. You remember."

Oet smiled.

"I do. Go on, though."

"The rest of the afternoon I didn't do anything! I got no closer to the village."

"Well, be frank, what happened?"

"I got no closer to the village."

"Tell me what the afternoon was like."

"It doesn't matter!"

"Yes, it does. You can't know all the ways your moments bring you closer toward your village," Oet said, filling up their cups, the bottle glugging away. "So what happened?"

"Alright, alright. I sat on the side of the hill and I watched the desert, and I looked for travelers and harpies and things I had never seen before but things that looked familiar, too."

"And you got to see the moon come and go?"

"Yep," Hariah felt ashamed.

"What a rare thing," Oet smiled.

"Those things aren't rare, they happen all the time. I'm horribly free and just have the time to see them."

"Do you know how many crafters and artists and builders like me would quit their trades to get a night like that? A morning with a fire and wild eggs?"

"You can do it whenever you want."

"You're right. But we don't. We just don't," Oet drank his drink.

"Why don't you if you're jealous of my fun and exciting life style choices?"

"Because we craft and create in the name of accumulating enough to get some time off, to relax, to do what you already do. Sad, isn't it?" Oet paused. Topped off their drinks. "Listen to this: your village and goals and everything else is a dreamscape. It's a dream, right? That makes it a dreamscape, a place you can live if you want. Where you live right now, the real world? I dream of that – that's my dreamscape."

"It's not that dreamy. Why don't you come join me for a night? We'll trade trades," Hariah wielded the word play back with a smile.

"People rely on me. My familiar relies on me. I'm familiar with my familiar. I rely on me, in this place," Oet ran his hand along the long bar. "It's not that sad, I think I'm being dramatic. I'm saying that appreciating the niceness of your day to day is, well, nice. More spream?"

"No, I'd better go. Lots of niceness to enjoy in my hovel on the hill."

Hariah left. Oet sighed. His familiar whirred. The Mason dreamed.

Chapter 5

The townsfolk were stationed behind the building,
about a quarter mile from the town. Most of them were garment
workers, and those who weren't were even happier to be out of
the acidic building they had been held prisoner in.

Leoric, Soranin, Porter and the four Caprican soldiers
had found the cache of clothes, armor and, most needed,
weaponry. Odd ends were there too, like bags and food and most
everything from the traveler's original goods. Even the gorgeous
stone which Porter had feared he would lose, still evanescent and
glimmering, the possibility of more and more oozing from it. Still
enigmatic and powerful because of that potential.

Shining and shimmering the stone sat in Porter's hand.
A young woman, brown black hair with sheen, touched his shoulder.

"Are you mute?" Porter asked, meaning it.

"No, sir, I tried to speak to you but you seemed away,"
she sounded hoarse and tried, and at a young age. Garment working, Porter supposed.

The soldier laughed as he placed the object in his
pack.

"I guess I was. What can I do for you? Did you lose the
group? They're camping not but a mile from here."

"No sir I...I'm not sure how to explain it. I have something I think is important for you to know. For anyone besides us
that saw it I imagine, since we don't understand."

"What's that, Miss?"

Even she didn't seem to understand the significance of
what she was saying, so Porter couldn't pick up on the importance.
There were black bruises on her wrists from her bonds. There
were invisble bruises underneath those, longer stained.

"After we had been captured, about two weeks later,
there was a day when the barn doors were opened and tengös
moved in enormous brown packages. They seemed like bales of
hay, except larger, and they were so careful with them."

"What became of these parcels?" Porter asked.

"They are here, on the walls of the factory, concealed

by the darkness and already so unimportant seeming. I know they mean something to the tengös, whether that means they are important to you I do not know. I don't know much." The girl's head drooped, and Porter lifted it with a hand.

"You know more than you know, and before this conversation, even more than me. Now go catch up with your people."

She smiled and ran off. Porter moved to the shadowy edges of the industrial building. He rose up the few steps and to the higher level, and then to the true wall of the factory. Upon reaching the wall, he was alarmed to notice that the "wall" he had once planned to move along was actually a long and high set of brown parcels, the size of bales of hay. Were it hay it could feed a thousand Billy Yaks for a thousand years, the second captain thought. The second wall made of mysterious packages traced the entire building, and as Porter surveyed the whole scene each brick of the wall became more dubious.

He opened a package with an industrial pair of scissors laying in a part of a sewing kit nearby.

Brown, nearly gold, roots stumbled out like a doofus waterslide. The roots were bigger and smaller and some had growths more gold than brown. There was a stink over powering the one in the factory, which wafted from the chemicals and sweat, and it was like a far too sweet molasses plus a thin ale. It was ellerwight, and it was ellerwight enough to kill Gelor seven or eight times over, and that's if everyone were addicts enough for twenty.

Porter's arms itched, and that was only one more omen pointing to the dire straits that they were in. The tengös may say they loved their summer vacation spot, but the bearded investigator was thinking now that it was the location of the town of on Diandre's Road, the prime thoroughfare for smuggling and dealing across the West Lands, that was the true draw.

The market? The West Lands. Diandre would be proud.

Tengös had frightened Porter enough, and had of course fractured his perception of reality not for the first and not for the last time. King Vonnidine, ruler of the Tengö nation had scared him witless. The same tengös as drug peddlers scared Porter beyond a reasonable doubt.

Porter showed Soranin, and they spoke about the

boxes.

The soldiers and knight of Caprica equipped themselves with their gear and huddled up, short one Duncan Day, who
was still serving as an ottoman. Tengö had missed the feel, and
more the weight, of Krude.

"Porter looks like a fairy," Leoric said, shoving his blades
into the sheathes on his hip.

"Tengö, Leoric," Soranin corrected.

"That's not what I meant."

Porter sighed.

"The wedding is soon. The people are free, but they
cannot reclaim the town without our help. What do you think,
Captain?" Porter asked Soranin.

"I think-"

"Not you, Leoric," Porter sighed again.

"This King Vonnidine has robbed us and de-robed us.
Caprica cannot allow such an embarrassment, nor a tengö city to
be established in the West Lands. That would shatter the façade
that the King has established," Soranin said.

And what, you agree with this? Porter thought, but
kept his piece to himself.

"And they don't need our help. Though, if we do it right,
we can be of great aid to our fellow West Landers. We are in their
fight, too. Have we got all our gear?"

"The horses," a younger soldier piped up.

"We truly would have an unfortunate journey without
our steeds," another mentioned.

"Our steeds," Leoric spat in a mocking tone. "Do shut
up."

"Easy, knight. They make a point. The stables are on
the opposite side of town, near the store we first visited in this
puppet's town," Soranin said.

"Then what do we do? We can't just leave with our horses, nor can we hope to take on the tengö king's family. There were
enough to replicate a whole town's worth of people. We cannot
hope to overcome such a force with such small numbers." Porter
wanted a drink. Didn't want a drink. It was fucking confusing now,
he thought.

Soranin thought. Leoric looked testy. The unimportant characters were still unimportant. Elsewhere, Duncan Day's back ached.

At last Soranin spoke.

"Porter you're getting married. And there's going to be a ceremony sure to make it into the tengö history books."

Chapter 6

The uncomfortable-walking Porter pushed the doors to the Fancy with the gusto of a, well, a man on his wedding day.

King Vonnidine was tending to a sheet of figures with two of his children, muscles and green hair, and the three of them looked up from the bar upon his entry. The monarch pulled his beak into a pseudo smile. So Porter thought, any ways.

"I figured we'd be picking your corpse from a buzzard's gnashy teeth in the mountains nearby, human, I figured we'd be."

"And miss marrying my dear Bunera? I think not."

Porter noticed a small and diseased-looking tengö in a chair at a table, alone. They looked like a solemn dried currant.

"You must be Aunt Finora."

The decrepit form's moon eyes lifted their lids.

"I am her, I am her."

The second captain kissed her forehead.

"A beauty you are, Aunt Finora."

If a dried currant can blush, Aunt Finora did. King Vonnidine sauntered in a waddle toward Porter and thumped him on the back, almost dislodging the jellyfish hat and shaking the golden rod. This drew the King's attention to the relic.

"Banged up the liora did you, banged up the liora?" The king spoke in a hushed tone as he ran his eyes up and down the tool.

Porter didn't speak, cursing himself for not having a witticism.

The king then smiled and this time it didn't seem forced.

"When you are not a human any more, you will under-stand how easy a mistake this was. You will make a fine prince, Porter. For a human. When you are not a human," The King walked away into the back of the Fancy, and the two sons, Porter's soon to be in-laws, strode forward and grabbed each of his arms.

"Time to go," the larger one said. "Time."

Porter was hauled into the sun.

The tengös chuckled and lugged Porter around the side of the inn, and they soon came to the back. Porter noticed this was the setting of his recent breakout, and was thankful nothing seemed out of place.

Where before he had mingled through the streets and the tengö population, there was now an enormous display of wooden pews. Pews upon pews covering the entire street, as far as Porter could see from his left to his right before the bend around the inn took them out of view on either side. Well-built white stone pillars bedecking the seating arrangement at tasteful intervals. Burnt flower-looking braids had been strung between the pillars, three pillars and three braids on either side, until they came to the front of the matrimonial scene where they looped onto two more pillars. These ultimate pillars were the most outward branches of a tree of the same white stone which was fashioned into the steps and the altar, all sitting right in front of "Gruff's Grains."

The altar contained some of the more bizarre decorations Porter had ever seen. He was remiss, terrified, to be approaching them now. He was lifted up, after his digging heels had unfurled a bit of red carpet that a disgruntled looking tengö had just finished laying down.

It wouldn't be safe to say it was a birdbath, and it wouldn't be wise to call it a torch, so somewhere in between the two lies the...

"What do you call that totem up there?" Porter asked his carrier, Muscles.

"The Tangalon, The Tangalon," he replied. It sounded average coming from him, but Porter had no frame of reference for this business.

A calm flow of orange, red and black ooze pulsed up and down from the basin of the five-foot odd inched structure, and its body of stone was the dark burning of the globule flower decorations. The ooze glowed bright, and faded in and out like a light at the back of a cave. Yellow quartz-like stones encrusted the head of the totem.

Also on the deck of the altar was an enormous golden wreath, which seemed to depict some amount of tengös making love and also fighting. Porter didn't realize this paid homage to the Tengö peace treaty that followed the Oilero Tengö conflict of historical year 15. It hung off of the stone altar's pillars. Two small stools with red cushions sat on each side of the wide set stage.

Along the pillars, surrounding the wreath, also protruded an enormous wall of the orange black globules. Once Porter was on the altar himself, he could see these decorative things also pulsated with a faint orange color like the slime in the basin.

Porter wanted a drink now. Some of the wight. Anything from that stash he saw earlier. He would have taken from there had his companions not been watching, their bodies as stone sentinels passing judgment on him.

What could only have been an hour or more passed, and Porter had to readjust his red hat and the liora a few times so that they wouldn't fall off and would not fidget his wrist constantly.

His former transporters were seated in a pew a few rows back and Porter asked them why he had to stand so long at the altar.

"Um, it's a part of the ceremony, um," Green Hair responded.

"Yeah, you not screwing it up that is, yeah!" Muscles added. The two laughed.

Porter shivered.

Evening crept on. The globules glowed in the low light like beacons, and three torches were lit on the pillars on either side.

Tengös filed in from every building in town. It would have been awe-inspiring to see all of these feathery orange humanoids flooding to a central location like bees from a hive, if the second captain wasn't so terrified.

They came from every building in what looked like a stream of dark, melted wax.

Except the factory. No tengös came from the factory, and none of the wedding-goers seemed to notice or care.

Had anyone caused alarm, run into the gathering as Porter had imagined they would for hours and hours, the plan to save everyone and escape to the mountains would have been trashed.

Since no one did, the wedding seemed sort of charming instead.

Light music began playing from behind Porter, some

J'doos, which are not native to tengö culture but to trolls, but once King Vonnidine heard their rich and boisterous sounds he had paid to have some play. They gave Porter a start. Two squat tengös flouted hors d'oeuvres on long, thin tables which they had slung across their backs like they had been either carrying water or locked in gallows. The snacks came on tiny plates, and they were tinier servings, tinier even than a child would have, but the tengö personage ate them and they smiled. Maybe this was because the squat tengös were finished bringing two large boxes to the front of the pillars, on each side but before the pews. When the boxes were opened, the sides of the construct became the floor of an impromptu kitchen, and small tengös in red hats similar to Porter's began dancing around an enormous cauldron on either side and tossing in whatever a guest ordered. Boiled and cooked to serve carrots, beets and meats that Porter had never even heard of.

"MY PEOPLE, MY PEOPLE," King Vonnidine's voice cracked the light cacophony as thunder might and each head turned from its conversational partner or its order-taking chef and swiveled to the altar. Porter winced.

"Today we see Bunera married, and we will see our one-day queen happier than anyone alive ever could be, except perhaps her father, today, we see Bunera," the king strode from behind the Tangalon, hand-in-hand with his daughter, who was her father's tone now, not that a non-tengö could tell the difference.

"We will see our one-day king transformed, we will see our one-day," the king said as he took Porter's hand.

Porter smiled and scratched his beard. Bunera looked gorgeous. A flowing red dress covered her and ran in a sweeping arc over her chest. A bit of the cloth was cut out covering her chest, inlaid instead with gold. She smiled, Porter thought, and it was kind. He could not explain his attraction to the tengö other than that in her he saw the parts of people that make people great. Cracked, orange or otherwise, a physical shell tells of a story so different than the story of what kind of relationship could be birthed.

She knew not of what was to come, and thought probably about her future with him.

It was a shame, and Porter was struck with the concept

of becoming the king of the tengö people. He looked at King Vonnidine and saw no real malice, and when he scanned the crowds
there was communal warmth Porter liked. In fact, loved.

"FINORA OF THE VONNIDINE RITE WILL LEAD US," the
king boomed, and the crowd responded in kind.

The dried fruit of a tengö was aided to the front of the
altar. King Vonnidine's shark grin lit up as he patted the woman on
her back, tender like a child, guiding her to the pulsating bird bath.
The bride to be grasped Porter's hand.

"You're going to make an amazing king one day.
Amazing," Porter felt the raw emotion in Bunera's voice. It wasn't
from her relationship with Porter, or lack thereof, it was simply a
conviction that only a young person can withstand and nurture. A
belief that this idea she had was reality, plain and simple.

Maybe she could just manifest things that way, Porter
thought, allowing her experience and world to be built by her
intentions.

Or Porter didn't understand the Tangalon and the mag-
nificence which it bestows.

Either way, Porter nodded, shaking the long hat, and
Aunt Finora took his other hand, and then both women plunged
his hands into the alive goo.

An itching, boiling sensation ran up to Porter's elbows,
and he screamed. It was still a deep scream, which he was thankful
for, but as the women then proceeded to lift his arms and dunk
them in to the gel, which also rose and fell with his hands, Porter
could see his hands. They were dark, cracked, and Porter's scream
became high and manic.

He grit his teeth and began to pull against their arms.
The king ushered his sons to the altar and, as Muscles and Green
Hair planted him in his place, Muscles lifted the liora from around
Porter's wrist and plugged its hooks into one of the globules on
the wall behind him.

It clicked in the Caprican's mind why the decorations
were sacks of this goo. As it shriveled, more decrepit looking than
Aunt Finora, the fluid dribbled down the staff and onto Porter's
rising and falling wrists. This matter spread quicker, and had a hint
of red, and raced up Porter's arm. His pores expanded and bristled.

In this aggressive scene, Porter could hear a humming coursing from the crowd. It wasn't the chatter that it was before, but an actual vibration that seemed to match the time of Porter's undesired splashing.

Porter recalled how stupid he looked in the royal garb, and then it occurred to him that this must be a part of his life flashing before his eyes, because otherwise it would be insane to have a silly thought as he was being transmogrified into some new being.

The plan failed, I guess, he thought as his shoulders began to itch and burn. *Perhaps I will be gorgeous*, he thought.

"That's enough!" Soranin cried.

"Yes, hold everything!" Leoric cried. His voice was a bit softer, and Porter assumed he must be a bit behind the captain of the army.

"He said that's enough," Duncan Day said.

"Quiet, Day!" Leoric said and a light ringing like metal on metal rang out.

The women let go for a moment, and Porter was able to retreat a few steps back. Like a madman Porter thrashed to and fro and the tengö ensemble released him. They stared at him as he scraped the ambient slime off of his arms and began scratching himself like a cat with mites in its ears.
In his flail Porter ripped the liora off of his wrist. It hung from the packet of tengö goo like an arrow in hay.

With a shove, Porter dethroned his squid hat, and it was then he saw that up to his shoulders, his arms were indistinguishable from King Vonnidine's. Well only in skin tone, King Vonnidine had a considerable amount of feathers in those chops. Porter only had tiny, bristling arm feathers which might look like arm hair from far away.

"Oh, fuck, then," Porter muttered.

"Who dares interrupt this ceremony?!" the king squinted out into the audience. At the very rear, in between the arcs of pillars, the three who interrupted this ceremony stood in shadow.

Soranin was in his full armor, as was Leoric. Duncan Day was in his soldier's attire, his lowly position as furniture behind him.

"My name is Captain Soranin Redbell, of the Caprican army."

"And I am-" Leoric began, but Soranin placed a hand on his chest. Though Leoric was upset by this slight, the captains came to understand that this was not the place to be divided on any matter.

"We are to liberate Gelor from your claim, King Vonnidine of the Tengö Nation. Leave now and-

"My claim is birthright, my claim," thundered King Vonnidine as he approached the front of the altar. His shadow was cast across the nervous guests like a zeppelin approaching earth. "It was promised to me. I cannot allow a few presumptuous fools to take it from me, it was promised."

Then from behind Soranin, Leoric and Duncan Day, from behind the stage itself, from the poorly lit corners of the event, came all of the people of Gelor. Women. Boys. Men. Girls. Any and all. Standing, some arm-in-arm and some as tall as they could make themselves, and all wielding a crude weapon of some kind. Their green clothes never looked prouder, their skin dark and blue in the night.

"What about a town of presumptuous fools? Fools whose livelihoods and families have been destroyed and mangled since you came to this land? You have been here too long, and in the name of King Ernhart and the Kingdom of Caprica I will be the one to show you your way home."

Soranin unsheathed his sword, Joi'den, and pointed it at the jiggly ruler.

Leoric managed to draw his blades and shove them toward King Vonnidine, too, shouting:

"AND BY THE KING'S SWORD I WILL VANQUISH MINE OWN OPPONENTS!" He shoved his way into the light of the torch that Soranin held, pointing his sword first in kind at King Vonnidine, and then, noticing his faux pas, sort of flung it around him to frighten the on-looking tengös. It worked, but he looked a bit the goat.

The six tengö guards stationed for the event and the three tengö princes readied themselves for combat, but King Vonnidine sat them down with a wave. The rest of the tengö soldiers and fighters who were attending leapt from their seats as well, but most of them had food in their mouths and wine in their bellies, and most of them had four or five Gelorans driving a pitchfork toward their throats.

The king held the audiences, human and tengö, in bated breath. Porter was ecstatic to see the orange tint to his skin retreating, feathers following, though where the liora had been clamped to his skin left was a thick tengö-orange band. Thankful again, Porter thought it looked hip.

Porter caught Bunera's eye, then, and saw the tremendous sadness growing there. This was no wedding, only an embarrassment, one which Bunera would not be allowed to forget anytime soon, Porter realized.

"Your demands," Vonnidine grunted. "Your demands."

"Father, you cannot submit. Let us rally our allies on Diandre's Road and retaliate, father!" the green haired prince shouted.

"Listen to me now, tengös. We got far too comfortable in this strange land; allowed ourselves to become contented and fat," Vonnidine started. He looked around and realized his congregation was in good shape, if not quite muscular, looked down at his impressive gourd of a stomach and sighed, then continued. "This was to be an easy coronation, a transformation for the human Porter and a husband for my fantastic daughter, all in the sanctity of our new home. But we must away, now, lest we lose the lives of every one of us here, listen to me now, tengös."

The hum of the seated immigrants returned, more nervous, and the king spoke to his sons who crowded near the front of the stage in hushed tones amidst the din.

"Your common sense is commended, King of the Tengö Nation," Soranin said. "And all we ask is that your people leave this town and return to your home. Leave the Gelorans alone – this is no settlement for you to conquer. This town is a municipality of the West Lands and shall stay that way. Be gone, now."

It didn't take long for the tengös to scurry from the ornate set-up, and most of them were out of their adopted homes and on the road within the hour. It occurred to Porter that they had a long journey ahead to travel, and they had their fill of bad puns and green clothes here and did not feel the need to take any with them. Porter also wondered where they came from, and if they would be alright on their travel home.

It struck him as odd that he cared what became of his would-be host community. Maybe it was the orange band. Tragedy forms some fashion of empathy, who knew?
Porter had returned to the inn after descending the stage and being given his possessions by Duncan Day.

"Captain Redbell says we are to keep watch and facilitate the exodus of the tengös, and follow them along the road, a few miles behind, until they are out of sight, since we'll be going the same way I suppose."

"Thanks, Duncan," Porter donned his familiar maroon shirt and saddled his armor in his arms like a bundle of wood, turning towards the inn. His eyes flickered toward the barn, the memories of high brush calling. "In the mean time?"

"Get some food, get some sleep, wash up and round up supplies for the road. That's what Captain Redbell said, but Captain Norrin said we need to rout these damn tengös."

"So, I'll just do that first bit, then?"

"Seems fine. Bye, Porter."

"Bye, Duncan. Great work, with the plan I mean."

"Of course, I-" Duncan tripped on an out-of-place, protruding rock near the door to the Fancy and tumbled forwards. "I-I, um, good night then."

Porter laughed and turned toward the inn. From the corner of his eye Porter caught two yellow eyes glisten in the distance, near the general store where they first stopped in Gelor, and he met the eyes for a moment. They were like beacons of knowledge, relics of truth, and then they were gone, leaving a longing for those chimmery doors to beyond in Porter's head Native power vibrated residually.

Porter shook his head, rubbed the new tengö tattoo he had acquired and entered the inn. In the darkness he constrained himself, wanting against desire to steal the wight he liberated. The bearded man proceeded to sleep all on his lonesome in the bed where he had made love to Bunera. She had let him feel a part of a family and identity, as dysfunctional as it all was.

Though many hit the trail just after the ceremony, the tengö king and his family were the last to leave the town. The Capricans were not surprised. They were surprised when the troop saw what the royal family intended to depart in.

The size of a Billy Yak and a half each, two beasts, which looked like the awful middle place between an ant and a grub with the same smoky, tengö orange color, thrashed at the end of enormous red chains slipping through their undulating mouths. Their mouths opened like ant mouths, collecting and gaping, but had no teeth of any discernable shape, like maggots. They seemed blind, but had feelers all across their hulking bodies. They were called murttens, and they smelled like pus.

Groggy, bachelor Porter came down after a few hours of sleep, and in this time the family had gathered their belongings from every nook and cranny of Gelor. Porter was munching on fried bread with a salted goose egg on top, curated from the remnants of the Fancy's kitchen, when he spotted the creatures. He felt like though his lot seemed to be cast in a lose-lose by the good King Ernhart, he seemed to enjoy each day better than the last. Things were exciting and new, even the less-desirables like near-death beat downs and forced-marriages. He thought even the peril of death and betrothal was sort of nice, too. Better than errands for Bord.

After wolfing down the remainder of his breakfast, Porter stood near the remaining members of his party and tried to look official. Soranin and Leoric always did a good job of this, but sometimes Porter felt almost as off-putting as Duncan Day, who stood sporting a fly in his jaw, circling the cave of his mouth.

The royal murttens were chained to a long red covered wagon. The wheels of the wagon were numerous and small, almost like treads, but the wagon cab was tall and plush on the outside, as ornate as King Vonnidine's general get-up. The king revealed himself from the Fancy to join his sons who were loading the wagon.

"Good morning then, good morning," the king said with a cold, political smile. Porter noticed his sons moving similar boxes over and over, in an assembly line way which seemed tried and true.

"What are you taking with you, then?" Porter asked.

"Our family heirlooms, opal and gold, provisions for the road. Nothing to worry about, good second captain," the king responded as he donned a brown, fur cape.

Not that I am well versed in these folk's customs, but did he repeat himself in this last bit? Porter thought as he watched the king stroke his precious beasts.

Bunera walked from the inn along with the three tengö wives, donned in a similar cape that was orange and yellow frilled. She smiled with a melancholy tinge at Porter, and Porter nodded, looked away. Was there any point in making them both feel sad by talking about it again, lifting the skeletons into the light?

The green haired son spoke to his father, his father nodded, fast as can be.

"We're off then, we're off," the king stated.

"Good riddance," Leoric spat. "And if we catch you this side of the Bastions of Tellor again so help me-"

With a loud oomph the most muscular prince dropped the crate he was carrying and his most muscular wife accompanied him to meet Leoric.

"Do not mistake our intentions, captain of Ernhart's sword. This is no defeat, nor retreat. You have met us on vacation, on a business venture of sorts," the mohawked prince was now not but a few inches from Leoric's face. "The tengö nation needs not bow. My father has spared our people bloodshed, but know that in doing so he has spared your slaughter," he spat.

The tension was thick like a glacier, and of course Duncan Day ruined it by asking quite audibly to one of his fellow soldiers what a venture was.

"I've had enough half-truths and conspiracy from your kind, Vonnidine," Soranin said as he moved to intercept the conflict, just as Leoric drew his short blades. "Out of kindness I will pry no further, but take these shaggy monsters of yours and go."

As the prince and princess entered the wagon, Soranin added:

"And whatever is pulling your wagon can go, too."

The king maintained his political visage and slammed the door to his carriage. From a small compartment at the front of the litter a small tengö, built to fit the small compartment, scuttled out and with two freakish, buff wings carried the chains and struck the murttens into action. The Vonnidines drew open the lavish curtains on their carriage as they carted away, and Porter caught again a fleeting glance of a much wanting to be loved tengö princess. Bunera was blue now, not any shade of orange or black or cracked skin making a difference in the shared-experience of a hue of loss.

"They changed their style of speech when they were certain they were unwatched," Leoric said.

"They operated in more secrecy and collusion than I initially thought, as well..." Porter agreed.

"No time to waste. Make a last check of your things then meet at the Geloran Gravy Barn. I'll speak with the leadership in town to see if they need anything from us before we make haste," Soranin said as he walked away. Soranin, as per usual, was bedecked in his armor and his purple cape spun behind him, cool like a hero.

"What's at the Geloran Gravy Barn?" Porter called out, with a knowing smile.

"I'm hungry, and I think Geloran gravy should make a fine breakfast is what," Soranin replied without turning his head to look back.

Porter was thinking about the wight again, and how glad he was to have that big, shiny rock back.

Gravy was indeed fine. King Kalan the Third had come to Gelor upon its establishment and had said that Gelor gravy is unlike any other gravy. He was right. The Geloran gravy was green. Green from cut chives and ground spinach. Green, savory and good. The eight men of Caprica discussed the ridiculousness of the night before, and how it had been a true debacle since they arrived. Some military men, they laughed.

"I thought Gelor was a boring place," Leoric said as he drained his dish of gravy, "now I see that it has been boring on purpose! For how many years again?"

"The tengö king said they had been here seven months," Soranin said.

Seven months? Tellor, I cannot fathom it," Leoric said.

"Fathom is a rather big word for you, Leoric, think you can fathom it?" Porter asked, reaching out.

Leoric looked up from his dish, considered a snide retort, but once he realized he had a mustache of green goop he laughed, and the seven travelers all laughed.

⬖⬗

Inside the royal carriage of the Vonnidine family, the conversation was less light.

"Father I believe we needed to uphold our image a bit better at the end of our time in Gelor," said the smallest of the Vonnidine princes. His wife nodded.

King Vonnidine looked at his son and said,

"I care not what you think, nearly at all, but I'll tell you why it doesn't matter. Our people had left, and are in Ollette by now, if I know our family. I do not want them to know of our evolution yet. Of our dealings with the ellerwight, how we can exterminate the Oileros who claim our home as their birthright," the king reached in his nap sack and pulled out three stalks, all a sick white with green tips. They looked old, were segmented at a forearms length long, and were brittle and shatterable.

"Father..." Bunera began.

"Bunera, quiet now. I know what I am doing," the rotund

royalty broke up the three plants and tossed his head back to catch the pieces. His skin danced to yellow and then red and then a bright nova of white, his feathers jittering and shaking between each shade, before relaxing to orange and cracked again. His brain skyrocketed, his talons grew and contorted then shrunk. This happened in the space of not even a minute. The murttens outside hawed and snorted.

"When will we reclaim Gelor? It is much more than the vacation spot you made it out to be and you know that," the largest prince who stared like a surly pup out the window asked.

His wife lay her head on his bicep, and she chewed thoughtfully on bits of Ellerwight too, her skin cascading in pigments and fonts and her eyes lulling and kicking. "We need to move the ellerwight to Ollette if we want to dominate as we did in this paltry factory town."

"Need you pretend that I do not know? It is a necessary objective, but it can wait until the West Lands settle. They know not what is coming, what has already come. Why do you think those men were traveling? It does not matter. He will keep his end of the bargain and deliver the ellerwight as far as Ollette, so there is no issue."

"The issue is that we lose profit and territory from this set back," the green haired prince spoke up now. "If we smoke, or eat, the stalk all ourselves then it was as hedonistic a vacation as-"

"Do you take yourself for a courtesan of tactics now that you have eaten the ellerwight, Yeunice? Do not think so highly of yourself. You've been daft since you first ate it, do you take."

The king's family all stared at him at his obvious faux pas.

"I-I'm sorry, excuse me," the king was embarrassed and remediated the issue by downing four more rods of ellerwight. His person exploded and imploded. "I'm in between codes, considering our impending meeting."

His daughter looked sheepish and gnawed her bottom beak. She missed Porter.

"No, the ellerwight will not cease flowing. The Tengö Nation will evolve and one day we will drop these facades, we will be free to flourish like anyone else, from the homeland to the coast. The violence will cease and we will be loved in our bodies. It is a shame they came when they did, those men of Caprica, though," the king said as he set his crown near his feet and raised them onto an ottoman. "Many great events are going to happen in their world this year, I should think."

The king paused. A moment later, the carriage came to a halt.

"We are beyond their gaze," his driver said. "And he waits at the large rock, as he said he would."

"I'm not so sure he's our ally," Bunera said. She squeezed her father's arm, hoping that it meant anything.

On a high boulder a squat man stood by a parade of yaks and horses, crates hanging from their thick bodies. He was wrapped in dark red robes, red like curdled blood.

"It's all right, Bunera," Vonnidine said, "Diandre's Road needed a new Diandre."

Book V

"Lords, how can we sustain? Our lives take and take and we wish they did not, we wish we were beings of air and could receive only the sun for our power, but we must live in the world as bodies first," The people asked.
"Expansion and beauty can be wed, their powers intermingling to lift you to this place of air and energy.
It takes your intention," Pyre said. "And your knowledge," Fauna said.
"To craft a life wherein you thrive, build and water the things you take of so you can thrive and build again." The obelisks of the universe said in unison.

of the First Book, Chapter 8,
from the bridged islands to the Northeast of Epic

Chapter 1

     The village was electric that day. Total jubilation. A light drizzle affronted the energy of the people who tumbled around the market, a market which had come together in the village center every fifth day since the founding of Third Maple. Pansen wasn't sure what the hubbub was about, but he enjoyed it. He smiled and the water was on his teeth.
     Old matriarchs populated the majority of the market's customer base, and balding men populated the seller base. The men could be young or old, one then the other was a normal pattern. It was because father and sons sold lots of things, and mothers and grandmothers bought them. These were not concrete roles, though, and some years it was inverted or different.
     It was not only alopecia sufferers and adolescence sufferers who frequented the market, though. Folk of every sort came through; the Indonobi, enormous mountain dwellers who have lived nearby since before the villagers, more ancient than Third Maple, had made Third Maple a tourist destination once it was

established. When a village was established, and the Indonobi said
it was cool, it became the nexus point for nearby settlements. It
felt natural this way, only because the Indonobi were taken care of
and loved. Otherwise it would be shameful to be jealous of their
ingenuity and take from it like uncreative youth.

The most exotic customer Pansen ever saw was a cyl-
inder shaped boulder elemental as tall as a quarter of an Indonobi
wearing a far too small hat, almost a sun hat, with a shaggy and
matted fur coat on. He was particularly exotic because he was
carrying, en masse, small birds.

Pansen was taking the family grypatin on a walk because the small creature enjoyed the emotional space created by
the affair. Being a cave dweller, this particular grypatin, though shy,
glowed a smoky orange and mewled happily as it skated, floated,
through the streets. It looked like a geothermal anomaly, some
volcano shrunk down, a tiny volcano with a big smiley face carved
into one side. Pansen's little sister, Fae, had found the four legged
sprite near the family home when she was much younger.

We were closer then, Pansen thought. He raised his
head and let the rain wash him clean again.

A hooded figure thumped into Pansen as he entered
a denser group of people. It was a serious thump. The figure was
wearing a blue robe with yellow trim, but masqueraded or no it
was clear this figure was strong.

As an acquestier, this didn't stop Pansen from wheeling
around, the grypatin yapping in accordance.

"Please be careful if you're going to run through the
market like that!" Pansen said. Small beads of rain dotted his
brown tunic, and in his shoes his toes mushed around in the
sogginess.

The cloak wearing bumper wheeled around as well, and
threw back their hood. A head of white and orange and gold
with a big set of sharp teeth roared at him. The roar was a screech,
too, and its eyes were dense brown with miniscule flecks of gold.
Tremendous arms beat upon its chest from under its robe, and the
market goer dropped the fruit and spices it had in its hands.

Pansen recognized him, and also knew this chap was a
griger. Beyond humans and elementals of various sorts, grigers

were always to be seen on market day. Indonobi had popularized the nearby griger village of Mandonizia, so when the escalated beings came to Third Maple so too did the grandfathers of Mandonizia.

A bald and mustachioed merchant intervened in the public and escalating debacle.

"Prince Hibla, please, please forgive this man. He is the son of our village acquestier. He meant no harm. Only to serve us."

The royal cat-ape began to pant heavily, and then set his long arms down by his side. He bared his teeth at Pansen as he approached him, brushing the merchant aside. A small gasp emitted from the seller and a few nearby shoppers.

"I remember you from your father's ceremony," the big biped was inches from, and above, Pansen's face, heaving in anger. "Are you any more of a man now, all these years later, I wonder?"

He began hooting and laughing at his own wit, or lack thereof.

"I guess I can't be the judge of that," Pansen said. "Have you stopped throwing your own feces, I wonder?"

The prince slapped Pansen upside the face. Another gasp from the halted crowd. The grypatin yipped and strained. Pansen cursed himself for letting his anger show, his discipline out of sorts.

Pansen steadied himself. An acquestier already would hold his tongue better than he had, and would certainly not do combat in the middle of a market. He composed himself.

"My apologies, Prince Hibla," Pansen said, bowing a shallow bow. "I'll see you at your coronation."

"You may, if my father still invites yours," the prince said.

In the pitter patter of weather, the two parted ways. "Ah, and acquestier-to-be?" Prince Hibla called out. "I'll be the judge. You are not a man."

Pansen felt cold, and was reminded he was no longer that young man in the village anymore. His anxiety sprouted in goose-flesh.

He had been reminiscing again, and who could blame him? The sun had abandoned him as he climbed higher and higher, and now he made himself comfortable under a tree. Large heaps of snow pooled on higher branches, slipping onto lower ones, and now just a few feet in front of the traveler's leather wrapped feet.

Am I a man now? he wondered.

The high mountains of this goliath range that cut the world in two crafted men. And it crafted graves.

He decided he must then be a man. It was his decision, in addition to his trial, not that of anyone else.

The tree shook with a new wind, and he longed for an angry griger and his funny looking grypatin and the beautiful Indonobi visiting his rainy market. He longed for the devastation of his youth.

Horseback riding seemed like a stale, told-too-many times joke to Porter now. Never that entertaining, and certainly overdone now.

The troop of seven men had been riding and they heard the caw-braying of the enormous creatures towing the bird royalty, but now the only sound was the rushing of wind on open plain. All around the horses and men was open field, some green grass and plenty tall and thick weed.

The sun bore down as it had for Porter so many days in Caprica, but now it was cloudier and only shone on the bridle of his horse. It hit also greener plants, dancing off a thicket lining Diandre's Road. The earth became wetter and less arid, and a greener scene dotted the land. The road wound through the handsome landscape and Porter admired it fully for the first time, pushing aside thoughts of the disturbing new tattoo, of making love to a species entirely not his own and of the stone he had found which now rested in his pack as best he could.

A rare scene too gorgeous to be missed for want of what has happened or may tomorrow unfolded around him, outside his invasive thoughts, and he knew he didn't want to miss it.

To drive the point home a herd of wild Billy Yak, a herd being four only, bull, cow and two calves, paraded not but a quarter mile off of the road. Weaving through the family of shaggy cattle ran some creatures Porter had only ever seen stuffed: Moltov Wolves. The thing Porter loved about these wild dogs is that except for the Mothers and Uncles, the matriarchs and much more violent brothers of those Mothers, they were herbivores. The blue and black dogs, looking like over-sized foxes with more traditional canine features and small horns, nipped at the sides of the yaks and skirted in between them as they walked, barking their jovial barks. Mothers and Uncles were not only assertive and defensive; they made sure the Mothers had meat in their stomachs while they gestated their young. Moltov Wolves cannot be born of simply flowers, after all. The dogs know their queens come first.

The lush landscapes and unreal wild kept astounding Porter, and he began to scribble in his journal. He glanced at the

shiny blue stone in his pack as he reached for his notebook. It was
secure there, and Porter was glad because he knew there would
come a time when he would want to sell it for ellerwight. He didn't
know that.

Yes, he did.

It was confusing. He wished he had robbed that stash
in Gelor.

Invasive thoughts coming back.

He inhaled, ran his hand through his hair, exhaled,
looked around.

Beyond the sight of his fellow travelers, and lying
straight ahead, was the tremendous presence of the Bastions of
Tellor, the Mountains. Stabbing and jutting through meek clouds,
the mountains couldn't have been more like earthen guardians to
the foreign and once impossible land to the East. The mountains
had roundness to some of them, some of the hills preceded the
true gateway to the Reef, but the larger mountains arced their
backs into tooth like formations that Porter swore were topped
with snow. He couldn't understand, because in his home city the
sun was bearing down and he could barely see.

Porter followed the line of natural ginormity to the
left and could see no end, and found the same to the right. He
felt faint, because he realized it was no longer concept but truth
he was riding toward, these once-dreams becoming actual. Their
picture became bigger and bigger every minute, and he hadn't
thought it possible.

As the soldier cast his gaze North, a duo of bergies flew
past his face, dancing in their synchronous way that they fly. It had
been a long time since Porter had seen the red creatures, always
with a partner, but he remembered his father saying a pair
of bergies was an omen of good luck. It meant there was joy in the
air, that's why they danced, he would say with Porter on his knee
and a smile across his face.

Porter could see in the distance Tunsworth, a fine and
industrious place. He realized he had never been, only assumed
from what he had been told and read. In the afternoon, there on
his horse, he laughed because the thought occurred to him that
he was only here, horseback and in the afternoon, because what

he had been told and read had been a lie. So what did that mean for Tunsworth?

"I see you looking to the North," called Soranin. "But take in the South for a moment."

The thicket of the land sprang higher to the South, so it was harder to discern the horizon, but Porter, then the entire group, looked South with squinted eyes and hands raised at a salute to sight, blocking the rays of day.

"Tellor has given us a beautiful moment, hasn't he?" Soranin said softly. "A million of them. It's odd to think of any people who can't see the world through his light, like those tengös. Their wedding ceremony was nothing like ours! Does it make it less so; I wonder?"

"Only different," Duncan Day muttered.

Whettle was Tunsworth's Southern compatriot of townships, making its name as a fine place for carpenters and woodspeople. It was a family place like Gelor, but harder than the green township. Whettle longed for the Ennabon Forest, but was stuck with a forest of maple instead. Ennabon Forest was a hair too far South for Whettle, a hair too East for Khu'Ron.

Before Whettle, further to the West and more North, sat exotic Vian. Behind Vian one could see the Bastions of Tellor well, and the small tribe had many rituals praying to the larger of Tellor's constructs to send them plentiful crops. This was from a book too, though, and Porter doubted any time spent in the library at this point.

He scratched his beard and swooped his hand down near Kettlestep's leg and plucked a long piece of Culture Grass, sticking it in his mouth to chew upon. It was named so because the thick grass was used for many a people's crafts all across the West Lands. When his nerves were at their jitteriest, and he found himself without vice, he looked to Culture Grass to relax.

There was a tale that Vian had a back path, a path known to only a few, made of cut stone dug into the earth so that one could follow the path straight into the Bastions of Tellor. A chink in the shield. Porter had not read this in a book, but had been told by Pod that it was the way he had once gone. They had been eating sausages at the Public House when he had heard the story. He was surprised, but was careful not to show it. His father had laughed, seeing through his son's guise.

Porter munched on his Culture Grass and stewed.

The afternoon bore on into night and the landscape evolved and morphed into something much stranger than the road to Gelor, which had been bedecked with signs and stories amongst friends. This path was winding, wild and without speech. Diandre's Road still, but its more primitive end.

The men had come upon a set of hills, rising and falling but ultimately falling, which brought them closer to the now looming mountains. The swaths of foliage off the path had calmed and receded into thin grass and rocks, more rocks than before. After maneuvering the horses down to the levelling of the hills there were more boulders than rocks, and the beginnings of large stone formations which stretched into mocking shapes, like jesters, curving high above their heads.

The mountains were so close that it made the air heavy. In distant Vian, evening fires could be seen. Porter saw fires far ahead on the tattered end of Diandre's Road as well, nestled in the fold of the Bastions of Tellor just to the South. Intimidation and discomfort prevailed as the horses became tired. Duncan Day suggested an end to the day's travels.

Leoric nodded.

Soranin hopped off his horse and pulled on his Skell Brew.

"Can we drink because we are afraid? Or would that make us not men?" asked a newt soldier who had begun unwinding some of the packs from his mount.

"Being a man invites fear," Leoric responded. "You just decide what to do with it. Like drink. Alcohol is an enemy of fear. So drink. Merriment is a friend of alcohol, and I am a friend of merriment."

A stifled pause in the dark.

"Believe it or not!" Leoric shouted, and the men laughed, their hollering echoing off of the granite statues and shapes surrounding them. "Ah curse you bastards, who is to start the fire? I'm hungry and Duncan Day's ineptitudes have caused my hunger to worsen."

Chapter 3

Dawn came to the sunken land later than it had in Ge-lor, and the first man to rise was Soranin. The captain stoked the fire back to life and sent the soldier, who had kept an eye through the sparse hours of early morning, to sleep. Soranin did not need or want company as he prepared the day's first meal.

The grass was dewy underneath his calloused feet and this was a pleasant change. Caprica can be as hot as Tellor's forge and it can feel as though the Champion himself were beating and bending a man into shape on the worst days. With that in mind, Soranin left a pot on the fire's coals and lifted himself to find water. Water, and to train.

Joi'den had an amazing purple gem centered in its sheath. The hilt was gold and the blade was gold, but the gem was unapologetically purple. Violet or indigo, not anything bright. Shirtless and shoeless, Soranin left one carrot near Kettlestep and began to explore the ravenous new land which they had descended into.

Geography was a field Soranin never studied. Nor cartography or topography, or any real schooling of any sort. It was unnecessary and uninteresting for Redbells because they were lifelong learners, learning with their hands. And in this way Soranin learned tactics, and how best to survive.

Still in early dawn and still under the impressive, deep shadow of the mountains, Soranin walked, gliding on the wet earth when he decided to entertain himself, until he heard the splashing of water.

To boil, Soranin thought, *these folk will devour as many boiled potatoes and grain as I conjure, I'm sure.*

An imposing and obtuse stone statue, the same opaque shade of gray and graphite as the rest, seemed to be in his way to the water behind. The stone resembled an Usul Tiger on its hind legs, muscle bound and lithe. There was a perceivable dip in the earth yet again as Soranin approached the animalistic stone to pass by it.

More elevation loss before trekking to Ollette? Soranin felt geography was useless, until right now when he may actually be able to use it.

The first captain scrambled across and over the idol, with Joi'den in his right hand. Puffing upon reaching the top, Soranin grinned and slid down the rocks back, and down into the bank of a stream.

Singing, not splashing, is what Soranin had heard. But it was also splashing, wasn't it?

Soranin called out:

"Is someone bathing here? I don't mean to intrude."

The stream was narrow, and long flowered trees curved over the stream. This land did not remind of the streams near Caprica, and the cool air and mud on his bare feet made Soranin wish he had spent his youth near a place like this. The water, he noticed, barely trickled here, though.

"I have been told my songs are like water against stone, and river hitting land is the sound of my voice," called out a voice from behind the trees. Soranin noticed that he deprived riverbed dodged its way through the gorgeous brush, and he scraped himself as he followed it through.

Curving up and into a small bay, the stream ended, and Soranin clutched Joi'den to his chest. He was afraid because he did not believe the lie his eyes told.

The pool was small, and seemed to be ill formed, and absorbing its entirety of space was a creature that was all at once an amphibian and a reptile, all at once a man and a woman. An ambient green frill sprouted from its head.

"You are-" Soranin started as he stepped forward without looking, an ankle plunging into mud.

"Callxn," responded the creature. It plunged its handsome visage under water, raising it out again and shaking the plumage on top of its head flippantly. It smiled as new frills branched out and water jumped off of them.

"I meant to say magnificent. I've never seen anything like you."

"That's alright – my kind are an affectionate but often over looked kind. I'm a Namiost, a spirit of fresh water. Fresh water is needed to sustain your human life, no?"

"No, I mean yes," Soranin gripped his blade and plucked

his foot out of the muck. "I don't mean to be abrupt but I have a task from my king. I need water to feed my allies; may I take some of yours?"

"Tsk, when will men observe before they ask? Look at your feet, then follow the bank to me and my pool."

Soranin saw the abundant amount of dirt and weeds at his feet, followed the trail of non-water. Between him and Callxn was a nest of felled trees and mud.

"Squor nest." Soranin said, then looked up to the pool. Callxn smiled, looking aged and weary.

"The architects of the ponds, the bane of my existence," the spirit chuckled and Soranin saw his gills ripple. "I am bound to this water, and those critters damned me into this pool nearly a month ago. Clearly my stream isn't much to marvel at, but I have lost many visitors to the new size and roundness of my host."

"Where do your visitors come from?" Soranin asked. Callxn sang, and lifted a hand towards the mountains at his back.

"Does not all water run down to the ocean? This must be a principle in your home too, no?"

"I-I guess it is," Soranin had never been caught by such beauty, but understood urgency. It had been at least an hour since he had woken and taken over watch. "I ask for some of the water from your pool."

Callxn laughed, and even this made Soranin weak at the knees. It was ephemeral and it was fluid.

"I do not live in a pool but a stream. If you can bring me a stream and not a pool, I may even let your party bathe in my host."

"Break down the damn?" Soranin asked. "I know it is large, but –"

Inspired by timeliness, but a chance to impress the natural naiad, Soranin further gripped Joi'den and leapt off of a rock near the bank. Catapulting to a lower branch from a willowy tree, Soranin raised himself and his blade high above the damn. In a terrible silence followed by a tremendous crack, he chopped through the damn in one swing. Once stagnant water turned fresh again geysered down the small hill and flowed happily through the muddy trail turned stream again. Soranin fell upon his knees into the stream, and as Callxn exhaled the breath they had been holding for what felt like hours. The red head grinned, laughed.

"I didn't cut it sooner because I thought you may be a spirit of the flora near these parts, too," this was a lie, but Soranin was feeling playful.

Callxn's look of shock softened into ease.

"Take what you need, and short of claiming the banks for your homes use this stream as you need," Callxn's frills consolidated into one bun-like afro, exploded into his prior flock and the Namiost sang their way into the unperturbed flow of its host.

Soranin walked back, his body temperature raised, smiling. Leoric called out as he approached:

"I thought we'd eat breakfast today, what about you fellows? Or were we all just hoping Soranin would have a nice dip?" Leoric elbowed Porter in the ribs and the second captain mustered a smile. The men were all awake, and they had removed the now blackened pot off the coals.

"My apologies, none of these statues murdered anyone in my absence?" Soranin asked as he gathered the pot and another pot for good measure, "No? Then follow me for a bath and a drink, but not in that order."

Soranin found the newt who had asked of masculinity. He told him not to concern himself with those sorts of things

◇◇

After a rousing breakfast of potatoes and a bit of jam, without a bit of meat, much to the company's disdain, or scones for that matter, and a bath in Callxn's home, the seven men saddled up in their respective regalia for their impending arrangements in Ollette. The natural statues seemed to wane and their presence become less bizarre and more routine if they did appear. The land was less open and plains-like, the green gone as well. The descent continued but barely, it was just the mountains that became more incredible and pervasive. To the South it was like they were already in the mountains, they couldn't be but three hours away. They'd be there by early afternoon, and Porter did his best to no longer worry about tomorrow and remorse yesterday.

199

His itches were being scratched by the adventure at hand, and it felt so much better than self-pity.

Porter also remembered some books he had packed. It had been so long since a moment's reprieve allowed him a chance to satisfy his hunger for a spot of reading. After rooting in his sack, he produced Heavy Waters. Soranin saw it, laughed.

The conversation tended to be more aggressive that morning, about sparring practices, which of them was the strongest fighter and how the Gelorans could have defended themselves better. All of the conversations were led by Leoric. Porter wasn't listening. He kept pace with Soranin at the front and the two discussed their journey. Soranin had divulged his morning's adventure to his most trusted ally, and Porter was inspired again.

"I reel every time we see something new, I swear it. How could we have lived so sheltered for so long? Golden souls, that's what my father said of the Ernharts, and what else is there more than that? What of my father's stories I mean-"

Soranin laid a hand on his friend's shoulder.

"I tell you one story and this is my payment? Your anxiety tenfolded? Porter, our journey may yet be just beginning, but it also may end here in Ollette. Release your expectation about this business."

"You are right, sir," Porter responded.

"Don't call me sir, now! Just gaze upon Jobelnon, now."

Jobelnon: Porter was not only not focusing on Jobelnon, he had forgotten it existed at all. Gazing to the North or gazing along the rift to the left of the Bastions of Tellor, in either case, Porter had passed right along the city to the East, the "gem of the land." Where Khu'Ron was historic and spice-ridden, Jobelnon was bustling and bizarre, where Caprica was agricultural and modest, Jobelnon was metropolitan and proud, and if Roiling Tide was the hard-working, non-unionized picker, then Jobelnon was the plantation owner in an easy chair. Hustling was the crop of Jobelnon, and it was ever in season.

Porter gazed to Ollette, there in the maw of the mountains, and asked why they would not stop in Jobelnon first. Porter felt foolish: if Ollette was only three hours away then Jobelnon was an hour. As they came to a bend in the now disintegrating road it did become much clearer how pointed they were for the Eastern city. As they turned to carry on toward Ollette, Porter cast a last look at the high rising enterprise of a city. The buildings were much larger than any he'd seen, and smoke billowed high from the titanic factories. Porter felt glad to not go that way.

Bringing up the rear, Duncan Day asked Porter's question again.

"We are on orders from the king and-" Soranin began from the front.

"And cannot dally. Bah, Day, do you listen at all? Your existence perturbs my very soul," Leoric finished from the rear. Leoric hurried his horse along to meet the others at the front, and Duncan swished his thick mustache around as his fellow newts chuckled. Porter cracked a smile.

The land kept rolling along with the travelers like a diorama crafted by some kind of post-modern madman. The stones became more gargantuan, the plants became more minimal and the well-watered green earth became pock marks instead of dotted patches. The stream they had bathed in ran far off to the right and into the mountains. The frequency of birds overhead increased, and their songs became enormous like the landscape. In the plains they had seen beasts and plants, but as they neared the trading town they saw flocks of birds going and coming from the peaks ahead.

On one particular curvy and disturbing stone formation to Porter's left, shaping itself like the end of a cane, a cane coming ten feet off the ground and as thick as a barrel of Lagoona Rum, sat a flock of fat brown birds. A flock, like the yaks, meant only five birds and not a swarm.

"Hee-ho. Hee-ho. Hee-ho!" came an eerie chorus from the group. It gave Porter a shiver. The birds were proportionally obese, and had blind eyes. Small gray beaks curved like a tropical bird's might, but tan bodies with white spots like a desert grouse. Their calling was hollow, a paper bag wheezing in the wind.

From the foot of their perch a form the size of a small dog scuttled into view. It was some form of insect.

Bone white and oblong, the head of the large bug spun and spun as it chittered. It approached the train of horses, but as

Leoric yelled at the mountainous bug it chittered a shriek and extended bone white legs until it was as high as the horses. The men all recoiled, but the bug shrunk down again and attacked the front of the cane. Its carapace was black, but became dotted red as it managed to claim the nearest fat bird to its mesh mouth. The other four hee-ho'd away and towards the mountains, and the bug extended its legs out. It juggled the dead bird above its elliptical head with its front legs, chomping down inevitably, then stilting away on its towering legs.

Porter was thankful they were making good time, because it was a disgusting sight.

"That'll make a man sick," said Soranin.

Duncan Day threw up. Soranin sighed.

Two of the soldiers rode ahead, Leoric joined them.

"Should we...do anything? Should we have done anything?" Porter asked, looking at the murder scene and the sauntering off creature.

"I fear that is just the way of things here," Soranin said as he pulled on his Skell Brew, passed it to Porter. "Mercy. What is Ollette like I wonder?"

Chapter 4

Shuddering was serving no one, and Porter was able to shake it off by stealing a swig of his superior officer's brew. Skell Brew toasted his throat, how much had Soranin brought on this damn trip, he wondered, and it was pleasant in comparison to the cold barricade left by the rotating, evil beetle.

Over his shoulder it was clear how far down they'd come. Jobelnon was a dot to the North, the hills were cliffs behind them, and Ollette was just ahead. The trail, which had dissipated and been replaced by rocks and more rocks and blind birds, now was reforming. It wasn't a strangled dirt path, though, but a brick path. The brick was a white rock, almost like that made of the odd formations which had accompanied them over the course of the last day and night.

Rising, slow at first and then all at once on either side of the somewhat wide brick road, came wooden poles. In between each pole was strung rope, like flags. It seemed as though the entrance to a gala event. It felt more Caprican than any other place between here and their home, but it was still mingled with a foreign scent. Porter didn't mind.

King Emhart can die in a bloody hole, Porter thought, *not in the damn tower of who-gives-a-hell.*

No time for malice, he realized. Just poison.

The horses had all fallen in line, two by two with Duncan Day at the rear, and the poles were climbing, their ropes dipping to the height of their the heads now. The mountains were no longer a day or three hours away. The entrance was just there, now. Just there.

A moment later, the ropes came in between two high walls of rock, and now the entrance was just behind them.

INSIDE THE MOUNTAINS

Book VI

Build and reshape and create and grant and craft and graft and
draft and allow the possibility you may fail in each of these
endeavors before you ever charge the earth with anything other
than your intention, your love and your power.

Inscription deciphered on the Mason's foot in the year 971

Chapter 1

Leoric reached up for the ropes above them, now
decorated with gold ingots here and there, and found he couldn't
reach them. They were parallel with the cut sides of the mountain,
and seemed a part of them now.

The knight wondered how it was possible a road could
be carved into such a monolithic mountain. Then he wondered
why a blasted trade post, too self-important to join the Westlands
to treat, had nestled itself so deep into the Bastions of Tellor. King
Dorigin should have extinguished these passionate fools years
ago, he thought.

*But, then I might never have seen this gorgeous earth
spike into the sky,* Leoric thought.

The mountains, the first two named Hurei and Bolai
(unbeknownst to Leoric) had been so close together that some
foreign client, an Indonobi (also unbeknownst to the knight) had
bolded them apart, cut a way in between them. As soon as high
stone walls were crowding the horses two by two over gray brick,
now they spread apart again, rounded out and the path felt more
like it had. Open, but bizarre in its foreign landscape.

The flora was sparse and consisted of things needing
no water or light, or were just shrubs, and the fauna of wolves and
yaks was replaced by a few of the disgusting birds who seemed
to hop more than fly. For variety, the strange flora and fauna may
combine every few hundred feet for a dead looking bush which
would all of a sudden begin squirming, and then four stumped feet

would explode from below it. Then a scaled turtle's head would poke out, and after spitting at one of the traveler's it would begin climbing up the mountains. Or something.

Resilient things, Leoric thought. *Gross, too.*

On the gold ingoted-ropes now came signs on either side. A few of the silent travelers read them under the breath in near unison:

"**Ollette!** ahead – the Bastions of Tellor/Gorbish Mountains Welcome You. Travel in pairs always."

"That seems a bit flashy."

"Tellor be saved, DUNCAN DAY ALL OF US WERE HAVING A MOMENT!" Leoric's voice bounced in their small traveling space. He couldn't stand that twitchy, old fool. If he had been left as an ottoman, he didn't think they would have lost much. Possibly, they would have gained much.

"He meant no harm," Soranin said.

"The road to the grave is paved with…meaning no harm," Leoric said. The group traveled on, glad to have folks to chat with in these strange new places.

An unremarkable hour later, Soranin called to Porter: "Have you got our paperwork for the mayor?"

"I have," Porter noticed scratches on his arm, trying to get in.

"Prepare it. I'd like to be on our way. And please, ride with me a moment as we approach the post."

Porter caught up to his captain.

"Porter, we haven't discussed it, but-"

"You mean to persuade me to return with the soldiers back to Caprica," Porter had known this conversation would come.

"And with me," Soranin said. He looked serious, his eyes pleading and hard. "You'd leave home to jaunt around for your vagabond? A ragged, bizarre traveler? I miss my daughters, man. My dog."

"Soranin you heard the king. His speech, his demeanor more bitter and uncouth. I don't think we'd be welcome, and yes, I trust Ortimer. Dogs aside, sadly."

"He's got a name? And what do you mean we wouldn't be welcome?" The horses whinnied, and Porter thought they may be sensing tension. He knew that he was.

"Yes he's got a name - he's a human being, isn't he? And look, I mean no offense, but I'll be going on. I feel awake for the first time, I feel-"

"Put away your boyish notions of fantasy and impressing your father! Or did you forget the mark upon your arm? That you were very nearly drafted into the Tengö Nation and all at once matrimony?" Soranin barked.

"Oh come now, it makes for a great story, doesn't it?"

"I meant only that this is more serious than trundling through the countryside," Soranin pulled out a scone. Hopejule, and he broke off a bit and passed it to Porter who nodded his thanks. "I've never been nearly this far. Not even on a patrol – only to Tunsworth. What about yourself?"

"I've never even been to Tunsworth," Porter realized he'd only ever been as far as Roiling Tide once, and it felt much like Caprica in its demeanor. Roiling Tide must have been lied to as well. "Is it like they say in the books?"

"I wouldn't know. I've only been there, not read about it."

"And I've only read about it. How about we discuss it more after we deliver our papers, hm? Once the mayor signs the zoning commission papers we'll take the men out for dinner, and brew of course, and we'll talk about it then. Is that alright, sir?"

"Don't you 'sir' me yet," Soranin gripped his reins, "there's Ollette. Come on men. Look official, in order, if you can."

"YES, OFFICIAL LOOKING, ON MY MARK!" Leoric could be heard calling from the back.

"He'll be the death of me yet," Soranin sighed, shook his head, smiled at Porter.

The rounded edges of the mountains were sloping up, and the road ascended into a wider path. Ollette began with wooden buildings, but not of the same hue and design as Gelor, Marryfarm, or Caprica, for that matter. The wood was redder, older to the eye, and softer to the touch. The buildings seemed to breathe easy, some thatched roofs signaling an older world.

The air was cleaner as the rounded edges all but disappeared in favor of a flatter, higher land. The mountains were all about them now, and they couldn't see the mythical and stony land from before. In fact, they hadn't been able to for hours.

Wooden buildings with glass-paned and homey looking windows with yellow curtains were behind them now, and as the mountains moved more to either side and the buildings got an expanse in between them it became clear Ollette was more than just a trading post. And it had been more than that for a long time.

The brick road became brick ground, and ran in all directions. The rope and poles had descended back into the earth, and any sense of being enclosed by the protection of Tellor the Champion was replaced with spaciousness, and a friendly, bouncy attitude. To top it off, a postman walked in front of them:

"Sorry, boys! You aren't at 444 Moonbeam are you?"

"Can't say that we are," said Soranin.

"Then I'll be seeing you!" The old man nearly skipped away.

Porter smiled at this pleasant omen.

Soranin's plated armor shone from the last bit of the day's sun staring from on high. The sky was about half its normal size because high reaching mountains occupied much of the once blue bed of clouds.

"Oh," Soranin had nearly forgot. "Which way is the mayor's office?"

The postman said he would be glad to show them: the government building was his next stop, anyways.

"Still eager to leave?" Porter asked.

"Remember Gelor, Porter? If we see any gorgeous women, I'm bolting home. And I'll be headed back with or without being taken hostage, this time."

"I'd be alright with being kidnapped," Duncan said. "I'm just plain horny."

The travelers had a laugh, but it was one of relief, not of Day's wit. The sight of the stilted creature eating the blind bird had disturbed them all, plenty, and it became memory now.

Chapter 2

The low lakes were gorgeous. There were many, and
there were few combatants. Sinéad was happy to let her hair
down, so to speak. Before all this running, she had had long hair
that was the envy of every girl in her town. Now it was choppy
and short, but she was growing it out as she could. Somewhere in
the chaos there was a beauty to her.

Chaos was one of the things that had made her so
beautiful. She didn't realize that yet.

The battle maiden hadn't seen or heard her pursuers
in four days. That's not to say that she wasn't being followed, but it
wasn't the familiars that had been attacking her. The only foes she
had brought her mace down upon lately were a few capituraptors.
They were pretty bird reptile hybrids, but easily surrendered themselves. It made her feel better that they were quite tender; perhaps
they gave themselves up specifically to be eaten.

Yes, she had lost her typical assailants. The lakes gave
her a chance to get creative with paths, and she hadn't had a fire
for two nights.

It was easy for her to know the difference between fan-
tastical adversaries of blue and cosmic light and the suppressive
noises they made, and the poorly-disguised, self-conscious noises
that humans make.

The battle maiden walked along the edge of a smaller
lake, a pond really, for only a moment more before stopping. It was
in the open, and to her left she could see a mountain that she had
already passed. She knew she had come so far.

"There's nowhere to hide, come on out now," she
called. The weight of her armor was temporarily lightened as she
stopped. Her mace rested along the leg plate of her too large
plating.

For a moment she thought she may have to do battle
after all. The follower made no move to reveal themself.

She slung her mace upon her pauldron and grit her
teeth.

"Wait. Fuck, wait," a suave voice called out from between
a few trees, behind some high grass. Sinéad was a little surprised.

Though, she really had no expectation.

"What's your aim?" she asked.

The figure stumbled forward out of the foliage, brushed themself down. The unknown agent had a brown and blue robe with an upturned hood. Their hair was long, she could see it from the edges of his shadowed body. A sword was at one hip and a satchel on the other.

They stopped.

The battle maiden began to walk at him, readying her mace.

"No! No please!" the person fell backward into the foliage, and with a sploosh she knew he had fallen into the edge of the pond as well.

"I'm Jayce, please don't hurt me."

"Why are you following me?" she said.

"I saw what you've done to those things following you. I need to get to Celian Yearning," the woman began to approach him again, "andIknewifIfollowedyouI'dbesafesopleasedon'thurt-meeee!"

The battle maiden threw his hood back. It was a man. A tall and handsome man at that.

She paused. In Koro'Scheen she had been unassuming; harmless. She knew she was strong now, of course, but to have another person commend her spirit, a human for that matter, confirms it. This was new, unnecessary, but it felt good.

She helped him up.

"You don't mind me tagging along until we part ways?" he asked, removing mud from his rear.

"That's what it's all about any ways, isn't it?" she replied. She started walking.

He jogged to catch up.

"That armor seems too big for you," he said.

"It is," she said.

"Isn't it heavy?" he asked.

"Yes, sometimes unbearably so."

"You're a strong woman, then."

A little stone idol was on a necklace he wore, and she thought the green eyes were unnecessarily eerie.

"I'm not that uncommon. You can just see my armor."

She thought Jayce would make a good companion, for the time being, so long as he didn't talk this much all the time.

Chapter 3

Ollette was thriving. It had an electricity to it, even though it was all in all plain.

How could we not have known it was like this? Porter wondered. Then he remembered how fascism worked, and a nasty frown curdled on his jaw.

The downtown, which happened to be where the government building was located, had a throng of people moving around even at this late hour, right before sundown. There were tall wooden buildings, each displaying a flag of with a stylized mountain centered on a yellow field. Inside the mountain there was a nest, more symbolic than detailed. There were four stars around the mountain as well.

The folk of Ollette were not like the folk of Caprica, or of Roiling Tide, and Porter thought not much like Khu'Ron or Jobel-non either. They were like the men who made rum for the Rough Bout, or the tengös or anything else living beyond the fringes of imagination.

Tall, gaunt men with earrings absorbing the side of their faces chatted with stout women who didn't seem to shave. Some folk had crimson bandanas over their eyes sat near a small, old man who had a caged griger. The griger looked like a very smart sabretooth tiger, and it was unclear why he was in a cage at all. It beat its yellowed chest and roared at its captors, making it the only of the vagabonds doing anything about their imprisonment. The others were only imprisoned by their loyalty to sin.

A man of slender build with skin gifted by darkness was playing a stringed instrument with a group of assorted folk, and he was drinking from a custom made, and handsome to boot, flask. It was a flask triple the size of any Porter had seen, and he was jealous. He was adorned in a coat camouflaged with greens and blacks, but that was fuzzy with brown hair too. There was a bandana around his head, similar to the ones worn by the others around their eyes, and his had a feather in the back of it. His pants were fuzzy brown too, and he had thick boots made of some material Porter had never seen.

It became apparent that Porter had been staring, and

the object of his stare caught his eyes. The man smiled and his teeth were unkempt, but his spirit poured through his music. He tapped his foot and sang, and it seemed the small corner of the square was their private dance hall.

If Jobelnon was exciting, then Ollette was outrageous.

There seemed to be a distinct community as well, one alive with the same electricity they had perceived earlier. Through the hodge podge of different people, a fraternity was born, through their separate backgrounds a congruent one designed for all of their sake's. It was the fact they had been run-off that brought them here and, therefore, together.

And the government building! It was wooden, too, and had long flags on either side of the face of the building. Easily the largest building in the downtown, the postman walked them by a statue of an enormous bird. Again, it seemed symbolic, but the bird seemed to have two long coils coming from the top of its head, and a scaled beak. The winged form, made of the same stone as in the descended land, had its wings cast in a gust in front of it, and its beak was shut.

"Tie them up here and follow me inside, please!" The postman was cheery, and was waving around the square like he himself was the mayor. "What business should I tell Mayor Jopples you're on about?"

"He should be expecting a party from Caprica..." Soran-in began.

"The zoning commission? Oh stars that's you? I wonder what he'll say, ha," the postman took his hat off and smoothed out his hair, looking more amused than anything else.

Outside the building was the typical hitching posts and pails of water, but there was a man standing by. He was dressed in a hat like the postman's, blue with a black trim that came across the front of his head.

"Are you a guard of the horses, then?" Leoric asked, expecting a laugh from his compatriots.

"Yes," the man replied as he patted Kettlestep's head, "that's me."

"Oh. Good then," Leoric said as he hopped off his mount. Caprica had no such posts, but then again, Ollette has been the mouth of the mountains much longer than Caprica has been the capital of the Westlands. And in Ollette the government building wasn't an ornate house for aristocrats. It was a community center where locals could be heard.

The sun fell down at their backs. Inside, there was a long hall bifurcating the building. The postman led them to the far end, and there they found a gold ingoted door, like the others before. The pommels of the door were curved and handsome, and the postman went in first, asking the travelers to wait.

Soranin dodged his eyes from Porter to the papers in the second captain's hand.

Porter nodded, nervous.

The postman stepped out and smiled, bowed, and his footsteps were heard as he walked away.

"Come in then," a sleepy voice beckoned from inside

Leoric stared at Soranin, but Soranin led the procession. Leoric muttered under his breath.

The room was wide and decorated. Artifacts and totems that Porter really couldn't have imagined sat in glass cases, and strange paintings were dotted across the walls, oaken and red. A thick rug was under their feet and under a square table taking up the majority of the room, spare a small drawer in the corner near the back of the room. At the far end of the table was a high ended chair, and a two-headed korkisdole, something Porter was quite sure was legend, because korkisdoles were extinct, and two-headed ones were used in stories to put kids to sleep at night, was taxidermized just to the right of the chair, slithering part of its once-fictional body under the table. A leathered hand stroked the fuzzy, and dead, creature.

An emotional arc played out by the man in the chair. First, a stare saying the man would be glad to be euthanized. Then, one to euthanize his guests. Last, a smile. It was political and lukewarm. And it was late.

"Mayor Jopples," Soranin bowed deep, and the rest of the party followed. "I am Captain Soranin Redbell, of the-"

"Do you have his papers?" Mayor Jopples interrupted, and he stood. "And don't bow to me. This is not the plutocracy you are used to, captain."

The atmosphere of the room was deflated with that one fell move. The mayor stood and crossed the room. Soranin looked stunned.

"Sir…" Soranin began.

"I'm no sir, nor am I worthy of a bow. I am a mayor; don't you understand what that is?" Apple Jopples had short, greying hair and a tight greying beard. He had a paunch belly and three earrings on his right ear. "Your king has prolonged this long enough. Let me see the papers and let us be done with this."

Soranin motioned to Porter who produced the papers.

The mayor took them and returned to his seat. He moved like he was on his way to having his teeth pulled, wincing and unwilling.

Plopping in his chair, the official set the papers on the table in front of him and spent a moment reading over them.

Porter noticed a folder of papers on the edge of his desk.

They were bound by a black tie, which read "Group F" upon the face.

Curiosity had no place yet; Porter only swallowed and had a nice sweat building in his pits.

"This is complete, Tellor-infused balderdash."

The mayor ripped the papers into shards, then into dust, his face turning redder than a rash and his tight hair frolicking out of control.

"Sir I don't-" Soranin began again.

"DO YOU HAVE WHAT I REALLY WANT? Did your king tell you why I haven't signed his papers? To promote his song-and-dance?"

Porter and Soranin glanced towards the soldiers who also did not understand what the mayor was referencing.

Leoric kept the coolest head of the party. Soranin's lack of understanding how to operate in a non-formal situation was driven home again.

"May we be seated?"

"By all means. It's the end of the day and all of the people of Ollette will be pounding on my walls in any moment," Mayor Jopples reached for the corner and produced a tall bottle and some small glasses.

"Lagoona?"

"Please," Leoric was slid a drink as the others were seated around him. "Why will they hound you so?"

"Our roc will not be visiting us at dusk, nor tomorrow's dusk or any dusk soon...." the mayor stared at the wall as he spoke, and then, snapping back to the room, "because of your greedy king. Who has kings anymore, anyway? You damn zealots are as aggravating as the elves. I cannot help but-"

"Please, Mayor Jopples, but just between us," Leoric raised a hand, a lazy flag of indifference. Porter was impressed with his negotiations. He wished he had had this gift when dealing with King Ernhart. "We all have our qualms with the king. Tell us yours."

"You speak so plainly about your distaste for your king," the mayor's face unreddened for a moment. "How unique! Your name?"

"I am Captain Leoric Norrin, of the King's Sword. This is my company: Captain Soranin Redbell, of the King's Army and his Second Captain Porter Rosset. The one with the mustache is Duncan Day, and these other three are...." Leoric's hand tumbled in the air as he stuttered for a moment, "well we are all on the king's business any ways. Which you seem to know plenty about."

"I do. Regrettably," Mayor Jopples drank and poured himself out again, the thick booze smelling of cloves. "I can only assume, as any of the folk that slip through the net surrounding your oppressive regime are, that you are only recently aware of our ways in Ollette?"

My father would have been one of these folk, Porter thought.

"We know very little, only that Ollette is one of our trading posts and the furthest Eastern settlement of the Westlands."

"That's what we are now? The stories change but there is a constant untruth: that Ollette is underneath Ernhart's rule. This has never been true, thank the stars," the mayor gripped a star necklace he produced from around his neck, under his shirt.

"Would you speak more, mayor?" Leoric clutched the bottom of his chair with one hand and animated his speech with the other, the party just as uncomfortable, if not more so.

"Ha, on what?" The mayor smiled. "You must forgive me, the naiveté of Westlanders never ceases to intrigue me."

"Why else would we be giving you these papers if not because you were a distant post of the royal family's property?" Leoric asked.

"Stars, that lunatic is demanding it of you, that's why! You do whatever he tells you to without question. Because he has to manage you to believe in this puppet show of his, so now you'll do his bidding without his even saying so. It's so hegemonic," the mayor paused, tried to regain composure.

"Because these aren't zoning papers. Well, now they aren't even papers, but prior to my outburst they were disclosure agreements. The king has us sign annual papers, which he signs as well mind you. I sure do grow tired of his self-righteous ego thinking he has us sign his papers. Has he ever heard of a contract? I digress. Both are cities, Caprica and Ollette. Show some balderdashing respect!" the mayor ranted. "Well, an inter-town if you ask around, but..."

"Cities? Ollette is a full-fledged city?" Porter interrupted, he couldn't help it.

"Doesn't quite fit your mold, eh boy? No, Ollette is no township or village, and certainly not a trading post. We're the first city of the Gorbish Mountains, or whatever you may call these goliaths, by entrance of the Sistered Pass. The first city before Yorenhuey and the best city besides Rolocheve, and that's only if you can appreciate proper Jilted Wine," the mayor said.

"The contract states we will refrain from contact with the Westlands, past the 114 Year Divide, and the Westlands will pay us back in kind," the mayor said. "Except for when contracts need signing. Which is why you're here. But I won't sign, because your king is an egomaniacal balderdasherer."

The soldiers reached for their swords.

"Don't, please, what a foolish thing to do with my life and yours," the mayor poured another drink. His fourth. "You didn't know the king dealt with thieves did you?"

Nervous glances passed amongst the company, and the mayor continued.

"The skunk knight came to visit me with papers once, when he was young and less fat," Jopples continued. "And while his party dealt with mine he must have romped off...but you don't know about the roc do you? That's where this rant got derailed in the first place, right?"

"I believe so," Leoric said, gaining composure.

"Ha, well the roc is Ollette and Ollette is the roc. It flies overhead, coming from its high nest, each day at dusk and cries out to the stars. It sings and Ollette cheers, and when we're lucky it's feathers rain upon us and we are healed. The roc is truly magnificent; it is one of many in the Atorlane Short Mountains, or so I've been told, but ours is enormous. I've come to calling it Jordan..." the mayor trailed off again. "But a roc needs a rock. Do you know nothing about them?"

The men shook their collective head.

"And what are the Atorlane Short Mountains? These few by your town?" Soranin asked.

"Well considering it is your head of state that ruined Jordan, I'll elaborate, but really there is no time to get into stories," the mayor was stinking drunk now, a stink of cloves. Porter hardly even wanted any rum when he considered the stench. "A roc is born along with a stone. As a fledgling we know it takes the rock around with it, and when it is old enough to build its own nest it becomes the heart of that nest. There's a heart to the place, you see."

"And you say your roc had its rock stolen? How can you be sure?" asked Soranin.

"A roc changes when its rock is not with it. It does not leave its nest, or in Jordan's case it does not visit the town. Some rocs are not quite as friendly or sociable as Jordan, you know...it becomes deranged, going mad. I cannot imagine the pain it is in and has been in for, stars, going on a year now."

"A whole year?" Soranin asked in disbelief.

"A whole year, since the last documentation," the mayor slumped. "I cannot believe that bastard king of yours either."

"Now just a moment," Leoric began. "Neither king nor knight would have done something like this. What did the rock look like?"

"I can show you a photo," the mayor stood and went to a cabinet on the wall.

"Sorry?" Duncan asked.

"My stars, you lot are true bumpkins aren't you?" The mayor slid a tan piece of paper with black etchings on it from within the cabinet. Upon it was a group of etched people, some government workers it seemed, standing in front of the building that they stood in now. Mayor Jopples, younger and with one less ear piercing, held a large stone, and even in the black and tan picture it shined a thousand nice hues.

"I think I've got that stone," Porter said.

The mayor gained even more redness to his face. "You do? What color is your stone?"

"It's hard to describe, sort of a blue and purple and-"

"Beautiful," The mayor butted in, sitting down with his eyes focused on Porter the whole time.

"That's it. Majestic, really."

"Oh my, my stars," the mayor was shaking. "Let me see it."

"I'll need to go to my pack..." Porter said.

"Go then."

A few moments later Porter came back through the enormous doors and set his thieved possession on the table. It sparkled.

"Did you think to tell us about this?" Soranin asked. His eyebrows were furrowed and his arms were crossed. "What in all of Tellor's might is wrong with you, man?"

Porter noticed the other men looking a bit disconcerted, and for the first time Leoric and Soranin seemed to agree.

"I didn't – I just grabbed it along with Krude on our way out. It seemed too fantastic to be set in a locked case."

The golden dream, the memory is all he had really thought of when he saw the rock in that case. Soranin and Porter had discussed his usage of substances before, and this had been his hope in keeping things quiet. Besides shame.

One particular day is when they had ever spoke about it in plain terms. Porter was late to his morning routes, which made him late to a speech to newts and the subsequent training and when he did show up his skin was near purple like a plum and he had food and grossness in his beard. Soranin had asked him if he was sick, Porter had said no, then Soranin had said there would be no issue then? Porter had said of COURSE no issue. For them, that was a plea and an affirmation and a rejection and an admonition.

So Soranin and Porter were the only two in the room with an idea of what had really happened.

"Well, I am betrayed, simple," Soranin said as he turned his gaze out the window.

"Look man," Porter said.

"Sir is fine," Soranin said curtly. "Is it the stone, Mayor Jopples?"

"Of course it is. It's Jordan's prized possession and her most tragic loss," the mayor was mesmerized.

Leoric broke the trance:

"We cannot give it to you."

"I'm SORRY?" The mayor nearly shrieked, his face a fat beet now, "You'd leave my people pounding their fists at my walls and down?"

"You've taken our fair share of a bargain clear out of the equation. You destroyed the zoning commission."

"I've already told you there was no zoning commission," the mayor said, maintaining his anger and pulling out more papers from his cabinet. "And I have my own copy of the paperwork."

"Then we can trade," Leoric said with a smile.

"There is one addendum to our agreement, I'm afraid," the mayor said. His hair was a wiry shrub, and he patted it into its original tightness. "The rock must be returned to the roc."

"Which rock to where?" Duncan asked.

"That rock," the mayor pointed across the table, "to that roc."

He then pointed out his window and toward the second closest mountain at the South end of the city. About half way up an indent could be seen on the face, and there were some large sticks and branches protruding off of the edge.

"We must take it to the nest? Can't your own people do it?"

"Some of our best and bravest have tried to go to

Jordan – to discern the issue on their own, stars know I haven't told them in fear they'll lose hope," a faint thumping began on the outside of the office. "Not that it has proven very helpful. In her deranged and depressed state, the roc has either regarded them in a nonsensical way and thrown them from the ledge, or less commonly, eaten them."

The newts exchanged nervous glances. One with a pin shaped head and a balloon body tittered, and the smallest, a boy with Khu'Roni style braids, wrung his hands together again and again and again.

"If you return the rock, to the...Jordan," the mayor glanced at Duncan as he spoke. "I'll sign those papers for you." Leoric raised an eyebrow.

"And give you provisions for your travel home," the mayor understood. "Would anything else be required of the brave adventurers who salvage the joy of the people of Ollette?"

On the door, a light thumping picked up force.

"I think we'd better discuss anything else upon our return – it seems as though the madding crowd is gathering for the evening, eh Mayor Jopples?" Soranin spoke as he turned and left the room.

"Yes," the mayor sighed as he poured another drink, the bottle having suffered from their visit. "Stars be with you."

Porter glanced at Soranin at the odd comment, Soranin shrugged.

Ollette was shrinking behind the seven men, but the distance amongst them had swelled greater.

Fighting the tengös had been an accident. It had felt sort of thrilling due to its hidden nature. Marching three miles out of town and a mile up a mountain to negotiate with an insane mythical beast did not seem thrilling. Only murderous.

Soranin and Leoric were taking the lead, but they kept a wide distance between each other. Their semi-matching armor was impressive to Porter who walked a long distance behind the pair. He had been shunned after the meeting, and the nerves the group held didn't provide the right platform to have "the talk." The three newts who aren't Duncan Day were huddled, but they were keeping safe distance. Duncan Day meandered between Porter and the three, and he rested a bit upon a walking stick he had collected from the ground.

The troop was a mile or so from the base of the mountain, night having fallen upon them ten minutes prior. They decided to approach the beast after a night's rest and with the advantage of day. They needed the creature to see the rock.

"Jordan," said Duncan Day as one of the newts stoked a fire. "I believe the mayor said its name was Jordan."

"The mayor said he called it Jordan," responded Soranin who was unfastening his armor, unraveling his sleeping mat. "but he also calls the king a thief. I see only one thief with us tonight."

Porter winced, but responded in no way but to poke the fire with his stick. Though their nerves were failing them, their military training didn't, and even so close to a city they kept a post. Tonight there was no conversation. It would be Porter.

"How did the rock end up in Caprica then, sir?" Duncan asked. The fire cast a hapless shadow on his wrinkling face. The stars upon the high, rocky terrain made him feel like he was in a desert, maybe near Khu'Ron. He'd never been there. He'd never left Caprica until this trip. But, then again, no one had asked Duncan.

"It doesn't matter how it got there," the captain replied as he wiped the plate he'd been wearing all day clean with a bit of cloth. He wore only a simple white shirt, stained with sweat and travel. "It matters that it was Caprican property until very recently."

"Soranin, I meant no harm," Porter said.

"Good night all, rest easy," Soranin slipped into his bag and soon into a dream, leaving Porter, Duncan, one newt who was too anxious to join his captain in slumber, and Leoric, who stared into the fire, finally speechless it seemed. Distress works wonders on vocabulary.

The fire crackled as all fires do, and the remaining journeyers stared into it as all men who have a burden in their hearts do. Looking to the stars is for the optimistic, a young man's gambit. It is in the fire that most passion can be personified and where a soul finds true company.

"I thought only that it should join me on my travels, I... I guess I wasn't thinking much at all. I felt a bit under a trance when I placed it in my bag," Porter said.

"It doesn't matter now, does it? No point in regret. At all," Leoric emphasized without looking at Porter. "But certainly not over taking a bloody rock. Let's see it again."

Porter brought out the rock. In the fire's light it was more radiant than anything the men had seen in the waking world.

"Maybe Jordan was calling it back," Duncan said, his green sun cap finding a place near his pack. Porter saw for the first time that Duncan was a few hairs short of bald, and the black head of hair which he had been imagining was only a monk's cut.

"Ha, maybe," Porter laughed. He feared Soranin's misplaced dedication to the Caprican bell would cause him to return with the newts after their hike tomorrow. It occurred to Porter that, given recent events, there was a new wrinkle. If they returned at all.

Then he remembered the papers, the Group F Easter egg in the office. He needed to speak with Soranin about it, but what would he think now? What might he say?

"Do you suspect the roc will be as violent as Mayor Jopples described?" he asked.

"Yes," the youngest newt, the one awake, squeaked.

Duncan chuckled, and his chuckling spread into Porter.

"It's entirely probable. I mean, he says some of his braver men have died trying," Leoric stood up and began to strip his armor as well.

"But they never attacked with seven men," said the newt.

Leoric laughed as he crawled into his bag.

"This task would be much simpler if we, or those who have tried before us, were attacking, newt. We're trying to treat with a roc. Killing it, or dealing any sustaining damage of any kind, is not a part of the mission. Consider it, then, like negotiating with a rabid dog who also happens to be a timeless, beloved mascot."

Chapter 4

The men picked at the remainder of some Geloran jerky they had purchased, on the king's Westlands credit of course, until it was gone, which just about finished their food. This was only convenient since they were in plate armor the remainder of their hike, an almost vertical hike, which promised to be hellish enough without packing snacks.

Soranin left his cape at the camp site, saying he'd retrieve it upon their return.

"A cape up there seems like as poor choice as going up there at all, snagging on things and getting raked apart," Soranin said to himself as they began the rest of their trek.

The newts lagged, with Duncan upon his walking stick, but they reached the trail that led to the nest, or so they assumed. They weren't sure what to expect. Porter was still processing tengös, and here before them was a roc.

Winding and switch-backing and dusty, the trail proceeded steep as could be right up the mountain. It wasn't long into their hike before all of the soldiers began to feel the heat of the day catching up.

From above them came a call like the first drink of a warm, chocolatey drink feels, but one spiked with the sound of a man cut down by steel that he did not expect. From the corner of the ledge they looked up to see the tips of a spread wing peeking over a higher ledge. Some of the shrub turtles from before began tumbling down, in true shrub fashion, from the ledge.

"Rude awakening for the cowardly fellows," Leoric said as the beasts rolled past.

"They may have been awake, but now they aren't alone on that ledge," Soranin said. "Jordan has woken for the day it seems. Porter, produce the rock. Understandably, you'll take point here."

"Understandably," Porter patted down sweat from his brow and moved up the last flight of rocks with Soranin behind.

Leoric went to draw his blades, but balled his fists and followed the second captain instead. The newts followed after him, and our eldest newt behind them.

The roc was everything the statue had been, but more.
And less.

The statue couldn't capture the color and fullness of its
wings, the brown with hues of yellow and gold. The brown tendrils
protruding from its head did not seem faulty like in the recreation,
instead gallant and swooping, laying back on the creature's head.
The beak of the creature was black and silver, and was a layered
thing. It looked like layers of iron, and little did they know it was as
hard as metal, too. The tail was cut by patterned feathers into the
shape of a fan, and the men were stopped in their tracks by the
bird's powerful and intelligent gaze.

But this is where the beast was less. Its stare was mad.
It was sad, it was spooked. Though its body was strong, its chest
rose and fell quickly, harshly. Jordan's claws were yellowed, and in
its mouth plaque had built up like a portcullis. Porter realized that
not eating, depression and anxiety were all diseases in their own
right.

The nest that the bird stood in was at the edge of the
ledge, a ledge no more than twenty feet across and thirty feet
long. It was sheer rock, with only sky beneath it on all sides. The
ledge was a fin into the otherwise unperturbed ocean of the sky,
and the nest a fantastic barnacle on the fin. Though it was the
roc that centered the scene as a force strong enough to halt the
Westlanders already uneven breath.

With its wings spread in a challenging position to the
day, the beast turned its body towards the party which had
approached on its left. It was more serpent like as it did this, low-
ering its body and hopping to close the distance.

Its eyes never moved from the group and it opened its
mouth, panting. After a while it roared again, and Porter knew it
was a queen here, in this place. The soothing crow underneath the
pained shriek was evident.

"Well," Soranin said. "Give it back."

Porter tried to lower his pack to the ground, and as he
reached for the draw strings on his bag the roc screamed again
and took three long steps toward the party, flapping its wings.

The last, non-descript newt lost his footing. He had

been second to last in the train, and as he stumbled he clawed onto an edge, eye level with his body flopping below. Without thinking he pulled himself onto the ledge and sprung up, unsheathing his short sword. Duncan Day gasped.

The roc did much more.

As soon as the newt had unsheathed his weapon, though an impressive reflex time for an apprentice soldier by Soranin's standards, his captain called out for him to retreat.

The roc was much faster than even his voice, though, and in with a lunge and a beating of its tarp-like wings, the roc picked up the newt in its talons. Then it ascended toward the sky, calling out again. Crazy to some, but in Jordan's madness Porter saw passion and defiance. Against the sun the huge bird looked like an eagle with prey in its talons, reminiscent of something ancient and terrifying.

Porter plunged into his sack for the stone and ran to the base of the nest. He thrust the stone into the air. Magnificent as it was by the fire, it was nothing in comparison to the unadulterated shine from the sun, and before Jordan could drop the soldier a reflection from the stone caught it in a powerful eye.

Instead of releasing the prey in the usual spot, the bird flipped and returned towards its original perch.

Leoric motioned for the group to get low, and they did, all save Porter. He stood as big as he could with his precious item raised like a prodigal baby above him.

The roc came in like a hurricane and threw its wings out to slow itself. As it reclined it released the newt. The poor fellow, wearing his Caprica trainee assigned armor, catapulted forward and was received by his superior officers, as best as they could receive an adult man flying into their arms.

Jordan touched earth and began to circle around Porter, back away at first and then settling into its nest. Porter saw its beak was dirty, and in its eyes it indeed was maddened. The bird clapped its mouth open and closed, and frothed a bit.

It slung a wing at Porter and shrieked, and the soldier was knocked down but held onto the stone. Then the roc lifted Porter.

They flew into the air and Porter felt free. Granted, the crushing talons around his middle weren't very freeing, but he looked down on the group of people who trusted him little, the city of Ollette that he didn't know and then over to the Westlands, the place where he'd been an ignorant peon for years. He wondered what Frogg would think of his character now.

Then he realized how high they really were. The roc lifted him far above the place where it had seemed the newt would meet his fate (I really should learn their names, Porter thought). The sun hit the stone in Porter's hands and the roc cried, but this time it was not with the pain and confusion it had been holding on to. It was mellow, a rich and beautiful noise echoing around the mountains that they now soared above.

A flock of bergies swirled near the aerial duo, and the roc tore through a cloud.

Porter saw the gorgeous landscape below.

He saw the landscape below.

He really saw the Bastions of Tellor for the first time, and it was like a map, not a pauldron.

I mean, this can't be all of it. I'm not daft, but this is incredible. Porter was flabbergasted, and panicked as he realized the creature was descending.

A village up North, by a trail from Ollette, and a roving trolley of some kind over there. There's a city, and that's got to be a city and by Tellor that is too. How many cities are there?! And they're splendid! Enormous and splendid! And what was that? And-

Porter hit the nest like a sack of heavier sacks and the rock popped out of his arms.

"Wait, don't-"

And into the talon of the roc.

The rock's colors magnified and blurred with the body of the roc, and as the beast clutched tighter on the stone it's claws gained color. Its feathers grew sheen and some of the plaque died away. It was searing with power. The roc ejected Porter from its nest and placed the rock in his stead in the nest.

The bird was nowhere close to back to its true potential, Porter imagined, but it had lost the twitch in its gait, the sadness in its eye. He looked at the big bird and his band felt heavy, the remnance of his matrimony. The connection from species to species and again to a new species had some depth Porter couldn't understand, but Jordan did and the great icon cooed at Porter.

He didn't want the rock back. His itching was subsided and mental screws weren't turning. He was in love with this big creature and the world he was learning about.

Jordan's antennae twitched and the bird cawed again. The men poked their heads up from the trail, and Porter smiled at them. He stroked the great bird's head, and the feathers felt holy.

"I think we can return now," Leoric said.

"Yeah, but first...what are your names?" Porter said, motioning to the three newts that weren't Duncan Day.

"Alaina," said the youngest, braided boy.

"Lentil," replied the obtuse and pin shaped one.

"Ganes, sir," said the soldier who was clutching his head.

"That was long overdue, and undoubtedly made things more confusing than necessary," Porter had hoped to spend more time with Jordan, but it had flown away while they chatted, down to Ollette, he thought. "Come on then."

The stone pulsed in the nest that it was at home in, and it was not disturbed again.

Chapter 5

It was a festive mood awaiting them in Ollette, except awaiting isn't the right word because the locals in no way cared if those strange Capricans ever came back, really. Their city was one again.

The many people who had crowded around the government building to harangue their elected official were now weeping on their knees, or dancing or just smiling into the sky. It was still early in the day when the group arrived back to the city, hungry and taxed, their bodies drooping in each step. Food vendors and merchants had moved carts to the square, and the mayor himself was outside, gazing up.

Jordan rolled and flipped and cawed, showering feathers upon the citizens hungry for the love of their beloved mascot and idol.

The travelers were aware of the festivities as soon as they neared the city's edges, and were accompanied by a blob of people who, packed close, were roving toward the heart of the city. The square itself housed all of the fun, and a fast-paced jazz band played somewhere Porter couldn't see. He was surprised when he felt a hand clasp his shoulder.

"You showed great courage, Porter," Soranin said. "Excellent work."

"Thank you sir," Porter replied.

"Don't you sir me quite yet," Soranin smiled. "You need to take care of yourself. You know that right?

"Yes," Porter felt vulnerable. "I know that. I think this thing is helping, whatever we're doing."

"We should get a dinner, flesh out what we mean to do here, speak with the men."

"Right," Porter said. "Will you go on?"

"For now let's just live loud and brash. For Caprica!" Soranin motioned to the great groups of people. The mayor, from the steps of the government building, cheered and pointed out the arriving heroes in the crowd. Without hearing him, Porter knew what he had said because the entire city seemed to turn upon them. Then an enormous cheer rang out, and a fresh shower of feathers, and some confetti, courtesy of Apple Jopples, charged down.

Duncan Day, Porter and Alaina were chatting with a group of gorgeous women, some human and some not, some not really women, while ordering scones and coffee.

Leoric and Lentil hotly debated the size of the roc up-close while their dancing partners smirked at their hot-headedness.

Ganes had followed Soranin to the foot of the government building to speak of recompense with the mayor. Jopples said they would have all the food and drink they could eat today, a credit from the city along with provisions like grain, clothes and gear, which would be supplied in the morning. After shaking hands, the mayor produced the signed disclosure agreement. Soranin placed it in the bag Nin'tei still had, then moved to join the party.

The still somewhat dizzy newt bowed, and Mayor Jopples laughed, telling him to follow his superior officer.

The mayor returned to his office to admire his korkisdole, reveling in pride for his community's wellness. His husband joined him, the two enjoying some Lagoona rum before parading around with the citizenry. It felt good to be in each other's company only, without feeling stuck between a roc and a hard place.

The day passed by, not a qualm or stress amongst the group of heroes. It was still exciting to be meeting new and strange people, some who had mewling laughs but were the size of houses. To play a bit of Sqwees Rat at the local public house and bet sums of money no one in the bar could produce. To dance with foreign people to stranger music, but it all feeling exactly right. Toasting to a job well done, to Ollette and to Jordan, and to the purple bell.

They had all slurred before finishing their last toast.

It was dark before the group decided to take themselves to dinner.

"Mayor Jopples is buying, Apple as he asked me to call him, since I believe it is still technically the day we freed Jordan from her pains," Leoric called out as they stumbled from the town square. They had all come to start calling her by the mayoral name. "So eat up!"

"But do be modest," Soranin said, slinging his arm around Alaina. "If we can."

They all laughed. Behind them the vendors packed away their goods, the band had ceased and all the citizens had gone home for the night. Or they had gone to the Fermented Forrest.

The FF, as many came to call it, was the best and the bravest bar in Ollette. The only twenty-four hour joint and the only spot the young hipsters and the weathered huntsman could find drinks and food that they both considered good. It was cheap, but not grubby. Boisterous, but not showy. Their breakfast was quality, and it was the newest spot in town in the second oldest building, the first being the library.

Many say it was because of the Fermented Forrest that such haste went into revamping the jail, but where else were travelers to go to swap stories and dish up?

Groups of dark and bright folks crowded the entrance, composed of two high, handsome doors like those at the government building. As the group approached in their simple clothes, having left their armor with the horse guard for the evening, they looked and felt like civilians for the first time in a long while. Ragged looking, but still civil looking. Porter sported a crimson doublet, Soranin a new white one. Leoric had himself a purple, Caprican doublet and the newts all had green. That is, except Duncan Day who wore a brown doublet and sported his walking stick which, at some point during the day's drunkenness, had been fashioned into more of a cane. Day had left his sun hat with the horse guard, and he'd combed his sparse hair over, but wetting one's hair and a touch of cologne didn't do much to mask inobriation and the exhaustion of dealing with an enormous bird.

They received woos and shouts, pats on the back and free drinks before they even got their table. Porter's head was swimming hard. The night was still roasting; they'd been keeping strong since they returned over seven hours ago.

A young man with a creature something like a squirrel roosting around his neck sat the seven down at the largest table, imposing and rectangular. They were not at the bar, but soon began getting the attention of everyone at the bar. Yellow banners, with nest symbols in their middles, strung from the ceiling were lined with a bloody red. There were lanterns along the wall, and a band in the corner. The military cadre did not see the emerald statues of dragons in all four corners.

It was impossible for the drunken crew to look at each other in this bar; the random groupings of people were astonishing. Only a few of them even read their menus. Drinks had been ordered right away and food items poked at blindly.

The incredible diversity was inspiring to the journeyers because every group, as different as they seemed, all shared a sense of cheer. No one was upset.

Leoric was pinching and grabbing nearly every gorgeous person who came by. Soranin laughed, he was less drunk and very amused. At least half of the passersby barely seemed human at all, though still gorgeous.

Seven tankards were placed around the table, all sporting a rich Fire Brew. Porter wondered if it was the same that came into the Rough Bout with those two eccentric men. His taste buds were not reliable at the hour.

"So," Soranin said as he clapped his hand on the table, throttled his brew. "Can we just say...CHEERS!"

Book VII

Chapter 1

The Mason Men out populated the locals at this point. Business owners – before the Setting there weren't so much "businesses" as there were artisan shops – teachers and warriors were near all Mason Men now. And of course builders were Mason Men, and there were far too many of those.

The Carskren desert blew its hot air over the hill as Hariah half slid and half ran down its edge. Better than at night where the hill became a frigid strait to Meinhah.

The geography of Meinhah was rural and simple. Tin Bin Hill lay a morning's walk from the city itself, and along a tiny path in between two smaller mountains. To get anywhere in the Tariyan Range one did plenty of walking along rural paths like these. Cjinoh, the nearest mountain of consequential size, overlooks all of the valley he once called home, but it is even a small mountain compared to others, he thought. The Tariyan is brutishly huge to the Meinhah people, and sprawls through rainforests and patches of sand and fog and mist.

The blonde outcast had never gone to the desert or to the forest or left the mountains at all, and he wasn't sure why. When he rejected the gift of the Mason, his people shunned him, yet he had never gone much further than Tin Bin Hill. The distance he could create felt scarier than the one created for him already.

Most days, unbeknownst to his former community, he could be found just beyond the Mason's Hope, or the Ruined Valley as he preferred to call it. He didn't meet many travelers, but he had met one in a red cloak who said its name before the Setting was the Ruined Valley, and he took the thick man's words to heart.

Hariah hated what had happened since the Setting, which included, amongst many other things, the renaming of his hometown to the Mason's Hope, so he preferred to call it the Ruined Valley. If that was its name before the Setting, it was even more appropriate a name now, Hariah thought.

The shadow of the totemic titan was not far away, so Hariah knew he was close. And, as the walls of earth rose beside him and the shadow drew nearer, there was the familiar shop near the edge of the valley. One place he could take refuge.

The shop was as plain as could be, and Hariah pushed the as plain as could be door wide open.

"OET!" Hariah called out, removing his helmet. His short blonde hair was sweaty, and his blue eyes darted along the counter for a drink of water.

"COMING!" Oet replied. The shop was small enough that they didn't really need to yell, but if Oet was smithing it could get noisy. The shop was only a smith in back, a small space behind the counter, and the counter. Oet's Smithery; 'nuff said.

The tiny mason floated over his shoulder when he stepped from the back room. It hummed and its little green eyes peered at Hariah. Like the one in Hariah's pocket, it was lifeless, but energy existed within it. Otherwise, it could not float.

"Were you on the hill?" Oet asked.

"A drink, please," Hariah said, and Oet understood. Hariah's totem did not float, because he did not pray to it.

The dust in Hariah's throat slid away as he slurped his regional brew. He finished his spream, tossed the cup to Oet.

"Thanks, man," Hariah said.

"Why are you back this time, Hariah?" Oet asked. "How could I not visit my good friend Oet Sun, son of Oet Sun?"

"I've never liked you, Pariah, you know that."

"Well you put up with me," Hariah rested his polearm along the wall.

"Why haven't you moved along yet?" Hariah stopped, but regained himself.

"I want to talk some sense into my people."

Oet walked from behind the counter and dotted himself with a rag. His workman's smock did not cover the hair that came from under his shirt. Oet was a man's man.

"What sense do you think they lack? Perhaps someday you will see that we are better off with him."

"It's a 'him'?" Hariah asked.

"Step outside with me," Oet said.

They walked outside. The shadow had grown longer as the day was coming into afternoon. The shadow spread over everything.

The Mason was the skyline. Its enormous golden and bronze head ate up most of the blue sky, and its broad shoulders, reaching out on either side, took most of the rain that would hit the cities below upon them like an incredible gutter. Its emerald eyes had once pulsated and now beamed day and night, proud, unrelenting, and were brilliant even underneath a bright sun. It had no mouth, and it sat like a monk on feet with no legs.

An inhuman, aberrant monk the size of five or six Tin Bin Hills. In the future it will go to war like it did in the past, disrupting the popular narrative of peace that surrounded it. But that is a story for another time.

The two men watched it, with one small Mason floating over Oet's shoulder.

"You know I have begun to pray each day," Oet said. "And the results are exactly as those Mason Men say."

Hariah turned on Oet.

"You're becoming a builder?"

Oet smiled.

"Would you like me to show you my new power?"

"No, I think I'd rather have hot forge stokers shoved through my nipples."

As they spoke, a Mason idol, perhaps the size of a bergie, flew in front of them. It was about twenty feet away, and it span around at the mouth of the road into the valley.

"Those things make no sense," Hariah said. "If it's a god

why does it need drones? What do they do?"

"They're protecting us," Oet said, his eyes cast to the sky.

"You're actually buying all this? I've only been away a month this time!"

"Three weeks. But I was studying him before that."

"Why didn't you tell me?"

"We're not friends, Hariah, maybe that's why."

"You just want more business. You're too far out and you want to give Meinhah some reason to see lonely Oet. Lonely, pathetic Oet who had no friends other than a pariah and that floating rock."

Oet began to walk inside.

"You're toxic, and one day you may see that the Mason saved us. Brought Meinhah into the future."

"What about Celian? Did homogenizing our culture with theirs under the banner of truth, no, terror, make us more advanced or did it make us simpletons? Is it a good thing that our culture takes second, nay, third, to travelers who trivialize our home as caricatures of their newfound lord? When will the Mason leave and destroy our cities in its wake?"

"He has already done battle and set, why would he move again?"

"You've ignored my points, and-"

Oet turned around and grabbed Hariah by his ailt.

"I'd say go home, Hariah the Pariah, but I know you haven't got one," Oet gave him a gentle shove, realizing his aggression. "So I'll just say leave me alone. You don't need to put this self-important quest upon yourself. There is no conspiracy and there is no heart break; Meinhah is happy. Our labor rewarded. Can't you see that?"

Oet went inside and his happy follower did too.

Soon his helmet was flung from the window and Hariah caught it. He was glad he brought his weapon and tool with him outside; Oet flinging them would have been a bloody thing.

He tugged his helmet onto his head. Then he pulled the figurine out of his pocket and turned it in his hand. It was lifeless, and had no energy in it. Keeping it out of obsession now.

"Can't you try thinking for yourself? Or respecting your culture enough to want it preserved in this decaying valley?"

The pariah ambled toward the city where he was born.

Where he had once been somebody.

He was hungry.

The whole bar roared, the newts standing with the officers following suit. Duncan sat, his bones whupped.

Porter noticed one of the band was the same man from earlier, the black man who had the exotic stringed instrument. He again was smiling, and his bandana had two new feathers now.

He was stomping his boot to the rhythm, and flicked his head to Porter in recognition.
The second captain raised his glass.

"What next, men? We've got our papers," Soranin said as they sat. smile.

"Right to business, eh, old man?" Leoric said with a "We'd best figure it out before I go ahead and black out, Knight's Swan!" Soranin guffawed and Porter doubled over.

"Anything to eat chaps?" the creature around the server's neck spun its head around and smiled at the drunken men, and they smiled back. Alaina seemed a bit less accepting of new creatures than the rest. His curiosity for novelty died when he went on his sky tour.

"Oh man, we haven't looked," Porter said, drunk in the way he ought to be. "You know, I forgot all about the journal I've brought. I will write ALL of this down, don't you worry."

Soranin ignored the ramblings, and spoke to the server.

"One of your best dishes for each of us, and bring a few extra plates? And a pitcher of beer," Soranin said, handing the menus to the black haired boy. Soranin promised a fat tip for the boy's work.

The three eyed rodent almost laughed, and the boy thanked Soranin.

"You know, I think my son might wear something like this," Soranin said, poking the giggling accessory the server wore. The server excused himself, and Soranin smiled.

"What happened to modesty, sir?" Duncan asked with a wink.

"Alcohol drowned it," Soranin laughed. "But so did curiosity! What are we to do?"

"Well," Porter mustered his courage. "Do you trust me

yet?"

"Aye, Porter, if I can be honest I have had great struggle in my heart since we spoke with the king," Soranin was drunk, but sober thoughts and all that. It was hard for Soranin to be so forward with his emotions. He pivoted: "Hey, let's see your tattoo, eh?"

Porter rolled up his sleeve and revealed his new smoky orange band.

"That's just absurd! I mean, I mean," Soranin began.

"No one told us about that back in Caprica," Leoric said. The newts looked uncomfortable.

"Look men, we've got something we should tell you," Porter said.

The officers lifted the veil for their compatriots, the secrets of the Westlands as they knew them, as they waited for the food. Porter went on to explain Ortimer, and the story which led to their discoveries. The mood at the table no longer managed to match the band's beats.

"So," Porter tried to reclaim the atmosphere. "You understand where we're at now. What's at stake."

"Allegedly," Leoric said.

"After what you've seen up until now can you doubt something like this? I find it easier to believe our journey, even a homeless stranger, over King Ernhart," Porter said, his tongue loosened by alcohol.

"I fear I agree with Porter, though it pains me," Soranin said as he polished off another tankard of beer.

"What does that mean for us?" asked Ganes.

The server came over with two plates on each arm, his neck piece carrying a side of fried vegetables, from the kitchen.

"Well at least one of you will need return with this agreement for the king," Soranin said. "But the rest may join us on our quest."

Our quest. Porter liked the sound of it, the way Soranin spoke like it was a reality and that there wasn't a chance they wouldn't all be adventuring to the other end of the world together.

"Couldn't one of us bring it upon our return? I mean, when does the king need it by?" Duncan asked.

"Day has a point," Leoric responded. "I'm not in the

mood to do any immediate favors for King Barnyard any ways. He'll get his papers when we return. Let's take these newts through the mountains with us, so they can learn something from their captains, I say!"

The men cheered.

"Ah," Porter recalled. "There was something I meant to discuss with you, Soranin. But now we can speak freely, considering our new quest."

Their server stumbled, on that precipice of revelation, and an enormous yak burger slid off his plate, fries and all, onto the chest of a local patron.

The patron was Kelingrande Muerti. Muerti had once been the mightiest and by and by the largest berserker in the berserker squadron of Reprico. Hannah had a long head of black hair, often in a thick braid, and was as copious as a house. That had been before he died and was buried in the Repricoan Graveyard three miles out of town, up the hill.

Muerti's dining partner, Horace Hannah, had been the one to bring him back to life. Hannah was a soul splitter once, following Daloshen in his homeland, and had become a magician in Reprico. As the city fell, Hannah found his opportunity to practice his most important spell: life giving. Muerti was a hero in the annals of Repricoan history, but since he was a berserker it was clear that his heroism came at the price of absolute gratuity and often decapitation. Hannah knew that in order spread the word of life after death he would need a convincing, and brutal, spokesperson. It was not a stormy day when Muerti was brought back to the world of the living, but there was a total darkness on the hill.

That was over a hundred years ago. The intervening years had been kind to the two companions.

Horace was small, with a black robe inlaid with green, a careful trim around the hood and in the seams. He had cast off his mortal shell and his skull was a bright ivory. There was a green glow somewhere inside his skull, perhaps his magic brain, perhaps his archaic soul. A chained and locked black tome sat by Hannah's glass. The glass was empty.

Muerti was, sitting, four feet taller than the server. His armor had been salvaged from the museum, months after the city's fall, and repurposed by Hannah. It was the blue and gold it once had been, Reprico's berserker squad's color combination, but with bone spikes running down his back, he had opted to sit on a stool. On his knees were skulls and on his shoulders a few vertebrae and sentry style skulls protruded straight up, and in their mouths were red crystals. Though his armor was polished, Muerti's bones were not: he was dirty and covered in blight. In his eyes was the same red held by the crystals on his armor. It was an enchantment of strength cast by Kelingrande. Judging from his size, it didn't seem necessary, though an overabundance of strength is not often brought on from necessity but from an interest in total domination.

Now, though, there was a mangled burger and potato fries on the chest of the skeleton. And Muerti stood up.

He clutched the server. The entire bar had been laughing at his expense in their drunkenness, but upon seeing his stature, and his dermatological state, they hushed.

He raised the young waiter into the air.

"Did you think you were a jester?" Muerti asked in a hollow voice. It was like some great baron had rumbled through a long dead hollowed out tree.

The server couldn't make a single word. His living neck piece expelled itself from the server and scrambled into the kitchen.

Horace watched, or so it seemed, without speaking. He looked like death, and in many ways he was. Though he considered himself life.

"You are a jester? Then dance, jester," Muerti set the boy on the table. Revival, and the absence of blood to be boiled, had taken some of the berserker's ferociousness from him.

"DANCE!" Muerti slammed the table and cracked it in two. For his sake, it was good Muerti had ferociousness in spades, easy to spend it on people and tables.

The boy began to step, unaware of how to dance almost at all, and a low, melodic rumble came from the skeleton.

Porter was frozen, but thankful that alcohol inspired his captain to action. It may have been the likeness to his son that prompted him to speak, or maybe he was just the kind of principled person who so many aspire to be.

"That's enough, then," Soranin looked no more imposing than the server in his doublet, and Muerti saw no threat as his skull rotated toward the captain of a land he hadn't visited in many years.

"No, it isn't, but your input is noted," Muerti rotated his head back to the scene at his table. The wizard's finger became a key and he unlocked his book, a wail escaping from its yellowed pages as it folded open.

"Porter, grab our weapons - there is a horse guard posted at all hours of the day and night, you must hurry."

Porter hurried out of the bar.

"Let him go," Leoric joined Soranin and stood. Leoric never let his blades off his person, sometimes paranoid and often wise. He drew them in the well-packed bar.

Again, Muerti swiveled toward them, his torso coming around this time.

"Do not irk me again," Muerti said.

He tore off more of the hard wood table, and the server screamed as he wobbled, almost fell.

"Do not terrorize him again," said Soranin. Porter returned then, since the building was only on the other side of the square, and threw Joi'den to Soranin. The newts gained short swords, and Krude was in Porter's grip, heavy.

Muerti reached under the old table, which held the dancing server still, and lifted two enormous glaives, placed them on the table. Moving with experience, and annoyance, the behemoth skeleton strapped the long, gold instruments to his forearms. Each was gold with red ingots, three each, and they were stained along the edge. Black, red.

The colossus stood.

"Kelingrande," Horace whispered. "Must you?"

"Horace," Muerti replied, standing and pushing himself away from the table. "They are peons to me. Beside, this is what our lord asks of us. Remember the scripture? Aid me or I will not finish his good work with you. You will finish it on your own, sorcerer. If you can."

The other skeleton stood as well, lifting his unlocked

book. With careful bending of his wrist Horace swirled his boney fingers above the tome, and as he finished, a black sheen came to the glaives on his partner's arms.

Muerti bent over, stamped his feet, and like a huge beast shouted:

"Criminals of life pay the soulless tax!" He roared like a bear and cannoned toward our heroes. Soranin only had time to shout to the other patrons of the bar to flee before he was bowled over by the berserker.

"Alaina and Duncan work with me, after the caster," Leoric shouted, leaping atop their table. The server had dashed into the kitchen for refuge while many others fled through windows and back doors. "Porter, Ganes and Lentil fell that ogre of marrow!"

The knight sprung forward into the air with the two soldiers following on either side of the table. Porter grabbed Soranin and pulled him up. Ganes and Lentil stood on either side.

Muerti had continued his charge into three more tables, and had since flipped back around. Roaring again, with thick red liquid snaking into the cracks in his skull, he lifted one of the cast-aside tables, spun himself around, then threw it at the ill-armored party. The newts leapt to either side and Porter was able to duck, Soranin backwards rolled towards the bar. The table sailed through and destroyed a portion of the bar and kitchen wall: the server scurried to a new unknown hiding spot, reunited with his three-eyed rodent friend in their joint terror.

The giant stood tall and clanged his glaives against each other, chanting, and stomped toward the bar. Porter stood and hung his axe back, then arced it above his head and swung down on Muerti. Muerti deflected with a glaive and kicked Porter in a kidney, and Porter was knocked into yet another table.

A black fireball whizzing over his head, Soranin shouted across to Porter to bring the fight outside. It wasn't Porter who obliged but Muerti. The skeleton grabbed Soranin by his doublet, smirked, and whipped around like a cyclone before launching Soranin through a window, and part of a wall, into the street behind the bar.

Porter yelled for Lentil and Ganes to meet him outside,

then took off to find Soranin.

The two newts had been near-frozen, a bit off to the right and left, and now began to run for the door. A yellowed bone hand grabbed each by a shoulder.

They glanced over their shoulders with a cartoonish gulp:

"Daloshen take you, criminals of life are forgiven again," Muerti called. The red scars in his skull glowed.

The environment had allowed for quick travel. The battle maiden felt the weight she carried these last few days begin to lessen. Talking to Jayce had been a great joy, and a surprise. More and more so.

Given the way she had lived, the way she had come up, she was uneasy with strangers. Strangers who wield rapiers even less so, but Jayce seemed to know his way through the mountains at least as well as she did. If not better. And he was handsome, his teeth nice and his hair in a little knot that she quite liked. She liked his passion, his zeal.

"I told him if he tried to pitch me on this Melinda character one more time, to go back to our true homeland as he put it, I said I was going to skin him and sell his ragged hide to a Tidecaller trading vessel!" he went on.

They were in a thicket of trees, but also in high grass, pushing their way along like rafters with a pole.

"You seem to know a lot about these religions and gods and cultists and such," the maiden said, her eyes ahead as always.

"It's just relevant in my work is all," he said. "So what's your name?"

"That relevant to your work too?" "Could be," he joked.

They were smiling and walking. The canopy above crowded out the sun. Their connection had been stronger since the second night when they had had a fire South of Old Yit. There was something novel about traveling together, and they had eaten squalor and baleel meat and fried some vegetables and it had been a good meal, the stars giving them entertainment plenty beyond what drink might give. They had sat by the flame, her skinning rodent and him shining his sword, both smiling. Ho had talked, mostly, attempting to prove himself an interesting and worthy companion. He had succeeded.

The next morning, they had bathed in another lake, a lake much like the one they had met at further back. They stood not near each other and looked away but Sinéad still felt an interest she didn't think she would. She loved women romantically, and had always felt the same way sexually, but was feeling an attraction to Jayce she associated only with her love for the female form.

"What is your last name, Jayce?"

"Corl," he called, scrubbing his scalp.

"Like Coral or like Carl?"

"The fine, fine line between that awful name and the beautiful ocean formations from my home," he laughed.

"Where's home?"

"Rolling Tide. I was a fisherman that way."

She didn't say anything, washed herself. It had been a good first few days and had gotten better since. The path was beginning to form again, amongst the grasses and trees, and all the plant life gave way to hills and the sheerness of mountain faces. They were walking deep into the mountains now. So many of them were in the mountains now.

"My name is Sinéad," she said. "Just a first name for you."

He paused. Laughed.

"Alright, Sinéad, just a first name," he said. "What do you do for work?"

"I haven't held many traditional jobs, but I practiced in forgery for a long time. Before Group F began to sack homes."

A pause.

"It has been quite bad, hasn't it? Azulana seems to have driven folks mad, except for in the Reef proper," Jayce kept on.

"Yes, Group F seems to have a bloody history across this country."

"They have been brutal in their efficiency."

"Yes, and-"

"Not even Tidecallers or Mason Men can rival the power of their soldiers when the azulana charges them in the right way. It's remarkable – Mason builders and Atorus starcatchers can't do a thing against them, either. It's tragic these major deities and their acolytes cannot recognize divinity in the lesser, those struggling to rise above the din and chaos presented by modern society, societies."

They walked along another lake, one of the last before the villages and towns in the mountains would begin to appear. Rural of rural, south of society. The wild.

"You sympathize with their cause, Jayce?"

"No no no," Jayce laughed. "No, I just think we need to find a way to live in peace is all. Right? It's not right they chase you like they do. Just because you, what, defended yourself in Koro'Scheen? It's lunacy, their quest needs stop."

A pause.

"I never told you I was from Koro'Scheen. Did I?" Sinéad felt a bit of her heart crunch, felt it get eaten. "No, I'm sure you did, at our fire," Jayce said. They
walked on.

"No, I'm sure I didn't," she tensed her biceps. Walked a little slower.

"Sure you did, you're overreacting," Jayce said. His pace matched hers.

"Do not tell me how to react, and if you mean to speak of lunacy..."

Sinéad heard him before she felt him, and was able to warp herself to block his shot. Had she not dipped her torso down, the point of his rapier would have wedged between her breast-plate and greaves.

She shoved into the sword and he staggered back into the lake, the water coming up to the lip of his crimson boots. He flicked a strand of hair out of his face, smiled.

"If I had access to that power, now instead of later, you'd already be out of the way," Jayce said. "I will have that power, though, once I prove the sole survivor of Koro'Scheen is dead and gone. Like the rest of these outer towns. Dead and gone."

A fisherman from Roiling Tide hailing from the Reef had been too convenient, she knew, but she had been willing to trust him. It wouldn't be a mistake she'd make again.

"I can't let you go alive, Jayce," Sinéad said, unsheathing her mace. "And you've seen what I did to your allies. Do not call me crazy again, and do not be so crazy as to believe you will leave that lake alive."

Jayce looked down, his lips curling for a moment, then looked up, his blade poised.

"My allies? How little you know of azulana," Jayce said. "How crazy you are."

She ran and jumped into the lake, mace above her head, and struck down at Jayce. He danced to the left, through the mud and kelp, and stabbed her in the thigh, shooting above the greaves again. He twisted the point and she screamed.

Raising her mace from the lake she swung it at him in a crushing arc, and he ducked, ripping the sword from her and vaulting backward. Sinéad came after him again, using her anger for survival like she knew how to do. She hadn't done it since her last battle, but she remembered how and she could never forget.

Jayce kept his blade up and Sinead moved right at it, grabbing it. Jayce was stronger than her and assumed he would win this tug of war, except Sinéad wasn't playing tug of war. She was attempting to kill him.

As he began to hunker down to keep his weapon, she let go and Jayce was thrown off balance for a moment. She thought this might happen – Jayce, being a fisherman or a rogue at best, was not the warrior he dreamed of being through holy gifts. His spiritual dedication may have been enough to make him a great warrior if he hadn't had to battle her to receive the fruits of his devotion.

In the teetering she approached him and grabbed his shoulders. He looked at her and she cupped her hands behind his neck and blasted his face into her pauldron, breaking his front teeth and concussing him. She let him fall into the lake.

The splashing was the only noise in the small opening. It reminded her of where they had first met, however many days ago now, and the difference, she noted, was that she wasn't meeting Jayce at this lake but murdering him instead.

His cloak looked silly now and his blade had fallen out of his hand, into the soft soil full of microbes and fish. He sputtered some pond scum.

"He'll catch you yet, he'll finish the purge and liberation will reign and you will know his-"

Her mace almost went wide, but collided with his head and the mass of his skull crumpled and broke. Jayce was a good looking Westerner no more, just a body with a lop-sided tumor.

"I know enough," the maiden said. She stepped from felt like nothing new.

the lake, her thigh aching, and kept walking. It was nothing new, felt like nothing new.

She walked for a few hours, getting within a few leagues of a town. She didn't know its name but was sure there would be someone who could take a look at her leg. It wasn't that it still hurt, necessarily, just that it...

She collapsed. It did hurt, and she couldn't tell why. She could only tell that it felt like her thigh was a burning log, full of embers and incendiary things. Her armor was a granite quarry on her tired frame. She sat down in between a lumpy rock and a splintery tree.

Her head was feverish. Her breath was shallow and it hurt to be alive. The straps of her armor were like snakes and she undid her greaves to look at the stab better.

Her wound was cranberry and blueberry and green like spinach left out for a week.

The tip of his blade had been poisoned, of course it had been. Who sits by the fire polishing their rapier? The sadness of it all is that despite winning the battle, gashes and wounds dodged and defeated, the man had still left her to die. And now she lay dying alone. Alone in the mountains, rotting slow.

The stars would be with her soon. She hoped some of them were from Atorus. She was willing to convert.

Chapter 4

Duncan cut through Hannah's robe. Straight through it.

Hannah grabbed the sword and began to pull himself along it, lower jaw clacking like a laugh but silent, toward the now piss-frightened man.

Captain of the King's Sword for a reason, Leoric leapt in between the two and elbowed Horrace back off of the sword.

"Shit," Leoric cursed. "I forget that they are made of just bone."

"Plans, sir?" Alaina asked. He was shaking, and Leoric felt pity. For only a moment though.

"Alaina run behind him, displace his book if you can. If not, then displace his legs," Leoric said. "Duncan with me on the front attack."

Leoric heard Muerti roar again, and a table whizzed by his head.

"Make quick work of him, the stronger one needs our attention I fear."

Dancing forward, with Duncan following, the Khu'Roni trained combatant struck out with his blades. Horace danced too, backward, and Duncan swung and missed the mage. Alaina made his way behind Horace and chopped at his arm, and bone bursting could be heard. The skeleton's arm, book in tow, fell to the ground.

Green light shone from inside Horace as he rose above the combat, and a wail bounced out from within him. His eyes turned to the book and it flew open, pages flipping like a hurricane. A green beam, holy in its rising, beckoned the arm, book in tow, back to its master. It attached itself to the undead man again, but now it was bound by magic and not bone.

Leoric was terrified by this power as it was, but Horace made it much worse. He conjured a ball of black flame, or it danced like fire any ways, in front of him like he was cooking a stew. He shot it at the duo in front of him and they were nearly hit by the shadowy blast. With cobra like speed the mage turned his head in the air and grew another spherical bolt, and in his terror Alaina was helpless to move as the black energy caught him in the chest.

"Daloshen forgives your crime," Hannah whispered. No one but his bright, dark lord heard him.

"Fuck," Leoric said. He and Duncan were hiding behind the bar as they saw Soranin exit the building. "Outside. Now."

The strawberry hair warrior ran across the combat zone, followed by a distant Porter.

Duncan rose to stand and, looking both ways, began his desperate dash too. A blackness, quick and lethal like a knife, entered his back. Crying, knowing he'd failed, Duncan fell on his knees and slung his head forward on his chest.

"Soranin!" Porter ran outside and lifted his captain. Soranin was battered but not beaten, and it wasn't long until Leoric met them there.

"Where are your newts?" Leoric asked.

"Right behind us. Yours?" Porter replied. Soranin was breathing heavy, reclaiming Joi'den from a nearby garbage can.

"Right behind me," Leoric said. "What the hell happened to make those demons so angry? And what are they blathering about, Daloshen?"

"I didn't want them teasing our server," Soranin said. He was still a bit drunk, they all were, and was regretting wearing his civilian clothes. They all were.

"Who the hell cares? What the hell, man?!" Leoric yelled. They could hear their opponents climbing over the debris to join them in the alley.

"We need to get them outside the city," Soranin said. "We aren't too far."

"I think the location of the battle will be on their terms," Leoric said, watching the hole in the wall and the torn asunder window. "Sadly."

Muerti bellowed again as he smashed down the rest of the wall, stepping out.

Horace trailed behind, floating a few feet off the ground like a morbid fairy.

Alaina, Ganes, Lentil and Duncan were with them too. They'd been forgiven of their crimes. Four handsome skeletons stood in their places, and it wasn't hard to tell which was which. Hannah cast his green gaze upon them and their clothes became thick leather, black.

The youngest of their cabal, Alaina's sword grew and rounded becoming a fighting staff like the kind he had used in training. He was most skilled with it, and he flipped it around himself like a propeller. The staff was stark white, with pommels of skulls on each end and a leather grip in the middle.

Ganes' sword curved, becoming the same white, until it was a U. Then a black string weaved in between each end and a quill materialized on his back. Ganes shot arrows with his sister in Marryfarm, after their schoolwork was done and was then double-checked by their mother.

Round and long, Lentil had a black leather helmet, unlike the others who had caps, and his sword simply grew. And curved. And grew more. He ended up resembling a black knight from Khu'Ron, scimitar and all.

Last and most-least, the once pitiful Duncan Day was the only of their crew who seemed to be smiling in his post life. A row of black spikes grew from his head in an ascending mohawk, and a thick black leather grip grew in his hand. Then a chain and spiked ball attached to the grip, and a hollow laugh erupted from him at the sight of his completed morning star.

"The living will pay the soulless tax," Horace said. Muerti roared and the new skeleton warriors cheered
with him.

The three officers ran. They stumbled and sprinted as their opponents laughed behind them, walking, with Alaina and Day pulling off only a shamble.

Porter rounded a corner and his officers ran with him. It led to a gate, and the gate led to what seemed to be a continuation of their path on the other side of town. It looked like Diandre's Road, except none of them had any idea what lay beyond Ollette. They had no map. They had very little hope.

They heard Muerti's feet picking up speed as he ran towards them, like a terrible battering ram.

No time or ability to speak yet. The officers just kept running. Short behind them came the six undead constables, collecting taxes. And another.

It was in the meadow of Yuvaton's great-descendant Roberto that the men lost steam. I'd say they ran at least a half mile off of the road, North, through the Olletian citizen's property. It didn't matter much how far they meant to go because there is no issue of maintaining energy for a berserker, alive or undead.

Muerti arrived first. It was a field of black, and a few flowers, all white, stood in the gap between the Caprican travelers and the huge skeleton.

"You look tired to me," Muerti said, cold as the night.

"Let me release you of your exhaustion."

"We're not tired," Leoric said. "We just wanted to finish this up without your wide ass breaking anything else."

Muerti's eyes flared red and he ran toward the trio. Behind him, not too far, came the rest of his dead crusaders.

He barreled toward them and meant to grab Leoric, not knowing how agile he was. Leoric leapt aside, Muerti spun his glaives around him in a frenzy, Soranin and Leoric deflected, Porter crashed his axe into the calf of the towering berserker.

Muerti tossed Leoric down like the knight was burning his hand, and clasped his splintering leg with the hand instead. It was then the reanimated newts and necromancer arrived.

"Kill them all, you worthless deviants," Muerti crowed, sitting down. It was clear his girth was not supported by the breaking leg. No muscle to lighten the blow.

Duncan engaged Leoric. His morning star had a good reach and it wrapped around the knight's leg fast, and the spikes dug into his skin. He cried out as Duncan pulled him toward the group of skeletons.

Porter ran forward with every belief he could disrupt Day. Alaina and Lentil met him first though, crossing staff and scimitar in his path. Soranin moved forward to help as well, and saw Ganes notching an arrow meant for Porter. With a powerful jump and thrust, Soranin met Ganes, and a fresh round of battle began.

Moltov Wolves brayed at the noise, and stray dlowers aiming for the Ennabon Forest chose a new path. One with less bloodshed.

Leoric was shedding blood then, but managed to snake his leg out from the chain by wedging his blade between his calf and the ball. He yelled as the spikes exited his body.

"Any quips for me now, brave sir knight?" the undead Duncan asked. His voice was no longer meek, his speech no longer goofy or naive. It had been burned away.

"I'm...I'm sorry, Duncan, I-" Leoric was shaken. He hadn't fought a sin made real before.

"Yes," Duncan said as he swung the ball and chain above his head. "But you're only sorry I'm going to kill you. That you're weak, and that in life you were a braggart and a child. In death you'll be forged new. . He will forgive you."

Leoric leapt away from the cannonball shot of the morning star, but was able to roll forward and in front of Duncan. He placed both of his swords below Duncan's head.

"No, that isn't quite it either," Leoric said. His voice was like tattered parchment paper, vaporizing when brought into fresh air. He crossed his blades up in an x and beheaded the former ally. Day's words still corrosive in their damage.

Duncan's head still smiled, muttering about the infidel Champion and the justiciers who would rectify, and Muerti was standing up.

Porter jumped backward as Lentil swung his obsidian blade, but couldn't dodge Alaina's staff as it came down hard on his shoulder. Porter cried out, and as he moved to swing at Alaina, Lentil swung and sliced across his ribs. The second captain coughed, hoarse, but managed to distance himself from his two undead opponents.

I've got to turn one of their attacks, Porter thought, *disarm one.*

Alaina, in his youth, leapt forward too soon and Porter found his mark. As the staff came down he notched it in his axe and yanked the staff away. It flew a great distance, and as the skeleton looked after the tool, Porter attacked. Another strong chop, like the one on Muerti's tibia, broke the newt. His body fell into pieces, but as Porter finished his attack Lentil slammed into Porter and all at once grabbed him by his throat.

"Who knew you were so quick and strong, Mental," Porter wheezed. "It was Mental, wasn't it? Or...Bento?"

There was no response from the blackness inside Lentil's eye sockets as he began to choke Porter. He wriggled, clawed at the firm grip, fruitless. He was near unconsciousness when Leoric leg swept Lentil in such a tactful way that he fell backwards. In another movement Leoric popped his elbow up, cracking Lentil's arm in twain. Porter was able to just pry the cold, dead fingers from around his throat.

"Help Soranin with the archer. I'll be there soon," Porter coughed.

"You're sure?" Leoric said. Porter saw his pants bleeding through tears in them.

"Yes, Thomas and I were always close," Porter said. "Lentil," Leoric said.

"No thank you, not hungry," Porter said with a ragged wink.

The adrenaline was getting him. It was in Leoric, too, because he seemed to understand this nonsense banter before running off.

Armless Lentil regained himself, as Muerti was trying to do, and shrugged his way toward Porter. Porter walked toward the stiff skeleton, kicked him hard in the stomach, and as he wobbled cut through both of his legs. Lentil fell upon his own remains, and watched as Porter followed Leoric.

The archer had been proving more difficult for Soranin than he anticipated. Whenever Soranin came to close quarters with an archer it was curtains for them, but Ganes was quick.

Leaping back between each attack he kept firing his arrows, and when Leoric and Porter reached the duel Soranin had received one in each shoulder, and another in his ribs. Their captain was quite near death.

"Soranin, retreat," Leoric cautioned. It was clear Soranin had fractured most of Ganes' nightmarish head.

"I must-"

"Retreat I say!" Leoric yelled.

There was no conversation about who had authority this time. The captain sat down, and Porter drug him away from Ganes who was aimed to polish him off. Leoric tried to dance his way toward the archer, but his wounded leg got the best of him in a bad step and he stumbled. He took an arrow, and if he hadn't put his arms out to shield his torso he'd have been killed. It was Porter who ran toward Ganes, distracted, who blew his body apart with his axe.

Muerti stood again, and had stuffed rocks in the hole in his leg to keep himself upright.

Horace, all this while, had been chanting a dark prayer. It came to fruition as the skeleton knights reached around and began to put themselves together, with a haunting glow like the one

Horace had used for himself, his minions using a sludge black in place of green. Alaina's body began to reshape and Duncan walked to his head. He placed it above his torso, letting it float above his vertebrae.

The Capricans couldn't make out that Horace was doing this, empowering the newts. They had been focusing on the clearer and present danger, but an ally in the shadows had not missed a second. He'd been biding his time for the skeleton warriors to fall. Now he struck.

In the moonlight painted silver meadow, the bard from Ollette rose from the grass. The bard took the three-stringed instrument from his back; his Kinbanian Troo. It was big and obtuse and fantastic for a dirge or a party tune or for combat. Drawing the string with a barbed arrow, the performer's favorite, he shot Horace through the middle of his head.

The caster's concentration broke, and soon after the undead minions followed suit. Duncan's head fell from atop his body, and Alaina was a pile of bones as soon as he had been put back together. Lentil hadn't moved much to start with, and Ganes exploded once again.

Horace turned around, his eyes almost as angry as Muerti's had been.

The bard smiled, then swung his Yolotanian stone flute across Horace's face. The Yolotanians are a vicious mountain tribe, located near the coast to the North, which prefer to gain the rich sound in their weaponry from hitting it against things. Often each other, or thieving criminals. Warlocks suffice in a pinch.

The undead caster sailed to the ground. Muerti was shocked, but gained himself the composure necessary to charge at the bard. In his fury he neglected to mind his calf, and nearing his opponent he began to falter. The bard side-stepped and cracked open the bone yet again. A hodge podge of stones tumbled out, and Muerti nose-dived into the earth, grinding up grass and dirt as he coursed into the pasture.

It was silent in the meadow spare cracks and grunts. A few stray yawps from the wolves, shallow breathing from the stunned Capricans and clacking from the undead warriors.

Horace began to raise himself again, but the bard dug

an arrow through his body and pinned him to the earth.

"What's in this, hm?" The bard was near invisible in the night, but his teeth glimmered in his familiar smile. Porter couldn't believe it was him, but he couldn't believe almost anything since they had left Caprica. The bard wrenched the dark tome form Hannah.

"It is not meant for the living! Muerti, stop him now!" Horace's muffled voice called.

The berserker struggled onto his arms, and swiveling his head around, roared at the bard.

The bard, still smiling, left the book shut. He set it on the ground at his feet next. Then, taking another barbed arrow, he plunged it into the lock and through the tome.

A vortex of red energy came swirling out of Muerti. Through the sockets in his skull he was being vacuumed into the book. The thick liquid in his cracks was harvested, and it came out of him like a funneled geyser.

"KLINGRANDE!" Horace cried. "I LOVE YOU!"

"And I you, Horace," the leviathan of dirty bone replied. He had reached for the bard, but his energy was disappating. "Return me again, if you can. I'll be waiting in the palace."

With an uncomfortable shudder, the red energy inside of the Repricoan warrior exited. A thud brought his empty vessel hard to the earth. Horace was silent. The bard's smile was gone, he still stood above the book. The lock on it had cracked, and falling from the book it became obsolete.

Soranin and Leoric were seated this entire time, watching and hanging on to their wounds. Porter was standing, but in similar disrepair.

"I will not beg," Horace said, still face down. "But I ask you release me."

"Why's that?" the bard asked, a glimmer of a smile returning. Everything seemed to amuse him.

"My tome was my only connection to my priest-hood," Horace said. "Release me and see."

The bard took his arrow back and Horace rose to his knees.

Horace shrugged out of his robe, it fell to the ground

near him. The green energy behind his eye sockets was flicker-
ing. It flickered in the canal that had been fashioned between his
scapula and humorous. It was becoming darker, black.

"I'll become like them," Horace pointed at the piles of
bones. "I've lost my right to Daloshen's grace." His voice was deep,
and hollow, but defeated now. There was no sinister presence, only
a collapsing sadness.

"I'm sorry for your sins, Horace Hannah," the bard said.
"What will you do?"

"I will stay here, near Kelingrande, and by dawn I will be
like him. A shell to be rested upon by carrion."

"The sun is not far away for you, then," the bard
reclaimed his arrows and turned away from the kneeling skeleton.
He approached the travelers. "Dawn take you all."

"I saw you earlier, and again at the bar." Porter said. The
bard reached for him, "What is your name, why did you come to
our aid?"

"I am Boretto, a bard from Yolotan. I saw you, and what
you did for our city. I wished to speak with you after your dinner.
You all seem to be having such a beautiful time, and I ask if I could
journey with your party."

"Our party of three now," Leoric said.

"Four," Soranin and Porter said at the same time.

The bard smiled.

"I will go and get help," Boretto said.

"Please do," Leoric said. "We won't be going anywhere
any time soon."

"Tellor's chasm, maybe," Porter said as he sat down.

"There is no such place," Horace said, eavesdropping in
his final hours.

"We'll see, wizard," Soranin said. "We have just begun
our journey in these mountains. It's feeling a lot like a chasm
already."

"Who is Daloshen?" Porter asked.

"One of eight," Horace said. "The only god with divine
power, a white love and a mind to save Epic."

"What's an Epic?" Porter asked. He coughed blood in the
shadows as he spoke.

He received no answer. Horace rose and walked away, but his conviction carried him only a few feet before he collapsed. He faced the mountain, his final act a silent butterfly pose.

The three Capricans gazed around them, seeing the next mountain just a half-mile to the south. In between Ollette and the next rise had been this stretch of grass, this silvery meadow, simple and on rolling hills. To their east and west were more mountains. Jordan's perch was not far from here.

Dawn came and stole away Horace Hannah for good. Three Capricans lay in a boneyard. Porter actually smiled beneath the grime and blood, his body at peace. The Bastions of Tellor churned along.

Chapter 6

Janniken fur was not suiting Pansen well today. Then again, nothing seemed to insulate him against his memories. It was because he hated what he was there to do.

"You'll have to kill one," Pansen's father, Hecho, had said. Not for a second did his inflection falter, stone.

The grypatin sat at the door, and Pansen's younger brother Yoncho went outside with him. Their grandmother was already on the porch. The rain was letting up, and she got a chance to watch her grandson play in the afternoon sun.

Pansen sat at the dining table. It was a roughhewn thing; the family of the acquestier gets no additional money or services. In fact, since one income is lost, they had less money than their neighbors. Being an acquestier also meant charity was expected whenever Hecho would leave the house, so they had little. Thankful for the community every day.

"Why?" Pansen asked.

"Because it is a part of our culture. Do we have to go over this every day?" Hecho said, busying himself in the other room.
said.

"I don't understand. It isn't protection anymore," Pansen

"An acquestier of Third Maple is more than it once was, son," Hecho found his way into the room and sat across from Pansen. "It's an icon. You are ambassador and leader, but you are the warrior of this simple place."

"A defender, you said."

"How old were you then, Pansen? Was I to tell you that you'd have to kill creatures far beyond your scope of imagination in the name of your people?" His father stood again and moved to the window overlooking the family fields. This season they grew ionbeads and Celian clams, neither of which may sound like plants, but both of which provide for their family, the others, when the seasons change.

"I remember you killing the janniken," the boy said. "It made sense. We needed the hide and we traded the meat."
Hecho's wife and daughter were in the field, rooting up the clams

and picking the beads, placing them in large sacks. There were hundreds more workers near them, and all of them were working like animals. He would join them once he motivated his son. Then his son would join too, and his youngest son as well.

"This too is important," he said. "It is tradition."

"I've never seen this thing I'm supposed to murder," Pansen said. "How can it be tradition?"

"The mystery for the acquestier is a part of the challenge. It is symbolic."

"How so?" Pansen stood and raised his voice, forgetting his discipline. "And how could you send me away from you and mother? From Fae and Yoncho and Grandmother? Will she be alive when I come home?"

Hecho said nothing and crossed his arms behind himself.

"How can you send your eldest son to the top of that mountain in the coldest season? Don't you know I'll die?"

"It's tradition," Hecho snapped. Then he softened.

"You won't die any ways. I didn't, and you are stronger than me. You've been fighting wolves and protecting our lands without even realizing it since you were smaller than Yoncho. You can conquer Bolo Khan just as I did."

Hecho began to walk to the back of his home, through the rear thatch door, and Pansen followed. He chewed his finger nails, and his heart raced: he could not escape his fate. His changing of season would not be spent teasing Alena in the field, her hair in the long braid running to the curve of her hip. The drying season would not be spent wrestling with friends and salting meat with his brother.

The mountain stole those simple delights. The mountain would change him from boy, to man, to acquestier. The word was ugly in his mind.

"Father, I-"

"Outside the house," Hecho said as he opened the door. "Ah, here it is. The janniken hide jacket we have all helped to sew and craft for you."

Pansen took it and tried it on. In the late summer it had been too hot, but trudging through the snow he wished it had a few extra layers.

"And this," Hecho said, reaching into the trunk on the porch which housed the coat. "Is from me to you."

The older man smiled and brought out a fantastic, brand new korekwood bow. His son was stunned.

"Yanche and I created it in his shop. We have a new quill with starbark arrows for you to fire, as well. I..."

Pansen was admiring the weapon while his father spoke, and now his father faltered, resolved.

"I know you'll lead this village to the future, Pansen. You must."

He was stony again, and the tears must have just been a trick of the light.

Hecho began to walk into the field.

Pansen admired the bow, beautiful and lethal. Fantastic and strong. In his hands it dappled in the sun, marbled, and shone a thick, royal brown.

Then it lay in his hands in a snow storm, his reality brought back to the now.

Pansen gripped it and slung it upon his back. No more time to think of fondnesses. They will kill him, he knew, this high on Bolo Khan.

But one more memory.

"Father," Pansen called from his back porch, it creaking under his shuffling feet.

Hecho turned. His white shirt was in contrast to his caramel skin, and his wrinkles were like carvings of sorrow on his forehead.

"I won't ask anything else, but can you tell me what they're like? The green dragons?"

Hecho looked down, took off his glasses and rubbed his eyes.

"Pray you catch one alone. They're indomitable as a pack," Hecho paused. "They're fantastic, and you'll have to kill one."

Book VIII

There is no helping it, the flattening pressure you'll feel when you
look at the stars and see all the love there.
All the power from each of those stars, shining on you.
Each is a story and a strong memory,
and let it be inspiration to you.
Because they are legion.

passage from Atorus' Celestial Journal

Epilogue

A rotted smile flashed from inside a bundle of robes. The Caprica Public House was in good spirits; the "Fantastic Footman Fish Fry Fever" was on in full swing. Ortimer had no money, but it was easy enough to start a tab with good Olaf. The noise of drunken rough housing militia and the sizzles and pops of breaded trout had grown old for the traveler. He sauntered to the swinging doors. Caprica's sun was blistering, hot and unkind, but Ortimer thought that what the sun wrought the moon would undo. Gorgeous, cool and calming. A good omen came with the night, he thought.

Ortimer strode to the surrounding wall of the city and looked across from the Southern exit onto the sprawling plains, noting each township and village with their unrecognizable shadowy features in the nightscape. The agriculture and farming of the West Lands struck Ortimer as something almost as gorgeous as the enormous satellite hanging over it every night. The West Lands during harvest season must be a commotion unlike any other, Ortimer pondered as he chewed on a small, fried Roiling Tide trout. Farmers running to and fro, collecting their goods and making preparations for the impending reaping. Ortimer slumped into the crook of the wall, a corner fashioned by the gate and the white brick. With fish crumbs in his mustache and ale sloshing in his gut, the vagabond schemed, dreamed and aspired.

Thousands of miles and leagues away, a monster shifts, its long hands causing the ocean and the land to perverse and to alter. A woman brings cities out of arid expanse into her modernity. Two beings of volcanic doom and flourishing life share jokes. An astronomer instructs his demagogy to missionaries and fools.

What will become of the party now that they have been devastated by the death knights Muerti and Hannah? Who is Boretto? Who is Daloshen?

What is the Mason? Will the Maiden make it to a sanctuary?

And where are these green dragons?

Look for more in

Eight Gods Book II: Divine Places

You'll meet a whole new cast of characters, adventure along with the party as they explore the mountains. You'll follow the Maiden (not like Jayce though!), Hariah the Pariah and Pansen as all of the world continues to mount to an earth-breaking confrontation.

Be ready to meet gods, elves, orcish tribes, wizards in training, old sherrifs, a talking cake and, maybe, gods. Be ready to see cities built on bridges, pinnacle cities in the mountains and brilliant obelisks in the flat lands.

P.S. How did you like the book? What do you want to see more of in the second? What themes can you identify?

Tell the author what you think at www.paolobicchieri.com

Let's create this together.

Thank you for reading.

"You are braver than you believe, stronger than you seem, and smarter than you think." - A.A. Milne (read Winnie the Pooh)